A FATAL TWIST
of LEMON

Wysteria Tearoom Mysteries

A Fatal Twist of Lemon
A Sprig of Blossomed Thorn
An Aria of Omens
A Bodkin for the Bride

A FATAL TWIST of LEMON

PATRICE GREENWOOD

Evennight Books
Cedar Crest, New Mexico

This is a work of fiction. All of the characters, organizations, and events portrayed in this novel are either products of the author's imagination or are used fictitiously.

A FATAL TWIST OF LEMON

Copyright © 2012 by Patrice Greenwood
All rights reserved

An Evennight Book
Published by Book View Café Publishing Cooperative
P.O. Box 1624
Cedar Crest, NM 87008
www.bookviewcafe.com

ISBN: 978-1-61138-184-9

First Edition July 2012
Second Edition June 2015

for the St. James Tearoom

Acknowledgments

My heartfelt thanks to the following people for their invaluable assistance with this novel: to Sherwood Smith, Jennifer Stevenson, and Judith Tarr for editorial advice; to Ken and Marilyn Dusenberry, Sally Gwylan, Kathy Kitts, Pari Noskin, D. Lynn Smith, and Jerry Weinberg for their thoughtful input; and to Chris Krohn for his untiring support. Thanks also to the members of Book View Café for their help with a thousand little details of bringing out a book, and to the founders and staff of the St. James Tearoom for inspiring me to write this story.

1

The first day my tearoom opened was wonderful—mostly. Funny how life can go swimmingly one moment, and fall to pieces the next.

The sun was starting to dip toward the west, filtered by the wisteria vines on the front porch, as I bade my guests farewell. My thank-you tea party had been a success, and the butterflies in my stomach had mostly settled down. After months of hard work, the Wisteria Tearoom was ready for its official grand opening celebration in two days.

"The tea was marvelous, Ellen! Come for dinner tomorrow," said my aunt Nat, giving me a big hug.

"Oh...I've got so much to do—"

"And you won't get it done if you don't take a rest now and then. Say 'Yes, thank you,' like a good girl."

"Yes, thank you," I said meekly.

Nat smiled. "Six o'clock."

I waved farewell to her and her perennial beau Manny Salazar, whose produce business was one of my suppliers. With a grateful sigh, I went inside and started toward the kitchen.

Claudia Pearson—a tall, older woman with snowy hair drawn into a tight bun and an aristocratic Roman nose, who always reminded me of Georgia O'Keeffe—stood in the hall putting on her gloves. She and Sylvia Carruthers, both from the Santa Fe Preservation Trust, were my most important guests at the thank-you tea. In fact, I'd come up with the party as a way of acknowledging them. Without their help, I wouldn't have been able to open the tearoom.

"Did Mrs. Carruthers go already?" I asked Claudia, who seemed in no hurry to leave.

"No, she hasn't come out."

We both looked toward the private dining parlor at the back of the tearoom, which doubled as a conference room and was where the tea had taken place. Vi, one of my servers, a stunning Juno of a girl with a tumble of flaming curls barely confined by a lavender ribbon, stepped out of the pantry across the hall, carrying an empty tray.

"Maybe she forgot something," I said to Claudia. "I'll go and see."

I went to the dining parlor door with Vi close on my heels. Dusk gathered at the windows and French doors, pushed back by the golden pool of light from the chandelier. I stopped short just inside the doorway.

Sylvia Carruthers lay sprawled on the floor beside the table, her huge heishi necklace tight around her throat, eyes bulging and her face a livid purple.

My heart gave a terrified thump.

"Vi, call an ambulance! Hurry!"

Vi made a small, startled sound, then disappeared. I rushed to Sylvia, dropping to my knees.

I lifted her by the shoulders and pulled her necklace loose. It wasn't easy—the heishi was practically embedded in her neck. As I tugged at it, some of the strands broke, sending tiny yellow beads dancing across the wood floor, a delicate waterfall of sound.

Sylvia didn't breathe. She didn't move. I tried to find a pulse, but there was none.

"Oh, no," I whispered.

Things seemed to happen in flashes after that. I remember Claudia Pearson standing over me, saying something wry, then taking out her cell phone.

I did what I could to revive Sylvia, but I knew in my heart

it was hopeless. Paramedics arrived in mere moments and confirmed that Sylvia was beyond help. I felt guilty and appalled and terribly, terribly sad. I also felt apprehensive, especially when the police began to invade.

Thank you for a wonderful afternoon.

Sylvia's last words to me echoed in my mind. I'd intended to honor her with this celebration. Instead...

The police wanted to talk to everyone. Vi and the other two servers, my chef Julio, and dishwasher Mick gathered in the kitchen where I asked them to wait. All young—college age—and looking rather shocked. I was not their peer, but I felt more divided from them than ever now as they clustered together, talking in low voices. I wished I could think of something to say to reassure them, but I was feeling none too assured myself.

Claudia remained, having called to cancel the meeting she and Sylvia had been headed for. I took her to wait in the Iris alcove in the tearoom's main parlor. With a resigned expression, she made herself comfortable in a blue velvet wing chair by the embers of the fire.

"Would you like tea, or have you had your fill?" I asked her.

"A pot of tea would be welcome, since I'm likely to be here a while."

"I'll get it. Oh—should I call Donna?" I said, remembering Sylvia's daughter, who had also been at the party. The thought of calling her dismayed me, but it could be considered my duty as hostess.

"I've already done so," Claudia said.

I breathed relief. "Thank you. I'm afraid I'm a bit distracted."

She raised an elegant eyebrow. "You've had a shock. Why don't you sit down?"

"I will, as soon as I..."

I stepped out into the hall and nearly collided with a police officer. She shot me an irritated glance, then headed toward the dining parlor with heavy, clumping steps.

Flashes of red and blue light spun down the hallway, reflecting on the polished oak floor. I felt a wave of dread for what this might do to my business.

I went to the kitchen. Julio had made a pot of coffee, normally anathema in the tearoom, but I was in no state to object at the moment.

The staff were all sitting around the small wooden table at the back of the kitchen with mugs in their hands. Vi huddled forward, cupping both hands around her mug, looking shell-shocked. Julio got up and reached for a fresh mug when he saw me come in.

"No, thanks," I said. "I'm going to make some tea."

Dee, one of the servers, jumped up, pushing a strand of blonde hair behind her ear. "I'll make it. What kind?"

"Assam," I said, choosing a tea with a warm and malty flavor, one I associate with comfort. "And two cups, please. Bring them to Iris."

Dee hurried to the butler's pantry. Her brother, Mick, the dishwasher, got up and followed her. Iz, the third in my trio of servers, a shy and soft-spoken Indian girl from Tesuque Pueblo, looked up at me, then laid a hand on Vi's back and started rubbing it.

"We going to be here a while, boss?" Julio asked. He was still in his white chef's jacket, but had unbuttoned the collar and freed his curling black hair from the hairnet and his customary colorful cap.

I swallowed. "I'm afraid so."

"I'll make some sandwiches."

"Bless you. And thank you for making the coffee, Julio."

"Cops drink coffee," he said, pouring the last of the pot into his mug and setting about to make more.

I smiled a little, thinking that cops probably didn't usually drink coffee of the quality Julio made. We'd had a tussle about that; I didn't want the tearoom to be pervaded by the aroma of coffee. Julio had promised not to make it during business hours, but he insisted on being able to have coffee early in the day while he was baking. Then he'd offered me some of his favorite Colombian blend, and I had given in.

Returning to the hall, I found more police arriving, bringing equipment into the house. I tried talking to them, offering to help, but they made it plain I was just in the way.

I glanced into the dining parlor, saw the flowers and crystal and china still on the table—phantoms of the pleasant tea party—but the room was filled with police wielding cameras and other paraphernalia. A flash blinded me and I stepped back, blinking.

The front door stood open, and a sharp breeze blew in along with harsher strobing lights from the emergency vehicles outside. Shivering, I went back to Iris to check on Claudia.

Dee was on her knees before the fireplace, building up the fire. She looked like something straight out of a Victorian painting, golden light from new flames glowing on her pale hair, white apron, and lavender dress. Such a lovely, comforting sight in the midst of all this chaos.

"Thank you, Dee," I said. "It was getting cold in here."

She gave me a small smile and stood, dusting her hands. Her gaze shifted to the hall, where police were coming and going, and intensified with interest. She went out, leaving me with Claudia, my last remaining guest.

A tea tray sat on the low table, with cups and saucers, milk and sugar. Hostess instinct kicked in, giving me something to do.

I seated myself across from Claudia. As I lifted the teapot, the lid rattled. My hands were shaking.

"Why don't you let me pour," said Claudia.

I yielded the pot and watched her serve us both tea, thinking it strange that she was so little affected by Sylvia's death. They were close colleagues, after all, if not exactly friends. Sylvia was a difficult person; I'd been terrified of her, myself. But Claudia seemed immune to her rants.

She also seemed unfazed by Sylvia's death. Could she have done it?

What a horrible thought! But there it was.

I hadn't really paused to consider who might have killed Sylvia Carruthers. It almost had to be someone at the thank-you tea. The only others who had been in the dining parlor were Julio and Vi, and neither of them knew Sylvia, as far as I was aware.

I frowned, trying to remember if I had seen anyone else in the tearoom. There had been a few walk-in customers, even though our first day open had been unannounced. Friday's grand opening was to be our official launch.

Dee returned with a plate of sandwiches cut into quarters, and two tea plates. She set them on the table, then left us alone again. Claudia leaned back in her chair with her cup and saucer on her knee.

"You should eat something, Ellen. You've had a tough day."

I realized I was still holding my teaspoon, though I had stopped stirring my tea. I set the spoon on my saucer, conscious of the small click of silver against china. I took a sip, then put the cup and saucer down on the table.

"I have a feeling it's just getting started," I said, reaching for the sandwiches.

Julio had made them substantial, with generous layers of sliced turkey and Swiss cheese. I offered the plate to Claudia, who shook her head. I took a sandwich and made myself eat a bite, even though I wasn't feeling hungry. Protein was a good idea, especially as the food at the thank-you tea had been heavy on the sweet and starchy.

I closed my eyes for a moment, remembering how pleased I had been with the tea, how hopeful that it would be the start of a successful launch for the tearoom. Now Sylvia's death had thrown everything into doubt. I couldn't bear to think of losing all that I'd worked so hard for.

A motorcycle engine roared to a halt outside, and the next minute I heard boots clomping on the porch. I glanced toward the hall.

"Is every cop in town going to descend on us?" I muttered, putting my sandwich on my plate.

Claudia gave a soft laugh. "Just wait until the media shows up."

I raised my eyes to her. "Oh, no!"

A crescendo of voices in the hall was followed by the appearance in the parlor of a uniformed policeman and a surly-looking Hispanic man in a black motorcycle jacket. The policeman pointed at me.

"This is the owner."

I stood and offered a hand. "Ellen Rosings."

The motorcycle man pulled an ID case from one of his many pockets and flipped it open to show me his gold badge. "Detective Antonio Aragón." He looked around at the parlor with a small sneer of distaste. "You got room where we can talk, Ms. Rosings?"

"My office. It's upstairs."

"Fine," he said, and headed out to the hall.

I glanced at Claudia. "Please excuse me."

"Ask him how soon we can go," Claudia said, taking her cell phone from her purse.

"I will," I told her.

Detective Aragón was talking with two of the cops. I started up the stairs, but he called me back.

"Say, Ms. Rosings, could you look in here a minute?"

He led me to the dining parlor. The police had now strung yellow "crime scene" tape across the open doorway, and I saw that they had brought in bright lights. Three of them were clustered around Sylvia's body.

My heart skipped a beat as I caught sight of her legs, sprawled with her green velvet skirt—classic Santa Fe Lady style—clumped awkwardly about them. I was thankful that I couldn't see her face, though I doubted I'd ever forget what it looked like.

Detective Aragón ducked under the yellow tape, then pulled it up with one hand and gestured to me to join him. I did so, albeit reluctantly.

"You were having a tea party in here, right?"

"Yes."

"Could you show us where the deceased was sitting?"

His smile was crooked, his eyes narrow, watching me. I swallowed and looked at the table.

"The farthest seat on the right side," I said.

One of the cops in the room glanced toward me. "This one?" he said, holding a hand over my chair at the end of the table.

"No, the one just beside that. Her name is on the place card."

The cop moved his hand over the chair that had been Sylvia's and I nodded, then turned to the detective. His smile was gone; in its place a look of speculation.

"Thanks," he said. "Now where's your office?"

I led him upstairs, trying to calm my nerves. My office shares a door with that of my office manager. It stood open, both rooms dark; Kris had left at five. I was grateful that she wouldn't be involved in this mess, though it seemed ironic that the only one of my staff who wasn't present when Sylvia had died was the goth.

Was murdered, I thought. No one had said that word aloud yet. I could still see the swath of yellow heishi tight around her neck.

It's lemon agate. Thought that would be appropriate for tea, ha ha.

The memory of Sylvia's jolly voice made the muscles in my shoulders tighten. Trying to shrug it off, I flipped the light switch and went to my desk. The stained glass chandelier sent a warm glow through the room.

"Please sit down," I told the detective, and tidied some papers on my desk.

He stood in the doorway looking around the office as he unfastened his leather jacket. The space is unusual; the upstairs rooms all have sloping ceilings, due to the house's design. His eyes moved restlessly as if trying to absorb every detail of the room.

Dark eyes, and I noticed they had long lashes. He was handsome in a very classic, Latin way, though the short, militaristic hairstyle wasn't my favorite on men. He would have been much more handsome if he ever really smiled.

He gave a disapproving glance at my reading couch, a green velvet chaise longue against the south wall beneath a bead-fringed lamp. "Nice setup," he said, pulling a visitor's chair up to my desk and draping his jacket over its back. He didn't sound as if he meant it as a compliment.

I folded my hands. "Have you any idea when my staff and Mrs. Pearson will be allowed to leave?"

"Have to interview them first. Okay if I use your office here?"

"Of course," I said. My voice sounded a trifle stiff, but I couldn't help it. I was tired and nervous and beginning to feel shock-struck.

"Great." Detective Aragón took out a much-crumpled pocket notepad and a ballpoint pen. "Now, you found the body, right?"

"Yes."

"When was this?"

"It must have been just before six. I'd been saying goodbye to my guests—"

"So some of them had left?"

"Yes, most of them."

"I'll need a list of everyone that was at the tea party."

I leafed through my papers and extracted the seating chart I'd drawn up. "Here you are," I said, handing it to him.

He blinked at it, then looked up at me in vague surprise. "You do this every time you have a party?"

"For every formal party, yes."

He laughed under his breath and shook his head, folding the page and tucking it behind his notepad. "Okay, so who was still here when you found the body?"

"My staff, and Claudia Pearson. They're all downstairs, waiting," I added.

"Anyone else? Any customers?"

"Not that I know of. Our grand opening is Friday, though we did have some walk-ins today. Iz was out front, she should be able to tell you when the last customers left."

"Iz?"

"Isabel. Naranjo. She's one of my servers."

"Did anyone else see the body?"

"Yes, Vi was with me. Violetta Benning."

He looked up. *"Violetta?"*

"Her mother's an opera buff."

Detective Aragón stared, his face incredulous. Finally he scowled and scribbled in his notebook.

"Benning. Okay, now could you describe the body as you found it?"

I did so, as briefly as I could while still mentioning the details I had noticed. He took notes without commenting, only looking up at me now and then with that appraising gaze.

"The necklace wasn't around her neck when we got here."

"No—I thought there might be a chance..." I swallowed, unable to continue.

"So you removed it. You realize that's tampering with evidence."

I glanced up at him angrily. "I was trying to save her life!"

He held my gaze and I felt like I was being weighed. Refusing to be intimidated, I stared back. A distant thumping testified to the activities of the police downstairs. At last Detective Aragón looked down at his notes.

"Did you know the deceased—ah, Mrs. Carruthers. Did you know her well?"

"Not personally. She was a great help to me in acquiring the tearoom."

"How so?"

"She knew of some grants that were available for historic preservation, and helped me meet the requirements and submit the applications. Without the grant money I couldn't have afforded to remodel and open the tearoom. She also put in a good word for me with the mortgage company."

He leaned back in his chair and cocked his head. "Why did she do all that for you?"

"She wanted to make sure this building was preserved. And she's—was—also a friend of my aunt's."

Poor Nat! I'd have to call her.

"Your aunt. What's her name?"

"Natasha Wheeler. She was one of the guests at the tea."

He unfolded the seating chart and made a note, then looked up at me. "So Sylvia Carruthers helped you."

"Yes. In fact I organized the tea to thank her, among others." I banished a momentary wish that I hadn't done so.

His glance flicked to the seating chart. "And these others. Can you think of any reason one of them would want to kill

Mrs. Carruthers?"

My heart seized with dismay. "So it's officially a murder investigation."

His eyes narrowed. "Suspicious death, until we get the autopsy results, but yeah. Looks to me like someone offed her."

I swallowed, thinking that he must be deliberately trying to provoke me. I would not, however, be tricked into incivility.

The silence stretched. Finally Detective Aragón leaned back in his chair.

"So how about it? Any reason one of your party guests would want to kill her?"

"I can't think of any reason," I said slowly, "but I don't know all of the guests well."

"Which ones do you know well?"

"My aunt, of course, and Gina Fiorello. She's a dear friend, who was here because she helped me get the tearoom ready to open. She doesn't know Sylvia Carruthers. Didn't," I corrected, exasperated with myself.

This was all so awkward! I wondered fleetingly if Miss Manners had any advice for proper conduct of murder investigations.

Detective Aragón kept taking notes. After a minute he looked up at me expectantly.

"I'm fairly well acquainted with Katie Hutchins," I said. "She's a neighbor, she runs the Territorial B&B across the street. Vince Margolan is another neighbor. He's in the process of setting up a gallery next to the B&B. I've only met him once or twice, though."

Aware that I was babbling, I stopped and watched the detective writing in his notepad. It felt surreal to be discussing the murder in such ordinary terms. A part of me felt like screaming.

"What about...Claudia Pearson?" he said, glancing up from

my seating chart.

I cleared my throat. "I've met her several times before today. She works with the Santa Fe Preservation Trust, of which Sylvia was president."

"And Manny Salazar?"

"He's one of my suppliers and a friend of my aunt's."

He referred to the chart. "That leaves Thomas Ingraham and Donna Carruthers."

"I met them both for the first time today. Mr. Ingraham is a food critic for the *New Mexican*, also a friend of my aunt's. Ms. Carruthers is Sylvia's daughter."

He nodded. "I'm going to need everyone's phone numbers."

"Mrs. Pearson is downstairs, waiting to talk to you."

"Yeah. How about the rest?"

I turned on my computer and read him the numbers from my organizer. I was beginning to feel impatient, but I certainly wasn't about to let Detective Aragón know it.

"What about the other customers? Do you have any names or numbers for them?"

"I wouldn't count on it. They were walk-ins."

Rudeness is a handy tool for the investigator, I suppose. Being subjected to a flat stare would make anyone restless and uncomfortable, anxious to fill the silence by talking. Perhaps it was stubborn of me, and perhaps unwise, but I was determined not to respond to such tactics. I waited, returning his gaze.

At last he spoke. "So, you have no idea why anyone would want to kill her?"

"I'm afraid not. She was a little abrasive, perhaps, but that's hardly enough to provoke a murder. I certainly wish whoever killed her hadn't chosen to do it here."

His eyebrows twitched into a slight frown, as if he'd been struck by a new thought. "Who else knew she was going to be here?"

I shrugged. "The people at the Trust, I suppose. I don't know who else. I believe her husband is deceased."

"Uh-huh." His eyelids drooped again. "So—did you kill her?"

I was stunned, then angry. I raised my chin, a subtlety that was no doubt lost on him.

"No, I did not! I have every reason to be grateful to her, and I'm horrified that someone—"

I stopped, aware that I was raising my voice. I took a slow breath before speaking again.

"Obviously, I'm upset that this happened. Will there be anything else, Detective Aragón?"

The corner of his mouth turned upward, though his eyes remained hard. "Nah. No offense, I hope. Gotta ask."

"Of course you do."

I turned off my computer and collected my paperwork, tucking it out of the way into a drawer as I sought to regain my composure. I then stood, and to his credit Detective Aragón got to his feet at once. His mother must have taught him the basics of civility, even if his manners were rusty from disuse.

I stepped out from behind my desk, indicating with a gesture that he was welcome to use it. "My chef has made coffee. Shall I send some up for you?"

"Not gonna offer me some tea?" His face revealed nothing, but I heard the disdain in his voice.

Two could play at that game. I gazed at him innocently. "Would you prefer tea?"

He held my gaze for a moment, and a sudden smile quirked up his mouth. To my surprise, this time it reached his eyes.

"Nah. Coffee's fine."

"Cream and sugar?"

"Black."

I nodded politely and started to go out. He called after me.

"Oh, hey, would you send up, ah—Claudia Pearson?"

He stood behind my desk, hunched a little beneath the sloping ceiling, notepad in hand, looking altogether out of place in his motorcycle gear amid my Victorian decor. Suddenly he was the one who seemed awkward.

"All right," I said, and left, relieved to be done with the interview.

I walked to the head of the stairs and stopped, heart pounding.

There was a dead body below. I did not want to return to face the upheaval.

I glanced toward my office, feeling an urge to ask the detective to escort me down, but that was foolish. I gave my head a brief shake and straightened my shoulders.

Cops drink coffee.

He wasn't part of my world, wouldn't understand my world. No doubt he wouldn't know what to do with a bone china cup and saucer. I was on my own. As usual.

I took a deep breath and went downstairs.

2

As it happened, I didn't see Detective Aragón again for hours. One by one he summoned everyone upstairs to be interviewed, then set them free. I sent the staff home as they were released, it being obvious that we would not be allowed to clean up the dining parlor for some time.

"I can stay, boss," Julio said, pulling off his chef's coat after he came down from being interviewed. He hung the coat on a hook by the door and went to the counter, looking lean in a muscle shirt and his festive chef's pants. I stared at a tattoo design circling his upper arm—I hadn't seen it before. It was high enough to be hidden by a t-shirt sleeve, and t-shirts were what he'd usually worn until that morning.

"No, go home," I told him. "You need to be here early to bake."

He started measuring beans into the grinder for yet another pot of coffee. "We gonna open tomorrow?"

"Of course we are."

If we didn't, we might never open again. We had to weather this. It would be all right. If I kept telling myself that, maybe I'd believe it.

I watched him, looking for a sign of rebellion. If Julio quit, I'd be in big trouble. He didn't say anything, just kept working.

A loud rapping at the front door made me step into the hall. The front door was closed at last; apparently all the cops who could fit into the dining parlor were already in there.

Bright, white light shone in through the small windows called "lights" that surrounded the door, along with occasional flashes from the emergency vehicles still parked out front. It looked like there were camera crews out on the sidewalk beyond the picket fence. I hoped they wouldn't come any closer.

I walked to the door, my steps echoing from the hardwood floor. Peeking out through the lights, I recognized the giant poppies on the dress outside, and pulled the door open.

"Gina!"

She caught me in a tight hug. I almost lost it right then, but I managed to step back, pulling her in with me.

"Thanks for coming back."

She grinned, cheeks dimpling deeply. "You kidding? I love circuses. Where's your TV? I bet this makes the ten o'clock news."

I closed my eyes. "I don't want to know."

"Yes, you do, it's important!"

I sighed, starting toward the kitchen. "It's in storage. Have you eaten?"

I had rented a storage shed for some of my parents' furniture that wasn't suited to the tearoom but that I couldn't bear to part with. The television had gone there as well, and I'd been so busy I hadn't missed it.

"Not since the tea," Gina said. "Come home with me and we'll get a pizza."

"No, I'm not leaving." I led her into the kitchen and looked around for the sandwiches. Julio must have put them away. He was nowhere in sight.

"You need to get away from all this nutzy police stuff. Hi," Gina added, smiling at a blond evidence technician who came in and reached for the coffee pot.

My hand went out toward it automatically. "It's still—"

The tech pulled the pot out of the coffee maker and held his mug over the burner, catching the stream. A slight smell of burned coffee rose from the little that had splashed on the burner.

"—brewing," I said.

The tech smiled at me, blue eyes behind wire-framed glasses. He was younger than me, looked like he should still be in high school. I felt tired, all of a sudden.

We didn't talk while the tech's mug slowly filled. He replaced the coffee pot, shoveled two heaping spoonfuls of sugar into the mug and stirred it with the sugar spoon, then went back upstairs.

Julio came in again, wearing a leather jacket and escorting Vi, whose shoulders slumped. "We're going, boss. Vi's gonna give me a ride home."

"Thanks, Vi. If you want you can take tomorrow off."

She gave me a wan smile that didn't erase the frown lines on her brow. "I'll be all right. Iz has a test."

"Okay. Get some sleep, though."

"You too, boss."

I nodded, though I doubted I'd be getting much rest that night. They went out the kitchen door onto the back porch, leaving me and Gina alone. I could hear Mick and Dee, still waiting to be interviewed, talking quietly in the butler's pantry.

"'Boss'?" Gina said, opening the door of the refrigerator and peering inside. "I thought you'd nixed that."

I sighed. "We're still negotiating what they should call me. Julio suggested 'jefa' but to me that sounds too much like 'heifer'."

"How about 'Madam'?"

"Too stiff. Besides, we're a block away from the Palace. It might suggest connotations that aren't appropriate for the tearoom."

The Palace Restaurant had once been a famous brothel. Gina guffawed.

"Right now it's 'Ms. Rosings,' but none of us like that

much," I added. "Trouble is, 'boss' is much easier to say. I'll probably give in and let them call me 'Ellen,' much as I hate to yield to modern informality."

Gina gave a gasp of mock horror. "What will Miss Manners say?"

"Scoff if you like," I said haughtily.

Gina looked at me over her shoulder. "Getting a little tired? I've got a nice, comfy spare bed, you know."

"I'm not going to leave while the police are crawling all over the place. This is my home!"

"Okay, okay!" She pulled a bowl of leftover chocolate mousse out of the fridge and put it in my hands, then took my arm. "Come on, girlfriend. Let's go sit by the fire."

We scrounged up two spoons and went back to Iris. The fire had died down again. I pulled a log from the carrier Dee had left and laid it on top of the coals, then sat staring at it, watching the first tendrils of smoke begin to rise.

Gina wrapped my hand around a spoon. "Eat your medicine."

I gave a half-hearted laugh. "Trying to make me fat?"

"Trying to get some sustenance into you. You didn't eat much at the tea."

"Too nervous."

"You need something in your stomach. It's going to be a long night, if you're staying here."

"Yes, Italian Mama."

Chocolate is such good comfort food. I took a spoonful of mousse and let it melt on my tongue. The energy of the adrenaline rush was long gone, and it was really starting to sink in.

There'd been a murder in my tearoom, in my beautiful dining parlor. A room I'd worked so hard to make inviting and peaceful.

Gina leaned forward and scooped up a spoonful of

mousse. "So who do you think did it?"

I shrugged. "I have no idea."

"Come on, you've got to have some suspicions."

"Can we talk about something else?"

"No, because that would be a stupid conversation, because we'd really be thinking about the murder."

She sat in the wing chair with her arms draped over the armrests, spoon dangling from one hand, looking regal and righteous, her hair a dark, curly halo. I pictured her reigning over a court of nineteenth-century Italians, all of whom cowered before her, and had to smile.

"Now," she said, "who can you eliminate?"

"You. Unless you're the killer?"

"No, I'm not so crude in my methods," she said airily. "There are legal ways to destroy people."

I laughed, shaking my head. Gina wouldn't hurt a fly. She's the sort of person who'd give her last dollar to someone in need.

"And Aunt Nat," I said. "She was friends with Mrs. Carruthers."

Gina raised an admonitory finger. "Ah, ah—friends can have fights."

"But did they look like they were angry with each other? No. Besides, Sylvia was still in the dining parlor when I came out with Nat and Manny and watched them leave together."

"By the front door?"

"Yes. I saw them drive off in Manny's car."

"And they never left your sight?"

"No."

"Good, that eliminates them."

"You're enjoying this."

She tilted her head and shrugged. "Might as well."

I ate another spoonful of chocolate. My stomach growled, probably from being clenched for hours.

"So, not me, not you, not Nat, not Manny," Gina said, frowning in concentration. "That leaves six suspects."

"Five. I don't think she strangled herself."

"Five, right."

"Plus the staff and the customers. And anyone else who might have slipped in."

She waved a hand in dismissal. "We'll worry about them later. The people who were at the tea are the primary suspects. They had immediate access to the dining room."

"You like watching cop shows, don't you?"

"Love 'em. Don't change the subject."

"That *is* the subject!"

"Who are the five suspects?" She ticked off the fingers on one hand. "That food critic."

"Mr. Ingraham."

"And Sylvia's daughter, Donna? Donna," she said as I nodded. "Then that guy who's opening the gallery..."

"Vince Margolan. And Katie Hutchins, but I don't think she'd do it. She's so sweet, and what would she have to gain?"

"We'll leave her on the list for now." Gina looked at her protruding thumb. "Who else?"

"Claudia Pearson."

Hasty footsteps in the hall made us look up. Iz came in wearing a long coat over her lavender dress, purse strap over her shoulder. Her cheeks were flushed.

"That guy is *so rude!*"

"What guy?" Gina asked, looking from Iz to me.

"Detective Aragón."

Gina turned to Iz, curiosity glowing in her face. "What did he say?"

"He asked all kinds of nosy questions about the customers. Then he asked if I killed that poor lady, and I said no. So he asked if I thought *you* had done it," she said, turning to me with an angry throb in her voice.

"It's his job, I'm afraid," I said. "I'm sorry, Iz."

"It isn't *your* fault he's a jerk." She tugged her coat closed and started doing up the buttons.

I had never seen Iz so emotional. Usually she's so quiet you don't even know she's there.

"Just go home and try to forget about it," I said. "Vi said you had a test tomorrow, so get some rest."

She looked up and brushed her dark hair back from her face. "I will. Sorry I dumped on you. Like you need it, on top of all this! I'm sorry, boss."

I stood up and gave her a little hug. "Don't worry about it, Iz. We'll see you Friday."

"Okay."

"Oh, you might want to go out the back door. There was a news crew out front."

She shot a glowering look toward the front of the tearoom. "Thanks for the warning. My car's out back anyway."

We listened to her footsteps die away down the hall. Gina looked at me.

"He thinks you're a suspect."

I opened my hands. "We're all suspects."

She didn't answer. Perhaps she'd realized it really wasn't a game. I passed the chocolate mousse to her and she ate a spoonful, looking thoughtful.

"You've eliminated Manny and Nat," she said. "Is there anyone else we can rule out?"

I sighed, thinking back to when the party had broken up. "When I left the dining parlor, Katie Hutchins was still there talking with Sylvia, and Vince Margolan was talking with Donna. You had already left, right?"

Gina nodded. "I came down to the gift shop. I saw Mr. Ingraham go out the front door."

"So he's accounted for." I frowned. "Trouble is, someone could have come in again by the back."

"Wouldn't Julio have seen them go past the kitchen?"

"I guess so."

"Or one of the servers might have noticed anyone in the hall."

I leaned back in my chair. "Maybe we should leave this to the police."

Gina put down the mousse and reached over to clasp my hand. "Sorry, honey. I didn't mean to get you down. I thought it might help to be working at the problem."

I gave her a feeble smile. "Thanks. But I guess the police know what they're doing. I hope they do."

"They could miss something."

"Speaking of missing something, if Detective Aragón finds out you're here you'll get grilled. You might want to slip away."

She shrugged. "Gonna happen sooner or later. Did he ask you who you saw in the room as you left?"

"N-no. But he'll probably ask everyone about their own movements, and then try to verify it."

I felt restless all at once. The suggestion that the police might make mistakes in this investigation made me uncomfortable. I picked up the mousse bowl and scraped the last spoonful out of it, then stood.

"I'd better check on the coffee situation. Want to come with me?"

"Sure."

We went to the kitchen, where we found Mick standing with the clean, empty coffee pot in hand, looking doubtfully at the coffee maker. His long ponytail hung down his back, blond like his sister Dee's. I took the pot from him and gave him the mousse bowl.

"Could you wash this, please? I'll make more coffee."

He looked relieved. "Sure."

"Thanks, Mick."

The simple task of making coffee was oddly soothing. Gina leaned against the counter, watching. As the pot burbled away I tidied up, sponging up spills, refilling the cream pitcher and putting a fresh spoon in the sugar bowl. I put some more clean spoons out along with a little plate to put used ones on, in an attempt to preserve the sugar from further violation. Probably futile, but I had to try.

Slow, heavy steps and a rolling sound came from in the hall. I stepped out and watched as two men pushed a gurney bearing a black plastic body bag out of the dining parlor. They went out the front door toward the waiting ambulance, which had shut off its lights.

"That'll look great on the evening news," Gina murmured behind me.

I shot her a glance, but before I could answer I saw Dee coming down the stairs. I went to the foot of the staircase to meet her.

"He wants to talk to Mick," she said, her voice full of repressed excitement.

I watched her. "You all right?"

"Fine. It's so interesting!"

"Interesting?" I said blankly.

"I'm taking a criminal science class. Actually, I'm thinking about making it my major."

"Oh."

"I can't wait to tell the professor about this!" Dee glanced toward the front door. "It's dark," she said, sounding surprised.

"Well, it's almost nine. Do you want a ride home?"

"I can take you," Gina offered.

"Thanks!"

Mick came out of the butler's pantry. Dee grabbed him in a quick hug, then went down the hall to fetch her coat.

"Detective Aragón is ready for you," I said to Mick.

He nodded, gazing after his sister as he took off his apron. He was two years older and had his own place, but they were still close.

"Shall I come back?" Gina asked.

"No, it looks like it's winding down," I said, stepping aside as two more cops emerged from the dining parlor.

"Sure you don't want to spend the night at my place?"

I shook my head. "Thanks, though."

She caught me in a swift, tight hug. "Okay. Call if you need anything, even just to talk."

"I will. Thank you for coming. Having company helped."

She smooched my cheek, then let me go and collected her coat. I walked her to the door, where Dee was waiting, and watched them hustle down the sidewalk past the news crews.

The house was getting quiet at last, though I could still hear people moving around in the dining parlor. I wandered through the front rooms: the parlors that I'd divided into the gift shop and eight cozy alcoves for groups having tea. Naming the alcoves after flowers now seemed frivolous, though at the time I'd thought of it I had felt clever. The flower theme reflected the wisterias that draped the front of the house, and they in turn had inspired the tearoom's name.

I'm especially glad you chose to celebrate the wisterias. We had the hardest time keeping the law firm from chopping them down. Had to take them to court once.

Sylvia's words, that afternoon at the tea. Just a few hours ago.

A wave of grief washed through me. It didn't matter that we hadn't been close.

Fighting tears, I collected the tea things from Iris and took them to the butler's pantry. As I returned to the hall, Mick came down the stairs with Detective Aragón on his heels.

"You want me to stay so I can wash up?"

I glanced at Detective Aragón, who shook his head. "No," I

said. "We'll worry about it tomorrow."

I followed Mick to the back door and locked it behind him. When I turned around, the detective was right behind me.

"Could you come upstairs, please?"

"All right."

He led the way, the thud of his motorcycle boots deadened by the carpet runner on the steps. I wondered if he'd thought of more questions, but instead of going back to my office he stopped and indicated the door opposite.

"This door is locked," he said.

"Yes, that's my private suite," I told him. "It's been locked all day."

"You live here? In Cinderella land?"

He sounded incredulous. I bristled, but kept my voice calm. "At the moment, yes."

He ran a hand over his short, dark hair. "Well, I need to look in there. Open it."

My private space. My last refuge.

"I'd prefer not to," I said. "It was locked, it has nothing to do with—with what happened here today."

His eyes narrowed. "Look, it's been a long day. Why don't you just make it easy on all of us and open the door?"

I'd had it. It probably would have been easier if I'd done as he'd asked, but I was tired of being helpful and receiving no thanks for it.

"I don't see why I should," I said, keeping my voice polite. "It has nothing to do with your investigation."

"I need to look in that room."

"Why?"

He didn't answer. His eyes just got meaner.

I was sad and weary and fed up with his bullying. I straightened my shoulders and summoned my best diplomatic voice.

"If you have a valid reason to search my private rooms,

Detective, then you'd better get a warrant. You won't set foot in there without one."

For a moment he looked so angry that I thought he was capable of anything. I was actually frightened, but I didn't want to let him know it so I held still and waited.

"Fine," he said at last, and turned away.

He clomped down the stairs two at a time. It wasn't until I heard the front door slam that I breathed a sigh of relief.

3

After that, I couldn't very well go into my bedroom, not while the investigators were still in the house. I fetched a book from my office, made myself a pot of peppermint tea, and went back once more to Iris to sit by the fire. The book couldn't hold my interest, though. Too much had happened, and I found myself thinking over the day's events.

Where had I been when Sylvia died? In the hall? At the front door?

I hadn't heard any sound of a scuffle, nor, apparently, had anyone else. My staff had been nearby, in and out of the butler's pantry and the kitchen. The murder must have been very quick.

The horror of it made me close my eyes, and I felt a familiar spiral of despair pulling me downward. I sat up and inhaled sharply, looking at the chair across from me where Gina had sat.

I could not, *dared* not let this defeat me. I had to fight it. It would be all too easy to give in to depression after something like this, but I knew that if I did, I would lose the tearoom that I'd worked so hard to create, and in which I had invested everything I had, financially and emotionally.

So I'd fight for it. All I could think of was to try to figure out who had killed Sylvia. The police would do their job, but they had no personal stake in identifying her killer. I did.

I half expected Detective Aragón to show up brandishing a search warrant, but he must have had more promising fish to fry. He didn't return, and soon I heard the remaining police coming down the hall. I got up to meet them.

The blond evidence tech was in the lead. He smiled at me. "We're though."

"May I go into the room to clean up?" I asked.

He nodded. "Got everything there was to get. Thanks for the coffee and all."

"You're welcome."

I saw them out and locked the front door. The street was mostly back to normal, only occasional traffic that late on a week night. The news crews had gone away. I watched the cops climb into a couple of SUVs and drive off, thankful for the silence left behind.

A breeze stirred the hanging clusters of wisteria blossoms on the front porch. Pretty, but in my present state of mind they also seemed melancholy.

I wasn't looking forward to clearing the dining parlor, but it had to be done. I wouldn't be able to sleep knowing the mess was still there, and besides, I needed to go into the room and face my feelings about the murder.

I went to the butler's pantry to fetch a tray. On impulse, I turned on the sound system that piped music into all the public rooms, and put on a lively Vivaldi mandolin concerto. Music filled the house, and I immediately felt less gloomy.

The yellow tape was gone from the door to the dining parlor. The furniture had been pulled all about, and coffee mugs sat on every flat surface including the floor, but beyond that the room didn't look too bad. I half expected to see a chalk outline of Sylvia's body on the floor, but apparently that's a cinematic trope. The only sign of where she had lain was the space that had been cleared around where she had fallen.

I stood looking down at that space, remembering. Poor Sylvia. No one deserved to die like that.

Swallowing, I turned to work. Everything on the north sideboard had been shoved to one end, no doubt to make room for some piece of forensic equipment. I put the tray down on the empty space and began collecting coffee mugs and china. By some miracle, not a single piece had been broken by the mob of police investigators, though everything was smeared with black fingerprint powder.

As I picked up each place setting at the table, Gina's game of whodunnit returned to me. I gathered the place cards and shuffled through them, looking at the names I'd calligraphed so carefully. I couldn't eliminate any of Gina's five suspects, though I felt pretty confident Mr. Ingraham wasn't the killer. Maybe I'd talk to Katie, ask her who was still in the dining parlor when she'd left it.

Of course I'd talk to Katie. She'd want to know all about the investigation. She was probably worrying how it would affect *her* business.

I fitted a teapot into the last empty space on the tray and paused. The saddest part of this mess was that the tearoom had been my salvation. Before I had decided to take the plunge and try to make it happen, I had been mired in despair.

The tearoom's genesis, though I didn't know it at the time, was a trip my family took to England—the last vacation we all took together. I was eighteen, about to head for college, and in love with English literature and history. My brother Joe was twenty-four and more interested in crawling pubs than visiting historic sites. While he was off exerting his independence, my parents took me to museums, famous buildings, and afternoon tea at the Ritz.

I fell in love. The dainty sandwiches and cakes, the scones, and especially the profound revelation of clotted cream—a food unlike any in America, so simple yet so sinfully rich— were such a delightful treat that I begged my parents to take me again the next day, and the day after that. We ended up having tea all over London, Brighton, and Bath. Even Joe got into the spirit of it, and found little places with no more than six elbow-rubbing tables that served cream tea and hot lunches. It was the trip of a lifetime.

The following year my mother was diagnosed with cancer. She never traveled again, spending the last two years of her life in a losing battle against that dreadful disease.

Dad was crushed when she died, and he never really got his spirits back. He passed on four years later, just as I was out of graduate school.

I spent a year in a tailspin after settling my father's estate. I gave all the cash I inherited to Joe in exchange for his share of the house on Stagecoach Road, in the hilly, northern part of Santa Fe. That house was much too big for me, though. A huge hacienda-style, single-story adobe laid out in a square around a center courtyard, what in a true hacienda would be called a *plazuela*.

That had been my favorite part of the house. I'd always thought of it as my secret garden, where I played and threw parties for my imaginary friends. After Dad died, I sat there for hours on end, trying to figure out what to do with myself.

Joe had moved to New York a few years earlier. Gina was away finishing a master's degree at Wellesley College. I wrote despairing letters to them both and burned hundreds of phone minutes, but even though they poured out love and sympathy, I couldn't shake out of my gloom. It was Aunt Nat who finally gave me a much-needed kick in the pants.

"Ellen, you need to figure out where you're going," she said to me over tea in my courtyard, wearing shades and a broad-brimmed straw hat adorned with yellow silk chrysanthemums. "You need to let go of the past, no matter how fond the memories are. You have a life, so get going and find it!"

"Where?" I asked her. Almost a year after Dad's death I was still numb. I felt as if I'd never have an idea again.

"Well, first question: do you want to stay in Santa Fe?"

"Yes."

Santa Fe was my home. Though I had gone away to school and traveled a fair amount, I never found any place I'd rather live.

"Next question: what career can you have in Santa Fe?"

I couldn't come up with anything. My degrees in literature and music probably weren't going to get me a job in Santa Fe. I could try for a teaching certification, but the best I could hope for was teaching high school English, and I couldn't drum up any enthusiasm for that.

"Can't we just have tea?" I said, knowing I was ducking the question.

"Certainly. That's an excellent idea. You remember the afternoon tea we had at the Biltmore that time in LA?"

I frowned. "Sure."

"You can do better than that," she said loftily. "You've done a beautiful job with this little tea for us two."

I blinked, looking over the cafe table I had set with my favorite china: teacups and matching plates, tiny silver teaspoons, a pair of tiny violet chintz milk and sugar servers, and a three-tiered tea tray loaded with all my favorite little comfort-food nibbles.

"It's just cucumber sandwiches and deviled eggs—"

"And these cookies, which are divine," Nat said, waving a thumbprint cookie filled with red currant preserves.

"I like to bake."

"Well, why hide it under a bushel? Share your talent with the world, darling!"

"What are you talking about?"

Nat took off her shades and leaned toward me, the skin at the corners of her eyes crinkling as she grinned. "You just want to have tea. So open a tearoom."

I stared at her. "Me?"

"Why not? You've always loved tea parties!"

"But, I—"

"You love planning menus, and you love English culture and tradition. Ellen, tea is an up and coming trend. If you find the right location, I think it would be a big hit."

"Wait, whoa—"

"You love the Victorian era, too. I think you should make all the decorations Victorian. In fact, there are some Victorian buildings in town—you should see if any of them are available."

"Nat!"

"What?"

She looked up at me, teacup in hand, all innocence. I knew what she was doing, and that I should be grateful, but I was too annoyed.

"I don't have any training or experience in the restaurant business," I said flatly.

"So what? That's the beauty of entrepreneurialism. All you need is vision and investment capital. You've got both. Hire good people to help you with the rest, and you'll be fine."

"A tearoom."

"You've been chattering about English tearooms ever since you and your folks took that trip. You've been throwing tea parties ever since then, too. You *love* tea and all its trappings. Why not take it a step further?"

I just shook my head. Nat put her teacup down and took my hand.

"Listen, honey, you've got to get out of this old house. Remember how you complained about the property taxes?"

I nodded. They'd taken a big bite out of my cash reserves. I still wasn't working, and I'd have to get a job soon if I wanted to keep my head above water.

"Let's go look at some Victorians in town, huh? Maybe you'll see one you'd like to trade for this white elephant. I'll call Jody and have her look at what's on the market. It'll be fun."

"Okay," I said, wanting to end the argument. "It doesn't cost anything to look."

Nat's friend Jody, a real estate agent, spent an afternoon showing us Victorian era buildings in Santa Fe. I figured it was just a lark, and made up my mind to enjoy the tour. Several were wonderful old adobe homes with soft lines, crooked doorways and uneven floors and yes, secret gardens. I had a nice time wandering through them, and was grateful to Aunt Nat for getting me out of my cocoon.

By the time we reached the Dusenberry house, I was tired. Nat and I stood on the front walk while Jody retrieved the key.

The house was neither large nor ornate, originally built in the mid-nineteenth century as officer's quarters for Fort Marcy. It was stuccoed in adobe-brown, and in fact was made of adobe, in classic Victorian shotgun style with a blue pitched metal roof. It was Territorial, really: the 19th century New Mexico style that evolved out of trying to make neoclassical structures with southwestern building materials. Early Victorians wanted their columns and Grecian dentations, but out here they had to make them out of wood instead of marble.

The place was vacant and looked a bit forlorn, the leaves of the wisteria vines that twined up the columns of the porch all fragile and withered in shades of gold, green and frostbitten brown (it was autumn). A sharp wind was kicking up, and when Jody got the door open and let us in I had a grateful sense of stepping into shelter.

Our footsteps on the hardwood floors echoed in the empty rooms and hallway. The southeast room on the ground floor was the kitchen, and the rest had been used as offices by the law firm that had most recently occupied the house. They had done some remodeling including the addition of pocket doors as dividers in the ground floor office areas (a nice 19th century touch, probably a concession to historic preservation

requirements). They had also added a restroom on the ground
floor and a remodeled full bath upstairs.

"It really isn't suited to be a home as it is," Jody said.
"You'd want to make some changes."

Nat hadn't told her about the tearoom idea, just that I
wanted to look at Victorian properties.

"Can we look at the upstairs?" I asked.

As we climbed the old wooden staircase, a curious thing
began to happen. I began to see things—a plush, oriental
runner covering the worn treads of the stairs, the walls painted
in quiet pastel tones with white trim, candlelight and
lamplight warming the rooms—all of it creating a mood of
peace. I was having ideas, for the first time in months.

As we reached the top of the stairs we turned to face west
down the hall, and I saw that the clouds outside had broken
up and late afternoon sunlight was streaming in through the
window at the far end. I had an impression of ascending to
heaven, and again a sense of peace.

I walked down the hall and stood looking out at the
withered garden and the roof of the porch below. A few
tendrils of the wisteria vines struggled for a grip on the ribbed
metal.

"I wonder how old those wisterias are," I mused.

"The Preservation Trust might know," said Nat. "They
keep track of the oddest little details. My friend Sylvia, who's
the president of the Trust, told me there's a wisteria vine in
Santa Fe that's almost ninety years old."

"Really? How nice to have flowers every spring for that
many years."

The door to the north side of the upper floor stood ajar,
and I went in and stood in the middle of the front room by the
big, brick shaft of the double chimney that served the
fireplaces downstairs. I felt safe there. Maybe not joyous yet,
but also not sad. It felt cozy, which was a much better

sensation than the vast emptiness of my parents' lonely old house. I looked out into the hall, where Jody and Nat were standing together, giving me space.

"What's the asking price?" I said.

That was the turning point. I didn't know if I could afford the house, didn't know if I wanted it just for myself or to share (it was smaller than my parents' place, but still too big just for me), or for this tearoom that Nat had suggested. Jody got me the specs and the owner's asking price. It was steep, which was probably why the house hadn't been snapped up. That and the funky oldness of it, and the historical designation that restricted remodeling.

I visited the house again, alone except for Jody who agreed to wait on the porch while I spent some time inside. I walked through all the rooms, trying to imagine leasing them out, but kept finding myself picturing tea parties instead. I thought back to my family's trip to England and the way I had fallen in love with English tea customs. *Those* memories made me smile.

After walking through the whole house again, I joined Jody outside on the porch. Fallen wisteria leaves blew around our feet and danced in little eddies in the corners. Snowflakes were just beginning to swirl down from a blue-gray sky.

"I'd like to make an offer on it," I said to Jody. "Can you list my parents' house?"

From then on I was caught up in a whirlwind of activity. I learned more than I ever wanted to know about real estate and mortgages and business loans. Nat introduced me to Sylvia Carruthers, who cheerfully bullied me into applying for a grant and agreeing to the Preservation Trust's terms for maintaining the historic character of the building. I acquired the Dusenberry house several months before Stagecoach Road sold (*that* was a nervous time), and was able to move in at my leisure.

I chose the south side of the upper floor, where the full bath was tucked behind what must have been two executive offices, for my suite. I brought only the items I most loved from home, along with those bits of my parents' furniture that would be appropriate to the tearoom. The rest I sold, donated, or put into storage. It was painful in some ways, but also very liberating.

At Nat's suggestion I took a class in tea blending and a seminar on small business start-ups. I needed to learn much, much more, but Nat said there would be time for that, and she was right. Putting the tearoom together was rather like assembling a jigsaw puzzle, only the pieces were not all provided. I had to go and find them. It took more than a year, during which time I attended a seminar at the Specialty Tea Institute in Seattle and began, slowly, to feel like I might really be able to pull this thing off.

It was expensive. I had to bring the kitchen up to commercial standards, *without* harming its historic character, and convert the neighboring room to a butler's pantry. I painted the walls myself but had to buy furniture for the tea parlors, along with rugs and gauze curtains and drapes for colder days. Computer system and telephones and cash register for the gift shop. And the china!

By that time Gina was home, and she and I had a grand time expanding my collection of beautiful teacups and saucers, teapots and milk and sugar sets, little silver teaspoons and tongs for sugar and lemon slices. We found a lot of things on Internet auctions, including some great bargains, but it all added up to a rather large chunk of change. And that was before hiring any staff or purchasing inventory and supplies. Suffice to say, I was motivated to make the tearoom a success.

And now, after all that effort, the Wisteria Tearoom was in jeopardy. I glanced at the disarray in the dining parlor.

My tearoom. My dream.

I could have wept with frustration, but I didn't want to slide back into the despair I'd felt after Dad died. I straightened my shoulders, carried my tray to the pantry, and began loading the dishes into the commercial dishwashing station. That little gem had been expensive, too.

As I rinsed plates and cups with the high-power spray, I wondered if the sound could have drowned out any noises from the dining parlor. It pretty well drowned out the music, though there were no speakers in the kitchen.

I paused, frowning at the Paragon cup in my hand, misty green with a medallion of poppies in the bottom. It had been Sylvia's cup. Probably the last thing she'd drunk from.

If only I hadn't arranged that tea party. Poor Sylvia might still be alive if I hadn't wanted to thank her.

"Stop it, Ellen," I said aloud. "You'll make yourself crazy."

I finished stacking the dishes in the washer and carried the tray back to the dining parlor to fetch the rest. As I moved around the room collecting the last of the china and straightening the furniture, I pondered why would someone want to kill Sylvia Carruthers.

She had been a generous soul, if a bit gruff. Her passion was history in all its forms, or so she had said. She certainly approached her work with the Preservation Trust with a passion. I remembered being carried along with it, rather overwhelmed by it, in fact. She didn't let anything stand in the way of what she thought was right for a property that deserved preservation.

Were there other matters on which she had the same determination? The usual reasons for murder were money, jealousy, lust. I couldn't picture anyone lusting after Sylvia, but she had an attractive daughter. What if she was as protective of Donna as she was of her beloved historic properties?

No, I'm not allowed to meddle in Mother's good works.

Donna Carruthers had said that in response to some polite

question I'd asked at the tea. She was a foot taller than her mother, and I couldn't remember having seen her smile. She had worn a tailored suit of beige linen to the tea, the antithesis of her mother's Santa Fe Lady style.

Donna and her mother hadn't conversed together at the thank-you tea, now that I thought of it, though that could have been because they'd been seated at opposite ends of the table. Could Donna have killed her mother in order to escape her?

Horrible, horrible thought. I rejected it, though a doubt whispered to me that it was possible. I didn't know Donna. She might have hated her mother.

Even if she didn't, she might stand to inherit from Sylvia. Money was a common motive for murder.

I didn't like thinking this way. My instinct was to feel terribly sorry for Donna. I knew how painful it was to lose a parent, especially the second parent. Even if they hadn't always seen eye to eye, there must still have been a deep connection between her and Sylvia.

I returned to the dining parlor to collect the linens. As I did so I heard a small rattling sound on the floor. I set my tray down, bent to peer at the hardwood, and found a tiny, lemon-colored heishi bead up against the molding.

Sylvia's necklace. The police must have collected the beads, and missed this one. I picked it up, rolling it between my thumb and fingertip. It was no more than three millimeters long. Who would have thought such a tiny thing could be deadly? Not by itself, but along with hundreds, thousands of others...

A necklace wasn't the best choice of murder weapon. Nor was a busy tearoom the best choice of location. I looked up sharply, my gaze falling on a reproduction of Monet's "Wisteria" that I had hung above the sideboard.

The murder must have been an act of impulse. I wondered if Detective Aragón had thought of that.

4

I awoke with a start after a restless night. The light coming through the tiny gap in the curtains of my bedroom was faint, a pre-dawn blue-gray. I sat up, listening, and heard the sound of the back door downstairs being pushed shut. Its opening had awakened me.

I pictured a faceless murderer creeping up the stairs to throttle me in my bed. A moment later the faint sound of salsa music dispelled that phantom. Julio was downstairs, gearing up to make his kitchen magic.

"Oh, good. He came back." As long as Julio stayed I had a shot at pulling the tearoom through this mess.

Profoundly relieved, I got up, showered, and dressed, choosing a gray silk dress with long, full sleeves caught into wide cuffs at the wrist. As I descended the stairs the smell of sautéing onions wafted up to me, making my stomach growl in anticipation.

"Good morning, Julio," I said, entering the kitchen.

"Morning, boss."

His pants today were burgundy with white pinstripes, with matching baker's cap and a plain white t-shirt that would later be hidden by his chef's jacket. It was the most subdued outfit I'd seen him wear yet. He scooped up a double handful of chopped mushrooms and dumped them into the skillet with the onions, raising a soft hiss.

"Figured you could use a good breakfast today."

"That's very thoughtful, thank you. Can I help with anything?"

"Nah. You cleaned up last night, no?"

"I needed to wind down."

He added chopped green chiles and chopped ham to the skillet, gave it a stir, then poured beaten eggs from a bowl into the pan for a frittata. My mouth started watering.

"Went through a lot of coffee," he said. "Have to order more soon."

"Go ahead."

"It can wait a couple days."

Meaning he had doubts about the tearoom's survival. I wanted to say something rousing and hopeful, but I had my doubts, too. We both kept them to ourselves.

Julio poured coffee into his mug, then lifted the pot, inquiring if I wanted some. I shook my head.

"Tea for me. I'll go make it."

"This'll be ready in a few minutes," he said, checking on the skillet.

"I'll be back."

By the time I returned with my pot of Irish Breakfast, Julio had set places for us both on the kitchen's break table and dished up the frittata with warm flour tortillas on the side. I took a bite and sighed with pleasure at the buttery onions and mushrooms, salty ham, and the sharp bite of green chile.

"Mmm, fantastic! Thank you, Julio."

"De nada. Get any sleep last night?"

"Some. The police cleared out around eleven."

Julio tore off a piece of his tortilla. "Tony Aragón hasn't changed much."

I looked up at him in surprise. "You know him?"

"My sister dated him in school."

"Maria?" She was a friend of mine—we'd been in the same class—but I didn't remember Detective Aragón from high school.

He took a sip of coffee. "No, Anna, my oldest sister. He was a senior when she was a junior. I was just a punk sixth-grader. They went steady for a couple of months, but he was too hot-headed. Got jealous if she even looked at another guy."

"That's believable."

"Got real bent out of shape when she gave him back his pin. I remember him standing out in the driveway yelling that she was a stuck-up faithless bitch. My dad finally had to chase him off."

"Wow."

"So be careful, okay? You don't want to piss him off."

Julio's dark eyes looked worried. I did my best to smile back.

"Right. Thanks."

No problem, I thought. I probably couldn't piss him off any more than I already had.

I ate some more frittata, concentrating on savoring it. I prided myself on being a good cook, but Julio was a magician.

A punk teenager, he'd surprised everyone who knew him by applying to a top culinary school in New York after barely graduating high school. Four years later he returned to Santa Fe, degree in hand, just in time to make the cake for his sister Maria's wedding.

I was in the middle of remodeling the tearoom at the time. When I bumped into Julio at the reception, congratulated him on the cake, and expressed a wish I could serve a miniature version in my tearoom, he perked up with interest.

Brand-new culinary graduates were a dime a dozen in Santa Fe; the best they could hope for was usually a sous-chef's position. We chatted over cake and champagne, and quickly came to a mutually-satisfactory arrangement: he would come cook some samples for me, and if I liked them, he'd be the chef at my new tearoom. It was a risk for both of us, but also a great opportunity.

Two days later he appeared at my tearoom with an armload of groceries, wearing a white chef's coat and flaming red pants printed with multicolored tropical flowers, and a chef's hat made from the same fabric.

"Nice outfit," I'd said, somewhat stunned.

"It's got hibiscus," he'd said proudly, pointing at a bright pink blossom on one knee. "Ties into the tea theme."

He then proceeded to take over my kitchen for three hours, producing four kinds of savories, a tea bread, and three sweets, all amazing. He had to have spent the two intervening days studying tea food, because everything he created that day was absolutely appropriate, not to mention delicious. I'd hired him on the spot.

I took another bite of my frittata and looked up at him. "Thanks for not quitting, Julio."

"Over this?" He scoffed. "I've seen worse."

No doubt he had. His family's neighborhood was borderline, on the edge of rougher parts of town. They were good, decent people, and had struggled to stay that way.

We finished our breakfast and I cleared away the dishes and built a fire in the kitchen fireplace by the break table, just for comfort, while Julio got started making scones. By then the sun was up, a pale, feeble glow through an overcast of cloud.

The phone started ringing at seven o'clock. I let the machine answer, then went up to my office to check the message. The call was from a television reporter requesting an interview. I left it, not wanting to deal with it yet, though sooner or later I'd have to. Before I could stand up the phone rang again.

I collected a couple of stray coffee mugs from my office and took them down to the dishwashing room. Ignoring the almost constant ringing of the phone, I walked through the parlors, making sure everything was tidy. The servers would check, too, but I wanted to be in the tearoom, to remind myself of the haven I had created and intended to maintain.

I picked up the brass firewood carrier Dee had left in the

main parlor and returned it to its place by the back door, then carried the book I had tried to read back to my office. I heard the back door open and close again, and glanced at my clock. It was almost eight. Kris had arrived.

She came into my office, shrugging off her long coat to reveal a black turtleneck and broomstick skirt. A graceful sandcast silver bracelet was her only jewelry. As always, her makeup was perfect and within business-world expectations, though the colors she chose were toward the goth spectrum, rather dark, accentuating her pale skin and black, cropped hair.

"I saw the news last night," she said in her quiet alto.

"So you know about the murder."

She nodded, blue-gray eyes gazing at me intently. "It looked insane with cops crawling all over the place. Are you all right?"

"Yes." The phone rang again and I glanced at it. "It's been going all morning. There are a bunch of messages for you to deal with, I'm afraid."

"Okay."

"I'm going to make a fresh pot of tea. Want some?"

"Yes, please. You sure you're all right?"

Kris has a tendency to view even minor setbacks as tragedies. The end of the world is always just around the corner. While that might be true in this case, I was determined not to acknowledge it. I made an effort and smiled.

"I'm fine. Thanks for being concerned. I'm glad you came in today despite this...unpleasantness."

She flashed an unexpected smile. "Oh, I think it's fascinating! I looked at the dining parlor on my way up, but it's hard to tell anything happened."

"I should hope so. I just want to get back to normal."

Her wry look told me she thought this impossible. I went downstairs, conscious of the dining parlor as I passed it on the way to the butler's pantry.

By the time I returned, Kris had been through half the messages. I set the tea tray on a credenza, hesitating as I noticed the picture above it, an ebony-framed reproduction of Millais's "Ophelia."

Kris had brought it in while we were decorating and asked my permission to hang it, and I'd had no objection at the time. Now, though, it bothered me a little. Lovely and ethereal as it was, it was still a picture of a woman drowning, and I was feeling a bit sensitive to the idea of death just then.

I poured tea for us both and carried it to her desk, sitting with my back to "Ophelia." Kris finished jotting a message, then hung up the phone and read from her notes.

"All four TV stations, the *Journal North* and the *New Mexican* all want to interview you," she said, "and you have messages from Katie Hutchins, Manny Salazar, someone named Willow, and two from a Detective Aragón."

"Drat. What did the detective want?"

"Didn't say. Just left a number for you to call back." She handed me a bunch of message slips.

"Thanks."

"Do you want me to return the calls from the media?"

I stood up and picked up my teacup. "Not yet. See what else we've got. Who knows, there might be a reservation in there."

"Oh, there already was. One."

I looked at her in surprise. "Well, that's good news."

She gave an apologetic smile. "And three cancellations."

"Oh. Well, carry on."

I took my tea into my office. As I sat at my desk, something seemed out of place. I put down the cup and saucer and the message slips and looked at the desk. I'd left it clean when I'd given it over to Detective Aragón to use.

The lower right hand drawer wasn't quite closed. It tended

to stick; I'd been meaning to wax it but hadn't gotten around to it.

I pulled it open. The papers I had stashed in there the previous evening lay in a tidy stack.

Too tidy. I remembered I hadn't racked them carefully when I put them away, but they were racked now.

"That bastard!" I whispered.

He'd gone through my desk.

Well, I hadn't told him not to. I'd left him alone in there. He was a cop investigating a murder, what did I expect?

I expected a respect for my privacy, and a little common courtesy, that was what. I took a deep breath, struggling to control my anger. It was going to be a difficult day, and I couldn't let something like this throw me into a bad mood before we even opened.

The phone rang again and I glanced up. This time it was my private line, so I answered it.

"Ellen!" said Aunt Nat. "I've been so worried! Didn't you get my message?"

"Oh—sorry, I haven't checked my cell phone yet. The tearoom's phone has been ringing off the hook."

"I can believe that! Why didn't you call me last night? I'd have come and helped."

"Sorry, I meant to call. There wouldn't have been anything for you to do, but thanks for thinking of me."

"Well, what can I do today? Do you need help with the tearoom?"

"Ah—maybe. Don't put off your own plans, but—"

"I have nothing planned today. I'll come right down."

I leaned back in my chair, surprised at how relieved I felt. "Thanks. It'll be good to have you here. I could use some moral support."

"You poor duck. You should forget all about it and go up to the spa and get a massage."

I laughed. "Not today. I'm sticking to my post until the fuss blows over."

"Brave girl. I'll come stick with you. About half an hour okay?"

"Anytime, no hurry. We don't open 'til eleven."

"See you soon, then."

I hung up, feeling rather better, and decided to check my personal messages. There were three, one each from Gina, Nat, and Jody Thompson, the real estate agent. I called Gina's number, got voicemail, left her a cheery message. Jody didn't answer either; she was probably out showing properties. Hers had been a courtesy call, so I left a message thanking her and assuring her that the tearoom was getting back to normal, and that I hoped to see her at the grand opening on Friday.

The next day. We had one day to pull it all together. I'd been counting on spending evenings getting ready, but Wednesday night had been a total loss.

I was about to jump up and get busy when my cell phone rang. I answered.

"Hello, Ms. Rosings, it's Vince Margolan. I just heard about what happened. I'm so terribly sorry!"

"Thank you, Mr. Margolan."

"Oh, Vince, please, we're neighbors, right?" he said in his hasty, New York way. "Listen, is there anything I can do?"

"No, no. Thank you. The police will probably want to ask you some questions."

"Yes, I just had a visit from a detective. That's why I called."

"Detective Aragón?"

"Yeah. Not very friendly."

I grimaced. "Well, I hope he didn't disrupt your day."

"No, well, not much. Just getting some paperwork together for the gallery."

"I'll let you get back to it, then. Thank you so much for

calling. I hope we'll see you at our opening tomorrow afternoon."

"Uh, if I have time. Busy week, you know. I'm hoping— well, I've got some big plans for the gallery. Lots to do."

"Of course. Thanks again."

We said goodbye and as I hung up I brushed aside a fleeting worry that no one would attend the grand opening. It was pointless to worry about that. Much more productive to get to work. Leaving the rest of my messages for later, I stood up and glanced into Kris's office before heading downstairs.

"Need anything?" I asked.

Kris shook her head, then held up a message slip. "That detective called again. You were on your cell."

I stifled a groan and stepped in to collect the slip. "I'd better call him back."

"Sounded kind of pissed."

"I'm not surprised."

I went back to my desk and dialed Detective Aragón's number, but got voicemail. I left a polite message, then went down to see how Julio was doing. As I came into the kitchen he was standing by the sink. I froze. His hands were up to the wrists in blood.

"Hey, boss," he said, smiling as he looked up at me.

He turned back to the sink, in which sat a colander of raw chicken livers. I relaxed, silently chiding myself for being so touchy. The smell of sautéing onions was back, and I went to the stove to stir them since Julio had his hands full.

"Starting on the pâté for tomorrow, I see," I said, proud that my voice sounded calm.

"Yeah."

He carried the colander over and started to dump the livers into the pan. On another burner a large pot of eggs was about to boil. I'd requested deviled eggs for the grand opening, a tribute to the day Nat had first suggested the tearoom idea.

"Anything I can do, or shall I get out of your way?"

"It's all under control. Oh, hey—that fruit basket in the fridge is yours, right?"

I nodded. "Manny Salazar brought it."

"Can I use a couple of the mangoes?"

"You can use anything you want except the raspberries. Those are mine."

"Got it. Thanks, boss."

He went over to the sink to rinse the colander. I stayed and stirred the simmering chicken livers.

"By the way, the candied violets yesterday were a delightful touch."

He came back, took the wooden spoon from my hand and glanced up with a small, wry smile. "I wanted to make your party really special."

"It *was* really special. And we're going to keep doing really special events. Don't you worry."

A muffled knocking sounded from the rear hall door. I gave Julio a reassuring smile as I opened the kitchen's outside door and looked out onto the porch.

It was the delivery girl from the florist, with cut flowers I had ordered for the grand opening. She and I carried bucket after bucket of white gladiolas, purple roses, blue iris and multicolored freesias and alstroemerias into the big, industrial refrigerator in the kitchen. I'd be up late that night, arranging them all in vases and teapots for the celebration.

Aunt Nat showed up as the florist's girl was leaving, wearing a handsome paisley dress in rich tones of burgundy, gold, and green. She caught me in a huge hug.

"Poor darling," she said into my shoulder. "What a horrible mess for you to have to deal with."

"Yes, well. I'm managing."

She leaned back, holding me by the shoulders. "Tell me

what to do."

"Come and help me move the dining table, if you don't mind."

"Of course not."

We went across the hall to the dining parlor, which I hadn't entered since the previous night. The chandelier was on, warm light filling the room. I must have forgotten to turn it off.

"It doesn't look too bad," Nat said, glancing around.

"I cleaned up the tea things last night and wiped up all the fingerprint dust, but I couldn't shift the table by myself. They moved it to make room to work."

Nat went to the foot of the table, where she'd sat the day before. We pulled the chairs aside and moved the table back to the center of the room, then tidied everything up. I put a fresh tablecloth on the table and retrieved the centerpiece from the south sideboard, placing it beneath the chandelier. Purple-edged white lisianthus, yellow rosebuds, and blue mist—a combination I'd chosen after long deliberation.

The dining parlor was back to normal, except that I couldn't help thinking about Sylvia whenever I was in there. I glanced up and saw my aunt gazing wistfully at the flowers.

"I haven't told *you* how sorry I am," I said. "You were pretty good friends, weren't you?"

"Oh, lunch now-and-then friends," Nat said. "We weren't terribly close, but I'll miss her. I've known her for years."

She shook her head, frowning. I went over and gave her a hug.

"I keep trying to think why anyone would kill her," Nat said. "She wasn't the easiest person, but she had a good heart."

"I know."

"She could come on pretty strong, of course, when she cared deeply about something."

I looked at Nat, trying to decide how upset she really was. She seemed bewildered, mostly.

"Did Sylvia and Donna get along well, do you know?" I asked. "I got the impression they didn't, but maybe they were just having an off day."

Nat sighed, and adjusted one of the hurricane lamps on the south sideboard. "Sylvia's always been a little disappointed in Donna. They're both headstrong, you know, and when they disagree...but they never had a serious clash that I knew of."

I nodded. "Well, let's go fold linens," I said, wanting to take Nat's mind, not to mention my own, off the murder.

We crossed the hall to the butler's pantry and got busy with the laundry. I had washed all the linens used the previous day, and now they had to be folded and put away. Nat took charge of the tearoom linens while I collected the tablecloth and napkins—my mother's lace—that we had used in the dining parlor.

"That's strange," I said. "There's a napkin missing."

"Maybe it's in with these," Nat said.

We looked through everything again. One napkin from the dining set was missing. I checked the washer and dryer, then around beside and behind them. No luck.

"Maybe someone snuck some scones home in it," Nat said.

I laughed and let it go, reaching for more napkins to fold. Nat began taking chores away from me, gently bullying me to go up to my office and answer the rest of my calls. I finally gave in and did so, reassuring first Manny and then Katie that everything was all right at the tearoom.

"I saw all those emergency vehicles last night," Katie said, sounding concerned. "I would have come over, but I had guests arriving and one of them got in late—"

"Thanks, Katie, but I'm glad you didn't come," I said. "It was pretty chaotic."

"You poor dear. I wish I could help somehow."

I picked up the pile of message slips and let them sift back to my desk like falling leaves. My gaze fell on the place cards I'd collected from the dining parlor and left on my desk. "Well, actually, you could clear something up for me, if you don't mind."

"Of course. What is it?"

"You were still in the dining parlor when I left after the tea," I said, my pulse speeding up a little at the memory.

"Yes, I was talking to poor Sylvia."

"What about?"

"Oh, just about the Trust. You know how she likes to go on."

"Do you remember who else was in the room?"

"Sylvia's daughter and Vince. They were talking about a gallery opening, I think."

"His gallery?"

"No, no. He's just getting started, he won't be ready to open for a while. I think they were talking about an opening this weekend, over on Canyon Road."

"And they were both still there when you left?"

"Yes. So was Sylvia."

"I see. Thanks."

"The detective asked me if I thought either of them would have a reason to kill Sylvia. Can you imagine?"

"Detective Aragón? He spoke to you already?"

"Yes, he was here this morning."

I frowned, wondering why he hadn't stopped by the tearoom if he was in the neighborhood calling on Vince and Katie. "What else did he ask you?"

"Well...I'm sure those kinds of questions are just routine—"

"He asked you if *I* had a reason to kill her."

"I told him no, of course."

"Thanks. I appreciate the vote of confidence."

"Sure thing. Let me know if I can help with anything."

"I will, thanks, Katie. Do come by tomorrow afternoon for the opening, if you have time."

"Yes, I'm planning on it. I think I can drag Bob over for a little while, too. We don't have any new guests arriving tomorrow."

"Bring your guests, if they'd care to come."

"That's so sweet of you, Ellen! Thank you, I'll let them know."

I sat musing for a while after we said goodbye, then glanced through the message slips to make sure I'd taken care of them all. The only call I hadn't returned was the one from "someone named Willow." I had a feeling that it was one of Santa Fe's woo-woo types, and didn't feel up to it at the moment, so I left that slip on my desk, tossed the rest, and went into to Kris's office.

"Do you have today's reservation tally?" I asked her.

She handed me three copies of a page printed from a spreadsheet. "Twenty-six."

I peered at the tally sheet and my heart sank. The tearoom could seat up to sixty at a time, and in order to break even we needed to keep it at least a third filled every hour. We had no more than three groups booked at once, and none at all from three to four. The bookings we did have were small, mostly two or three customers.

"Maybe tomorrow will be better," I said.

"Speaking of tomorrow, you had put a cap on the grand opening at sixty."

"That's right. Are we booked up?"

"No, we're at nineteen, including your invited guests. What I wanted to know was should we cap it at forty-eight, and not use the dining parlor?"

I bit my lip. "Yes, I guess we'd better."

The phone rang again. Kris answered, punching the button for the business line with a perfectly manicured, silver-frosted fingernail.

"Wisteria Tearoom. May I say who's calling? Thank you, please hold." She looked up at me. "It's channel seven. Want to take it?"

I shook my head, and escaped downstairs with the tally sheets while Kris sent the call to my voicemail. In the kitchen Julio glanced up from glazing a beautiful poppyseed bundt cake.

"Twenty-six," I said, sticking a tally sheet in a clipboard mounted on the wall by the door.

"Okay." Julio nodded, but his brow creased in a slight frown.

"We may get some walk-ins," I said hopefully.

In the butler's pantry I found that Dee and Vi had arrived and were helping Nat fold the last of the clean linens. Relief flooded me at the sight of them.

"Good morning!" I said, trying for cheer.

"Morning!" Dee smiled. "Any interesting developments?"

"Ah—none that I can think of. Here are today's reservations."

Dee pounced on the tally sheet and started getting out china and place settings for the setup trays. I watched Vi, who was uncharacteristically quiet. Usually I think of her as "Vi for vivacious," but that was not her present mood.

"Fires today?" Dee asked.

"Yes," I said. "Looks like it may rain."

I beckoned Nat out into the hall and led her down to the gift shop, where I put the last copy of the reservation tally on the hostess stand, next to the diagram of the parlor alcoves. "Can you play back-up hostess? I'll be here as much as I can, but I've still got some calls to return."

"Of course," she said, looking at the sheet. "Looks like it won't be too busy."

"No, unfortunately."

"Now, don't you get discouraged. This is only your second day, remember? It takes months to get a restaurant going."

"Years," I said. "Or mere weeks for it to flop right out the gate."

"It won't flop. Chin up, Ellen."

I met her gaze. Neither of us mentioned the elephant in the dining parlor.

I gave her a smile I didn't feel and headed back down the hall, passing Dee, who was carrying a set-up tray of china and linens. I peeked into the butler's pantry and found Vi absently sorting the tiny silver teaspoons and knives that I'd washed the night before.

"Vi? Could you come upstairs for a minute?"

She glanced up and nodded, following me. I led her through Kris's office to the small storage room behind it, where I picked up a big basket filled with tea samplers—three varieties of tea, enough to brew one pot of each, tied up with pretty ribbons—that I'd been putting together in my spare time.

I handed the basket to Vi. "Could you take these down to the gift shop?"

"Sure."

"But first come with me for a minute."

I led her out, past Kris who was on the phone, and down the hall to a small sitting area I had set up by the window at the end of the hall. This was at the front of the house, overlooking the garden and the street. The space wasn't really practical for office use, but I wasn't about to let a window go to waste, so I had set it up with two comfy leather chairs and a low table, as a place to have private tea with a friend.

"Have a seat," I said, taking a chair.

Vi set down the basket and sat in the other chair, folding her hands on her knees. Her posture was stiff, leaning forward as if she expected to have to jump up at any moment.

"Did you get any sleep?" I asked gently.

She gave a little, surprised laugh and met my gaze. "Not much."

"Me neither."

"It's so awful. I kept seeing her face."

I nodded. I'd had my own nightmares, including one where I'd wandered through the tearoom, finding my guests one by one, each dead. I shook the memory away.

"It's a slow day," I said. "You could go home."

"But that would leave only Dee serving!"

"I can pitch in if need be."

She sat up straighter and shook her head. "I won't abandon you. It wouldn't be right."

"I'd much rather have you go now and be rested for tomorrow. And by the way, thank you for not quitting."

She surprised me by bursting into tears. I handed her my handkerchief and waited for the storm to subside, which it did quickly. I'd indulged in a few tears myself, the night before.

"You've worked so hard for this," she said, wiping at her cheeks.

"So have you. So has all the staff."

"And you made such a wonderful p-place, and beautiful and everything. I *love* the tearoom!"

"Thank you," I said, smiling.

"And then *this* happens!"

I swallowed. "It's hard right now, but we'll get through it. Everything we worked for is still here."

I knew I was trying to convince myself as well as Vi. She gave a couple more sniffs and dabbed at her face.

"Is my makeup ruined?"

"No. Just needs a little tidying."

She nodded, dabbing beneath her eyes, then heaved a sigh. "I'm all right."

"You sure? It really would be fine for you to take the day

off. My aunt is here."

She sat gazing out of the window at the street below, blinking. "No, I'm okay. Thanks, though."

A distant rumble of thunder made me glance out the window. The sky to the west was mostly clear, but our weather usually formed over the mountains to the east.

"Have you heard back from the Opera?"

Vi shook her head. "Not yet, but it should be soon. Rehearsals start in May, they told me."

"Let me know when you find out the schedule. We'll adjust your hours as needed."

She smiled. "Thanks. It's great of you to put up with the uncertainty. You're the best boss ever."

I felt myself blushing. "Well, I did music in college. I know how crazy it can be."

Vi stood, smoothed her apron, and picked up the basket of samplers. She looked at the crumpled handkerchief in her hand.

"I'll take that," I said, standing.

She handed it to me with a last, small sniff. "Thanks, Ms. Rosings."

"Why don't you call me Ellen. It's not so stiff."

She looked at me, blue eyes wide. "Really?"

"Yes. You can pass that along to the others."

She smiled, and caught me in a quick around-the-shoulders hug. "Thanks, Ellen!"

I fetched a fresh handkerchief from my suite, then returned to the gift shop to close out the cash register, which I should have done the previous night but had forgotten. I pulled the large bills and the checks, printed out the credit card transactions, and put everything into a bank bag for Kris. I was about to take it upstairs when a loud knocking on the front door made me look up.

"Drat. I bet it's the press."

"I'll go look," said Nat, who had been straightening the gift shop merchandise. She went out and came back right away.

"It's just one woman," Nat said. "No cameras. Might be a relative of Sylvia's—she's dressed in black."

I sighed. "I'd better talk to her. Would you take this up to Kris, please?"

I handed Nat the bank bag, then went out into the hall and to the front door. The woman Nat had described was standing outside.

She was indeed all in black, an elegant wool dress and suede boots. Her hair was a carefully cut waterfall of platinum. She wore gold wire-framed glasses, and a necklace of turquoise beads interspersed with tiny bird fetishes set off her outfit nicely, a touch of Santa Fe style without going overboard. Not, however, something I would have chosen to wear if I were in mourning.

I unlocked the door and opened it a crack, peering past her looking for reporters. "May I help you? I'm afraid we don't open until eleven."

"Good morning." Her voice was surprisingly low. "Are you the owner? I'm Virginia Lane, but please call me Willow. Everyone does."

Someone named Willow. I summoned a smile. "How do you do? Yes, I'm Ellen Rosings."

"I heard about last night, and wanted to tell you how sorry I am."

"That's kind of you. Thank you."

"It's quite ironic. I've been so anxious for you to open. May I come in?"

"Well...certainly."

She stepped inside, and while I locked the door again she stood gazing around the hall and up at the ceiling. Her black ensemble tempted me to invite her upstairs to meet Kris, but I figured neither of them would appreciate the joke.

"I've wanted for years to see Captain Dusenberry's house," she said, stepping to the door of the main parlor and looking in.

Captain Dusenberry was the army captain for whom the house had been built in the nineteenth century. I'd learned about him from the folks at the Santa Fe Preservation Trust. Since the house was historic, I'd had to sign a preservation easement that specified I couldn't alter the character of the building. It had made remodeling a little tricky.

"When it was a law firm they didn't allow visitors," Willow said, "but now that it's open to the public—well, here. Let me give you my card."

She opened her small shoulder bag. I glanced surreptitiously at my watch, then accepted a glossy black business card with silver lettering: *Spirit Tours of Santa Fe.*

"Oh. You're the guide for the ghost tour."

"No," Willow said with a dismissive gesture. "That tour is aimed at tourists. Famous landmarks around town with spooky stories thrown in. My tours are focused on the spirits themselves. We visit places where they are verified as active, and have known histories."

Ooookay. I smiled politely, wondering how to escape.

"That's why I wanted to meet you," she continued. "Of course, now that...well, I'm sure you wouldn't want to do this right away, but eventually I'd like to include Captain Dusenberry in my tour."

"Well, I..."

"This is a bad time, I know. I don't want to intrude. Would you mind my just taking a look at his study?"

"Study?"

"Yes. That's the room where he was killed."

My heart skipped a beat. "How interesting," I said faintly.

"Has he manifested for you?"

"Ah...no."

"You do know that he haunts the house," said Willow, looking at me over her glasses with a very serious expression.

"Does he? I hadn't noticed."

"May I look at the study, Ms. Rosings? You needn't escort me, I know which room it is."

"Well—"

"I won't disturb anything, I promise."

She looked at me expectantly. I gazed back.

"Certainly," I said slowly.

She smiled, and walked down the hall. I followed, feeling like I was floating through a bad dream. Willow went straight back to the dining parlor, stood in the doorway for a moment gazing at the room, then turned to me.

"Do you mind if I go in?"

I shrugged and gestured that she could. It wasn't as though a herd of elephants hadn't already been through there.

She walked all around the dining table, looking at the walls, the ceiling, the floor. Finally she went and stood against the north wall, behind the table, and closed her eyes.

I watched in horrified fascination. Was she trying to commune with Captain Dusenberry? Was Sylvia getting in the way? She did have a tendency to interrupt...

I shook my head to clear it. I should probably find out exactly what had happened to Captain Dusenberry. Maybe the Preservation Trust would have some records. I didn't feel like asking Willow.

Willow inhaled sharply through her nose, then let out her breath in a long sigh. She opened her eyes and nodded, as if agreeing with something someone had said. At last she came out of the room.

"You might want to keep this door closed," she said, gesturing at the dining parlor's door. "I think the spirit is active."

"Oh?"

"Yes." She glanced at me, then back at the dining parlor. "May we talk privately?"

"Of course," I said, stifling a sigh. "Would you like some tea?"

"No, thank you. I have to meet a tour group at ten-thirty."

I glanced into the dining parlor. It seemed perfectly normal, but still I turned off the light and closed the door.

Willow smiled in approval. "Best to leave it quiet for a while. It may be that all the recent activity has stirred the spirit up a bit too much."

"Mm."

"Many people find that they can coexist peacefully with resident spirits," Willow added as I led her down the hall to the front parlor. "Over at La Posada they get along pretty well with Julia Staub."

"Do they?"

"There's no reason why that can't be true for you as well."

I invited her to sit in Lily, by a window overlooking the porch. She leaned forward, lowering her voice. "I just wanted to tell you that it's possible Captain Dusenberry's spirit is responsible for what happened last night."

"Are—are you suggesting that a *ghost* killed Sylvia Carruthers?"

"It's possible," she said, her pale eyes wide behind the wire frames. "Physical manifestations are rare because they require a great deal of energy, but they have been documented. A restless spirit, one with pent-up hostility, might very well be able to attack and kill a human being."

I leaned back in my chair. "Forgive me, but I find that very hard to believe."

"Do you?" Her faint smile returned. "Would you also have trouble believing that no fingerprints were found on the murder weapon?"

5

I stared at Willow in astonishment. Behind her the lace curtains stirred, though the window was closed. Stray draft, I told myself. Old houses are drafty.

"How do you know there were no fingerprints?" I asked.

"I have a friend in the police department. I'd better not mention who."

"Well, the killer could have worn gloves," I said.

Willow tilted her head, blue eyes gazing at me with steady curiosity. "Wouldn't you have noticed someone wearing gloves?"

I would, and in fact I had, but I didn't care to discuss that with Willow. "My point is that there could be any number of reasons for a lack of fingerprints," I said.

Not the least of which being that the weapon was a necklace of tiny beads. I was surprised that none of my prints had been found on it, but then it had broken, and even if it hadn't, getting all the strands to line up again...

"True," Willow said. "I don't know that the spirit is responsible, I only wanted to alert you to the possibility. Do be careful, Ms. Rosings. There *is* a presence in that room."

"And you think it's Captain Dusenberry."

"Yes."

"You know, we've been here for months, and no one has noticed anything unusual."

"Until last night."

Her gaze was steady, her voice matter-of-fact. If it weren't for the outrageous things she was saying, I would have found her completely credible.

"Have you shared your theory with the police?" I asked, wondering what Detective Aragón would make of her.

"No. In general the police tend not to credit theories of paranormal manifestation. The only time I talk to them about such things is if they come to me."

"And do they? Come to you, I mean?"

She shrugged. "I've been consulted on a couple of missing persons cases. They only turn to a medium if they're desperate, of course."

"Of course."

I wondered how successful those consultations had been, but didn't quite have the guts to ask. Willow might respond with a lecture on communicating with the spirit world, and I didn't think I could face it just then.

She took a wristwatch out of her purse and looked at it, then put it back. "I've got to meet my group," she said, standing up. "If the presence becomes troublesome and you decide you want help, give me a call. I can offer you a couple of recommendations."

"For exorcists?"

She gazed at me, eyes calm. "Not exactly. The people I know are more attuned to manifestations of energy than to religion. Of course, your personal preferences would be respected."

"How considerate," I said faintly.

"In the meantime, if you feel like making a gesture of conciliation you might try visiting Captain Dusenberry's grave. It's in the National Cemetery."

"Oh. Thank you."

I stood up to show her out. Willow turned to me as we reached the front door.

"I'd still like to discuss adding your tearoom to one of my tours, after things have settled down of course."

"Yes. Well, thank you for stopping by." I unlocked the door

and opened it. Outside the sky was heavier, and a breeze had come up.

"I'm not a nut, Ms. Rosings. In case you were wondering."

"No, I wasn't wondering."

Willow gazed at me as if evaluating my honesty, then gave a brief smile. "Good luck," she said, and went out.

I closed the door and watched her stride down the steps and along the path to the sidewalk. She went through the gate and closed it behind her without a backward glance. I watched her out of sight, then my gaze strayed to the wisterias on the porch.

Big, drooping clusters of pale purple flowers—they had come to symbolize the dreams I had for the tearoom. Dreams that were worth fighting for. I wasn't going to let Sylvia's murder kill the tearoom too.

The back door banged. Turning around, I saw Gina striding toward me, radiant in a ruby-colored dress with a fringed shawl printed with roses swathing her shoulders.

"Hola, girlfriend! I came to see how you're holding up."

"Thanks. Doing okay so far."

"You open at eleven, right?"

"Right." I glanced at the clock behind the hostess station, which showed ten-forty-three.

"Good," Gina said, grinning. "You'll have time."

"For what?"

"For the interview," she said, pointing toward the front door.

I looked out and saw a news van pulling up to the curb. "Oh, no."

"Oh, yes. Better get it over with, or they'll just keep bugging you."

"But I don't *want* to be interviewed."

"Yes you do." She pulled me away from the door and started smoothing my hair and my dress. "Listen to Mama

Gina. You want that nice man to ask you questions standing on the porch surrounded by wisteria, with your beautiful lace curtains in the background."

"Gina—"

"Because half a million New Mexicans will see it and they'll want to come here. Where's your lipstick?"

"Upstairs. You don't think all those people will mind that there was a murder here?"

She took a lipstick from her purse and grabbed my chin like a grandmother inspecting her grandkid. "No," she said as she carefully touched up my lips. "In fact a lot of them will find that intriguing. How could such a pretty place be the scene of a horrible murder? Blot," she added, grabbing a tissue from the hostess stand and handing it to me.

I blotted, feeling rather unhappy about the whole thing, but it was too late. The news crew was heading up the path.

"Let me answer the door," Gina said, pushing me into the gift shop.

"Why?"

"Because you're too important to answer the door!"

She ducked back into the hall, leaving me to reflect that it was too bad I hadn't known how important I was before. I'd been answering the door all my life.

I tidied the hostess station to pass the time while Gina greeted the media people. A minute later she breezed in.

"It's channel four, Ms. Rosings," she said grandly. "Do you think you could spare just a couple of minutes to talk to them?"

I mouthed "No," which she ignored. She caught my arm and propelled me into the hall.

"This is Carla Algodones, Ms. Rosings," Gina said, smiling as she presented me to a sleek newscaster who looked familiar. Ms. Algodones wore a beige trench coat over a blue dress, and her shoulder-length hair was perfect, dark brown and curling.

"How do you do?" I said.

"So sorry to hear about the tragic event, Ms. Rosings. Do you have a few minutes to tell us about it?"

"Well, I—"

"Out on the porch would be best, I think," said Gina, shepherding us outside to where two young men waited next to several cases that probably held electronic gear.

"I only have a few minutes," I said. "We open at eleven."

Ms. Algodones smiled. "This won't take long."

It was a bit chilly outside, and I stood with arms crossed to keep warm while the two men flung open their cases and hauled out floodlights and a shoulder-held television camera. To give them credit, they were ready in a very short time. With the lights supplementing the feeble daylight, I stood beside a column draped with wisteria, a lace-curtained window behind me, while Ms. Algodones held a microphone toward me.

"Ms. Rosings, can you tell us what happened here last night?"

Broadly put. I hesitated, then said, "I don't think I should talk about the details while the police are still investigating."

She looked impatient, then the bright-eyed newscaster smile returned. "Tell us what you can."

"Well, several guests were attending a private party in the tearoom yesterday evening, and unfortunately one of them died shortly afterward."

"And the police are investigating it as a murder?"

"Suspicious death," I said.

"The police haven't released this person's identity, but can you tell us a little about them?" asked the reporter.

"She was an older woman, a long-time resident of Santa Fe."

"Respected in the community?"

"Oh, yes. We are so very sorry for her family and friends."

"Was there any sort of altercation at this party?"

People just don't respect history as they should!

Sylvia, her voice vibrating with passion. There had been a couple of awkward moments during the tea, but I didn't think they could be called altercations.

I shook my head. "No," I said with confidence.

I saw two ladies out on the sidewalk, dressed in coats and hats. They paused at the gate, then after a moment's hesitation they opened it and started up the path.

"I'm so sorry, I have customers arriving," I said to Ms. Algodones. "I have to go now."

She looked disappointed. "Okay. Thanks for your time," she said, and turned to the crew. "Where do you want to do the lead-in?"

"Out in the yard," said the one with the camera. "Get a shot of the whole house."

Ms. Algodones cocked a suspicious eye at the sky and produced a collapsible umbrella from the pocket of her trench coat. I escaped into the tearoom, where Nat looked up at me from the hostess station.

"Two customers coming," I told her. "Make them feel at home, please. I think the camera crew made them nervous."

"Will do."

Gina pounced on me. "That was great! You looked wonderful."

"I need a cup of tea."

I headed back to the butler's pantry with Gina on my heels. Dee and Vi looked up as we came in.

"We're open," I said, reaching for a kettle. "Customers on the way."

Dee gestured at two cozy-covered teapots on the counter. Nearby stood two double-tiered serving trays on which sweets were already arranged.

"We're all set," she said. "Just need the scones."

"I'll get them," Vi said, and darted out toward the kitchen.

I put the kettle to boil and went upstairs to fetch down the teapot I'd been using. Gina followed me, still burbling over the news crew.

"Maybe we can get the other stations to come, too."

"I'm sure that wouldn't be a problem," I said drily. "They've all been calling."

"Wonderful!"

"Is it?"

She smiled at me, shaking her head. "Honey, you can't buy this kind of publicity!"

"Gina, I *wouldn't* buy this kind of publicity."

I took the teapot into the kitchen, intending to rinse it. Mick jumped up from the break table and took the pot out of my hands.

"You're here early," I said.

"Thought there'd be a bunch of dishes to do."

"Oh, no, I did them last night."

"Yeah, I saw. I put them away."

"Thanks, Mick. You're a gem."

He smiled, and I felt a sudden rush of gratitude toward my staff. Julio was at the stove, humming softly over something savory. Dee and Vi were fussing over the tea trays in the pantry. They were all sticking by me, despite the whole awful mess. They were terrific, all of them.

Mick insisted on washing the teapot. Not wanting to deprive him of feeling useful, I took a clean one and made a pot of Darjeeling. After checking with Nat to make sure the customers were doing all right and that the second party with reservations had arrived, I went up to my office with Gina. Julio had made more than enough scones for the day, so we took some up with us and had a cozy munch while I caught Gina up on what I'd figured out about the murder.

Gina licked a little lemon curd off her fingertip. "So when Katie left the dining parlor, Sylvia was still alive, and Donna and Vince were still there."

"Right."

"So maybe Donna and Vince were in it together!"

I shook my head. "It wasn't premeditated. It was impulsive. A premeditated murder would have been much better planned, I think. Actually, the killer took a tremendous risk."

"A crime of passion!" Gina said, her brown eyes going wide.

"Well, some kind of passion anyway. Oh, and there's another suspect."

"Who?"

I picked up a scone and cut it open. "Captain Dusenberry's ghost."

I described Willow's visit and her theories of paranormal manifestation. Gina guffawed, enjoying every minute. I played up the ridiculous side of it, but I wasn't so sure Captain Dusenberry could be ruled out. I wasn't sure of anything.

"What about this Willow lady?" Gina asked.

"What about her?"

"Could she be the murderer?"

I blinked. "Well—I guess that's possible, if she snuck in somehow. I don't know what reason she'd have to kill Sylvia, though."

"What do you know about her?"

"Not much, actually."

I showed her Willow's business card. Gina tapped the card against her palm, looking thoughtful.

"Let me copy this down," she said. "I know some people in tourism, I can ask around a little."

I handed her a pad of sticky notes and a pen. "Okay, but watch out. She has a friend in the police department."

Gina looked up at me and grinned. "I'll be subtle."

"That'll be a first."

She laughed, then scribbled down Willow's information and handed me back the card. "Gotta go. I have a client meeting at two. You going to be all right?"

"Yes. It's slow today, but I'm hoping it'll pick up tomorrow."

"Do some more TV interviews and I guarantee you it will."

"Okay, okay."

I was resigned to doing more interviews. Having talked to channel four, I couldn't very well refuse to talk to the others. I walked Gina out, then stood on the small porch at the back of the house, gazing up at the Sangre de Cristos, blue mountains with white snowcaps that blaze pink at sunset.

All my life I've looked to those mountains when I need comfort or inspiration. Today they were half-shrouded with wisps of cloud, pale scraps drifting against the blue pine forest.

By one o'clock it was raining, a steady downpour that drummed distantly on the steel roof and made me want to curl up by the fire. Instead I dutifully returned all my phone calls, even Detective Aragón's. I got his voicemail again and didn't bother leaving a second message.

I called the papers and the TV stations, did phone interviews for the former and made appointments for the latter. I promised each of them fifteen minutes, which I thought was fair and about all I could stand. The first crew would arrive at two-thirty, the others at three and three-thirty, during an hour when we had no reservations that day. I planned on using Hyacinth, a small seating tucked in the corner behind the gift shop, because of the rain.

At one-thirty, everything went to hell.

I had just seated some walk-ins—tourists who thought a cup of tea sounded nice on a rainy afternoon and who apparently hadn't seen the evening news—when an imperative knock fell on the front door. Since we were open for business and anyone could have walked right in, I took this as a bad sign, and I was right.

When I opened the door (my importance having momentarily slipped my mind), I found Detective Aragón standing outside, his leather motorcycle jacket dripping with rain. Behind him stood two city cops, not dripping but undoubtedly wet, and looking grim.

The detective handed me a folded piece of paper, and my heart sank. He'd done it, called my bluff. Not that I had anything to hide, but I had hoped he would respect my last remaining shred of privacy.

"I don't suppose I can talk you into coming back after business hours," I said, glancing at the search warrant.

"Nope," he said, and brushed past me into the hall.

I followed, determined not to let him upset my customers or bully my staff. At least he didn't intrude into the parlors. Instead he tromped straight up the stairs with the two cops behind him.

I hurried down the hall and poked my head into the butler's pantry. "Two walk-ins in Marigold," I said to Vi, then went upstairs after the cops.

They were all waiting outside my door. I took the key from my pocket and unlocked it, then followed them in. Up here, right beneath the roof, the rain was louder.

Detective Aragón pushed past me as soon as I had the door open, cast a glance around my suite, and headed straight for my wardrobe. He pulled the doors open.

"Hey, be careful!" I said, following him. "That's an antique."

He pushed the clothes hangers back and forth. "Where's the dress were you wearing yesterday?"

"In the laundry."

"Get it for me."

"Excuse me? What for?"

"Evidence. Fiber samples."

I frowned, but I understood what he meant. I went into the master bath and took the dress out of my laundry basket. Turning, I found Detective Aragón right on my heels. He almost snatched the dress from my hands, then gave it to one of his sidekicks. I winced as the cop bunched my dress up and stuffed it into a plastic bag.

"You can go back to your business if you need to," Detective Aragón said rather unkindly.

"I think not," I answered. "I have some fragile antiques in here. I'd rather stay and make sure they aren't harmed."

I waited, arms folded, while the three of them pulled on latex gloves and started tossing my suite. As I watched, my patience thinned and I wondered if Detective Aragón had gone to the trouble of obtaining a search warrant just to spite me.

I was annoyed, but I wasn't about to let him know it. Not for nothing am I a devotee of Miss Manners. Courtesy is the best weapon against rudeness.

They started with the little sitting area I had set up north of the chimney, looking beneath the chair cushions and rifling my bookcase. Detective Aragón made a show of looking underneath the furniture, even turning my wing chair over to poke at the bottom.

They glanced through my kitchenette, opening all the cupboards, the mini-fridge, the counter-top convection oven, and even the wine cooler. Having exhausted that side of the suite, they moved on to the bedroom.

One of the cops started poking through the drawers of my low-slung dresser, stooping beneath the slanting ceiling as he did so. The other pulled apart the pile of throw cushions at the head of my canopy bed, shot me a hangdog glance, poked at the pillows a couple of times, then moved on to the nightstand.

Detective Aragón made a disgusted noise and pulled back all the bedding, scattering cushions on the floor. He lifted the mattress and peered underneath it, went to the far side of the bed and lifted it again, then carelessly threw the covers back over the rumpled bed and stomped through the sitting area to the master bath.

I strolled to the bathroom door and leaned against the frame, where I could keep an eye on the whole suite. The cop going through my dresser reached the lingerie drawer, turned bright red, and shut it again after a cursory shove this way and that of its contents. The one at the nightstand opened the lower drawer as if expecting a snake to jump out of it, and looked positively relieved when all he found was the novel I was currently reading and a bottle of melatonin tablets. He moved on to the wardrobe.

Meanwhile, Detective Aragón had poked through my linen closet, stuck his nose into the shower, disarranged the magazines in my small bathroom reading rack, and opened my medicine cabinet. He stood staring at the contents, which consisted of my makeup, vitamins and herbal supplements, and a few basic first-aid items.

He turned his head to look at me. "You one of those health-nut freaks?"

"Freaks?"

"Yeah, vegetarian new-age herbalist bullshit. I got a sister who's into that crap."

"I'm not an herbalist, I just keep a few home remedies," I said evenly. "You know, you've given me a great idea for a special tea event, though. Would your sister know a *curandera* who might be willing to come and give a little talk on traditional herbal medicine?"

He glared at me, eyes narrowing, then slammed the medicine cabinet shut and stalked back to the bedroom. I followed. Both cops looked up nervously.

"Anything?" Aragón snapped.

They shook their heads. The one at my dresser pushed the bottom drawer shut and stepped away from it.

"Maybe if I knew what you were looking for I could help you find it," I said sweetly.

"I got a better idea," said Aragón. "Why don't you come in your office and give us your fingerprints. Leo, go get the kit."

One of the cops bobbed his head and hustled out of the room with lightning speed. The other followed the detective out into the hall. I locked the door, thankful that the search was over.

"We need to fingerprint all your employees. We'll use your office again," Aragón said, starting across the hall. He stopped short when he saw Kris appear in the shared entrance. She gave him a cool glance, then looked at me.

"Channel two's on the phone. They want to know if they can come half an hour early."

"No," I said.

"Who's this?" demanded Detective Aragón.

I took a steadying breath. "Kris Overland, my office manager. Kris, this is Detective Aragón."

"How come I didn't see you yesterday?" Aragón asked her.

"I leave at five," Kris replied coolly, and turned back to her office.

"We'll need your prints, too," he called after her, then went into my office.

I followed him, scooping up a fresh pile of message slips from my desk as he sat down behind it. He glanced at me with a narrowed gaze that told me he was looking for a reaction.

No doubt he was wondering if I'd noticed he had searched my desk. I chose not to pursue that. Instead I took my time glancing through the messages, then looked up at him.

"Why do you need fingerprints?"

He wiggled my computer's mouse and peered at the

screen as if hoping something juicy would pop up there. Tough luck for him, the computer was off.

"So we can identify everyone whose prints we found at the crime scene," he said, opening my pencil drawer.

That was deliberate. Yes, he wanted me to know he'd searched my desk. But why?

It occurred to me that he *wanted* me to be guilty of this crime. I felt a flush of indignation rise to my cheeks.

"What good will that do?" I asked, though I knew he was right. I was annoyed enough to want to poke back. "You already know who was in the room, and there weren't any prints on the murder weapon."

Detective Aragón looked up at me, eyes furious. "And just how do you know that?"

6

A friend told me. A friend who has connections in the police department."

I hoped Detective Aragón wouldn't pursue it. I really didn't want to have to tell him I had learned about the lack of fingerprints from Willow.

He watched me through narrowed eyes. "Or maybe you know it because you destroyed any prints there might have been."

"What? I would never do that!"

"Sure you did. You told me so yourself." He leaned forward in my chair, his dark eyes intense and accusing. "You pulled the necklace away from the victim's throat."

"I was trying to save her!"

"You know CPR, Ms. Rosings?"

"Yes, and I tried. I tried everything I could. So did the paramedics."

"We might have been able to get some prints if you hadn't moved the necklace. Those little amber beads, though—"

"Not amber. Lemon agate."

He blinked. "What?"

"They were lemon agate. She mentioned that."

He frowned as he looked at me, as if he were trying to place a piece in a puzzle. "Whatever. When you pulled them away from her throat, any prints that might have been on 'em got jumbled like a jigsaw puzzle."

"Well, I'm sorry about that, but I couldn't just leave her there! I didn't know she was beyond reviving!"

The cop who had gone for the fingerprint kit came in with

a metal case about the size of a briefcase. Aragón glanced at him and gestured for him to put it on my desk.

"Okay, we'll need to get everybody in here to be printed. We can start with you," he said to me.

"Why are you bothering, if there are no prints on the murder weapon?"

He gave me a look that said he thought I was a complete idiot. "Because we dusted everything in the room for prints—"

"I'm well aware of that! It took me over an hour to clean up all that black powder!"

"—and we need to match them up to the people we know were in the room. If we find a print that doesn't match, then there's another suspect."

"Oh."

Feeling foolish, I submitted to having my fingers pressed onto an oily stamp pad and rolled around on a large card printed with boxes. As I got up to go wash my hands, Detective Aragón glanced up at me.

"Send in your office manager. I need to interview her."

I left, pausing on my way out to look into Kris's office. I told her the detective wanted to talk to her, then went downstairs to use the public restroom to wash up.

By this time I was wishing I had taken Nat's advice and gone to the spa. I was tired and cross, not having a very good day, and the television crews were about to start arriving. I glanced into the kitchen, realizing as I did so that I hadn't offered Detective Aragón any coffee. Well, he wasn't being particularly courteous, so I didn't feel obliged to treat him as a guest.

"Everything okay, boss?" Julio asked, looking up from stirring a large pot on the stove.

"Yes. The police want to get everyone's fingerprints."

Julio rolled his eyes. "Okay. I made some chicken soup for lunch. Want some?"

I couldn't resist going over to the stove. The heavenly smell of the original comfort food rose from the big soup pot.

"Smells fantastic, but I'll have to wait. I've got to deal with the press."

"I'll save you some," Julio said.

The noon hour was long since over, and the tearoom had quieted down. Only one party of two sat in Iris, sipping tea and enjoying the fire while they watched the rain out of the window. I went across the hall to Hyacinth and found Nat there ahead of me, shifting the low table aside.

"Hello, dear. I thought I'd make a little more space in here for the camera people," she said.

"Thanks." I picked up a petite, lace-draped side table and put it against the far wall.

"Are you all right, Ellen?"

I summoned up a smile. "Fine. It's just that Detective Aragón. I think he's deliberately being a pest."

"You can file a complaint if he's harassing you."

"If he keeps it up I will." I shifted a fragile antique lamp to the mantelpiece, where I hoped it would be safe out of the way. "Julio's made some soup. Why don't you go back and have some?"

Nat straightened up and brushed her hands. "That sounds wonderful. I was just getting a little peckish."

"You know, you don't have to stay. I'll be all right, and the afternoon looks quiet."

"What about four o'clock? Won't it get busy at tea time?"

"We have no reservations."

"But you might get walk-ins. I'll stay."

She gave a nod of cheery determination, as if her willing business to pick up at four would make it happen. I hugged her, then sent her off to the kitchen for soup while I went to the gift shop to keep an eye out for the news crews.

The shop was sparkling with light glinting from twin

chandeliers and gleaming off the displays of china and knick-knacks. Outside the rain was coming down a little heavier, making me glad to be cozy and warm. I stood at the hostess station, looking over the woefully empty reservation chart and thinking about everything that had happened in the last twenty-four hours.

Dee looked in, wiping her hands with a paper towel. "Hi. Just checking there was someone here. Boy, that fingerprint stuff is yucky, huh?"

"Yes. I'm sorry about that."

"It's OK. It was interesting to see how they do it."

I smiled. "You're really interested in police work? You know it isn't like on television."

"I know. I've read some books about forensics. Mick thinks I'm nuts."

I tried to picture Dee, with her cheerleader looks and sweet outlook, as part of a crime investigation team, and failed. "Well, it doesn't matter what he thinks. Follow what interests you."

"Oh, I will!" She grinned, then left.

I glanced at the clock. Dee had reminded me of the whole fingerprint fiasco, and I realized I'd been wanting to follow up on something. I just had time to make a phone call, and since Detective Aragón was still in my office, I used the phone at the hostess station.

"Santa Fe Preservation Trust," said a young woman's voice after a couple of rings.

"Hello, this is Ellen Rosings. May I speak to Claudia Pearson, please?"

"I'm sorry, she's in a meeting."

"Oh. Well, I'd like to come by and see her this afternoon. Would four-thirty be all right, do you think?"

"I don't think she has anything then. I'll let her know you'll be coming."

"Thank you," I said, and gave her my number in case Claudia needed to cancel. As I hung up I saw a news van pull up to the curb out front.

The interviews were more or less the same as the one I had done in the morning, except that there seemed to be a lot more equipment involved. Each station brought in its own assortment of lights, sound booms, and cameras, taking up most of Poppy, the neighboring alcove, as well as Hyacinth. Fortunately I was able to close the pocket doors between them and the gift shop and keep the fuss confined.

As for the actual interviews, I'm sure the reporters were disappointed. I refused to give any details or speculation about Sylvia's murder, confining my comments to what I'd already told channel four.

I was just ushering the channel seven bunch out when Detective Aragón came tromping down the stairs with his two cops. He took one look at the camera crew and went ballistic.

"What do you think you're doing?"

The reporter's face lit with delight. "Detective Aragón! Got time to answer a couple of questions?"

"No! No comment." He turned to me, looking fit to burst a blood vessel. "What the hell inspired you to invite the media in here?"

"That's not quite how I'd put it," I said calmly.

"If you've told them anything that compromises the investigation—"

"I haven't. Ask Mr. Rodriguez," I said, gesturing toward the reporter.

"*That's* the truth," Rodriguez said, shaking his head. "Maybe we'll get a few seconds before the weather, but heck. It's yesterday's news. C'mon, Dirk, we got that school break-in to get to."

They trundled out, followed by the cops, but Detective Aragón stayed. He stood glaring at me like a bull in the chute until the front door closed.

"If you have compromised this investigation I will bring you up on charges," he said in a tight, angry voice.

I answered calmly. "I have done everything I can to assist your investigation—"

"Bullshit! You forced me to get a warrant to examine the crime scene!"

I drew myself up. "My private suite is not a crime scene!"

"This whole *building's* a crime scene!" he yelled, waving his arms. "And now you've turned it into a media circus. I ought to book you right now!"

I'd had it. Gloves off.

"Fine," I said, "then I'll file a complaint for harassment and illegal search!"

"You forget the warrant."

"You didn't have it when you went through my desk last night!"

He didn't have an answer for that, so he just glared at me, nostrils flaring with each angry breath. He looked rather magnificent actually, though I wasn't in an admiring mood.

"I have been very patient, Detective," I said with what calm I could muster, "but I do have a business to run."

A corner of his mouth curled up in a sneer. "Yeah, you look real busy giving press conferences. That'll give your sales a boost."

I was stung, partly because of Gina's pushing me to do the interviews for just that reason. I took a careful breath before answering.

"Contrary to your obvious belief, I am not talking to the press because I want to. I'm talking to them because they won't leave me alone. When they ask for details I refer them to the police."

"Oh, thank you very much, your highness."

"I beg your pardon!"

He stepped toward me, thrusting out his jaw. "It's all a game to you, isn't it? You come in here and fill this place with Victorian crap—"

"It's a Victorian house!"

That just made him madder. "You people don't give a shit about Santa Fe, you just think it's fun to move in here and play tea parties! Play gallery owner or antique dealer—"

"I was *born* in Santa Fe!"

"Yeah, but was your grandmother?" he said nastily.

"Yes, as a matter of fact!"

He stopped short, blinking in surprise, then scowled. His jaw worked for a moment and I thought he was about to say something else, but instead he brushed past me and stormed out the front door.

I watched him go, stunned by the strange turn the argument had taken. A moment later the roar of a motorcycle engine sounded, swiftly fading into the muted noise of traffic and rain.

A smattering of applause made me turn around. Julio, Mick, Dee, Vi, and Nat stood gathered in the hall near the kitchen. Kris was on the stairs just below the landing, one hand on the banister, peering down at me.

"Well," she said, sounding highly amused, "you gave him what-for, didn't you?" She showed a Cleopatra smile, then went back upstairs.

Nat hurried toward me. "Brava, darling. That man's had a chip on his shoulder ever since he walked in here."

"Well, I didn't set out to knock it off," I said, trying for a laugh. "I'm just glad there weren't any customers here."

In fact, I was shaken, and when Nat pulled me into the main parlor I didn't resist. She led me to Rose and nudged me toward one of the wing chairs by the fire.

"You sit down and relax for a minute. You've been on your feet most of the day."

"There's one more TV crew coming—"

"They can wait. You haven't eaten anything, have you?"

"A couple of scones, and I did have breakfast."

"That was hours ago. I'll go fetch you something." She bustled off, leaving me to frown at the raindrops running down the window.

I hadn't intended to argue with Detective Aragón, and I had a feeling I was going to regret it. I knew he considered me a suspect for Sylvia's murder. Would he carry out his threat and charge me with obstructing the investigation?

Nat returned almost at once with a tray bearing a steaming bowl of soup and half a grilled cheese sandwich. I thanked her and set about devouring them while she went out to watch for the news crew.

Julio had done something wonderful and subtle with the soup, some combination of herbs that made me think of French cuisine and New Mexican food at the same time. I felt better almost at once, and when the last news crew arrived I was able to face them with a good grace and answer the familiar round of questions.

"I understand this death is now being investigated as a homicide," the reporter told me in the glare of their lights.

"The police haven't informed me of that," I said blandly, hoping that little soundbite would make it onto the evening news and into Detective Aragón's awareness. As my equilibrium returned, I was feeling less frightened and more annoyed with him.

I shooed the news crew out the door at ten to four and heaved a sigh of relief at finally being done with the interviews. I hoped Gina would be satisfied. For my part I doubted it would bring us any business, but at least now maybe the media would leave me alone.

Yesterday's news.

I glanced at the seating chart. We had two reservations at

five. I was beginning to give up hope for Friday, but maybe Saturday would be better. Or next week. People who didn't know Sylvia, who only saw the story on the news, would have forgotten about it by then, even if the rest of us hadn't.

Poor Sylvia. To be relegated to the back page before she was even in the ground.

What had she done that had made someone want to kill her? Was it something she'd said at the tea? I couldn't remember her saying anything that provocative, though there had been some undercurrents in the conversation that I hadn't fully understood.

If her murderer was someone at the tea, and I felt pretty certain it was, then he or she had decided to kill her during the tea or as it was breaking up. Someone impulsive, who had a reason for wanting Sylvia dead.

The bells on the front door tinkled as a party of three women in business attire came in. I greeted them warmly, by this point feeling profound gratitude toward every customer who crossed the threshold. I showed them to their seats in Jonquil and informed Dee and Vi of their arrival, then poked my head into the kitchen looking for Nat. She was at the break table talking with Mick and Julio.

"I'm going out for a bit," I told her. "There's a party of walk-ins, and two reservations at five. You can let the servers handle it if you want."

"All right, dear," she said, getting up. "I do have to get ready for dinner. Manny's offered to take us out, given the circumstances. You are still going to join us?"

I stifled a sigh. "Can I take a rain check? Sorry, but I think I'd better make an early night of it. I was up late last night."

"Of course," said Nat. "Maybe tomorrow."

Julio stood up and reached for his jacket on the corner coat rack. "Think I'll go, too, if it's okay. The pâté and the brioche are done. I'll come in early to do the last minute stuff for the opening."

I suppressed a groan. I still had all the flowers to deal with, not to mention straightening up the mess Detective Aragón and his flunkies had made of my suite. Maybe I wasn't going to make an early night of it after all.

"Thanks, Julio," I said. "You want a ride to your place? It's still raining pretty hard."

He glanced toward the window. "If you've got time."

"Sure. I'll just get my purse."

I ran upstairs to my suite and grabbed my wool coat and a scarf as well as my purse. I locked the door again, then looked into Kris's office.

"I'm going out. Might not be back by the time you leave. Any important messages?"

She shook her head. "It's been quiet all afternoon."

"How does tomorrow look?"

She gave a small, rueful smile. "Pretty quiet."

I tried not to wince. "Cancellations?"

"A couple."

"Hm. Well, thanks."

I hurried back downstairs, shrugging into my coat. Julio met me at the back door and we walked along the *portal* to the back of the kitchen, where I parked my car.

Julio was silent as I drove out to Marcy, then took Washington north toward his apartment.

"Is your roommate coming to the opening tomorrow?" I asked.

"Yeah. He's always up for free food."

I had given each of the staff one free pass for a friend to attend the grand opening. Now I wished I had given them two each, but it was a bit late for that.

"I thought he was a chef."

"He is." Julio glanced sidelong at me and grinned. "We've been having a little competition to see who can come up with the best dessert."

"Oh. You're not going to surprise me, are you?"

"Don't worry. Nothing that isn't appropriate for the tearoom."

"Okay," I said, suppressing a twinge of concern.

Julio was sharing a place with a fellow culinary graduate. I worried that he'd be offered a position he liked better than the tearoom. My hope was that he'd be satisfied with the creative range of our menu, especially the afternoon teas.

We'd even talked about trying a high tea eventually, though with Julio's talent and flair it would be a far cry from the traditional hearty evening meal of a British laborer. Welsh Rarebit, yes, but it would be Welsh Rarebit with a difference.

I pulled into the parking lot for Julio's apartment building. Before getting out of the car he gave me a serious look.

"What did you say to get Tony Aragón all steamed up?"

"I have no idea. One minute we were talking about the media, the next he was screaming at me about my grandmother."

Julio rubbed a finger down the dashboard in front of him. "See, his folks are pretty poor. I think they lost their house or something. He's always been touchy about rich people."

"I'm hardly rich—"

"To him you are."

"I see. Well, thanks, Julio."

He nodded. "See you tomorrow."

I watched him into the building, thinking about what he'd said. I didn't consider myself rich—not at all, if you looked at my mortgage. But the fact that I had such a mortgage in the first place was due to my inheritance. The Dusenberry house was not cheap, being both historic and in the midst of old Santa Fe, a short walk from the plaza.

So Detective Aragón was touchy about money. That explained some things.

I drove east on Paseo de Peralta to the historic neighbor-hood where the Santa Fe Preservation Trust had their offices. Their building, a comfortable, sprawling adobe, had once belonged to a rancher who had served a term as governor of New Mexico.

I parked and hurried through the rain to the shelter of the *portal*, pausing there to look westward across downtown. The sky was darkening, though it was still hours to sunset. A huge storm was blowing up out of the west, promising more rain. A distant rumble of thunder followed up the threat. I went inside, glad to be out of the chill.

Shelly, the pretty brunette receptionist whom I'd met a few times during visits to the Trust, looked up with a smile. "Hi, Ms. Rosings. She's on the phone. Would you like to warm up by the fire until she's free?"

"Sure. Thanks."

I took off my coat and strolled over to the kiva fireplace, sitting on the cushioned banco beside it. The fire had fallen to coals, and I took a stick of piñon from a rack nearby and propped it against the back of the roughly conical fireplace. After a moment flames began to lick up its sides.

"Thanks," Shelly said. "Sorry. It's been a little crazy here today."

"I'm not surprised. I'm so sorry about Mrs. Carruthers."

Shelly looked at me with wide eyes. "Poor Claudia's been a wreck all day. It must have been awful for you, too!"

"It wasn't the best of days," I admitted.

"I think she feels extra bad, because...well." Shelly picked up a stack of papers and began to sort them.

I moved to the chair by her desk. "Because why?" I asked gently.

Shelly glanced toward the closed door behind her which led to a series of rooms, the last of which had been Sylvia's. Claudia's office was next to last, I knew from having passed through it on previous visits. Shelly leaned toward me and lowered her voice.

"They argued yesterday morning, and I don't think they had sorted it out before they went to your tea party."

"Oh, no," I said. "Poor Claudia! She must feel awful."

Shelly nodded. "They worked really well together most of the time, but every now and then we'd see fireworks. It's just too bad it had to happen yesterday."

"Do you know what it was about?"

Shelly shook her head. "All I know is Sylvia won. Please don't mention it to Claudia. She's upset enough."

"Of course not," I said, though my curiosity was aroused.

"There, she's off the phone now," said Shelly. "Go on back, I'll let her know you're here."

I fetched my coat and opened the door, passing through the conference room and a records room before pausing to knock on Claudia's door. The building was arranged on the old hacienda design, with no hallways. Instead there was a central *plazuela*, like the courtyard at my parents' house on Stagecoach Road. As I glanced out a window at the rain pouring onto the little garden, I felt a pang of homesickness for the old house.

Claudia opened her door and looked out at me. She was wearing a dark brown dress and a dark patterned scarf caught to her shoulder with a silver and turquoise pin. For a second she looked apprehensive, then she gave a stiff smile and waved me toward a chair.

"Sorry I've been hard to reach. Busy day."

"Mine, too," I said, draping my coat over the back of the chair.

It was an old-fashioned chair, leather on a blocky wood foundation with lots of big brass studs. The rest of Claudia's office decor was similar. Solid woods, a few well-chosen ornaments like the classic Navajo rug on the wall behind her desk and the polychrome pot on the mantel of her small kiva fireplace. There was no fire burning there. Probably she didn't have time to fuss with it. She was a no-fuss kind of person.

We both sat down, and Claudia put aside some papers and leaned her clasped hands on her desk. "What can I do for you?"

I took a deep breath. "I'm hoping you can—well, give me some peace of mind."

Claudia frowned. "What do you mean?"

"The police have talked to everyone, but they haven't told me anything of course, and I've been trying to puzzle things out on my own."

"You mean about Sylvia."

"Yes. I know you were in the room when I left. Can you tell me who else was there?"

"I left right after you did."

I didn't remember that. What I did remember was that when I came back from showing Nat and Manny out, Claudia had been in the hall, putting on her gloves. I remembered that clearly, because I'd found it so charming and old-fashioned. Claudia had been the only one who'd worn gloves to the tea.

Gloves, of course, would leave no fingerprints. When Willow had told me about the absence of prints on the necklace I'd thought of Claudia at once. But I knew the lack of prints was due to my moving the necklace.

"I went into the restroom," Claudia added. "When I left the parlor Sylvia was talking to Kate Hutchins, and Donna was in the room talking to Vince Margolan. When I came out of the restroom I glanced in and saw Sylvia and Donna talking, then I went to get my coat."

That fit with what Katie had told me. I nodded.

"All right. Thank you."

"Did the police ask you about me?" Claudia watched me intently.

"No," I said. "That is, they asked if I knew of any reason why any of the tea guests would want to kill Sylvia. I told them no."

She seemed to relax a little, and looked down at her clasped hands. "Sylvia and I didn't always get along very easily."

A tingle went down my arms. I answered with polite interest.

"Oh? I thought you worked together well."

A small unhappy smile curved Claudia's lips. "As long as I let her have her way, yes. Now and then we differed, and it usually led to harsh words. I'm afraid that happened yesterday."

"Oh. How unfortunate."

"Sylvia always thought her own opinions were right. She didn't like being challenged."

"And you challenged her?"

Claudia sighed, picked up a pen and began to twirl it between her fingers. "Yesterday morning. We disagreed about the acquisition we were to make that afternoon at the title company, after your tea."

"An acquisition for the Trust?"

"Yes. In your neighborhood, in fact. I thought we were paying far too much money for it, but Sylvia was determined. We had been bidding against another party who wanted the property, you see."

"Oh."

She straightened up suddenly. "I'm sorry—would you like some coffee or a soda or something?"

"No, thanks," I said, waving a hand. "I had a late lunch. So what happened with the property?"

She went back to twiddling with the pen, doodling a little on a notepad by her phone. "The price got so high the Trust couldn't afford to buy it. Sylvia wouldn't let go of it, though.

She arranged to put up half the money herself."

"Goodness! That must have been a lot of money for her to just donate."

Claudia nodded. "A big chunk of her savings, I believe. She was adamant, though. Kept saying there was no better use for her money than to preserve an endangered historic building. The more I tried to reason with her, the more stubborn she became."

"I can believe that," I said. "She does—she did—come on like a steamroller sometimes."

Claudia laughed. "Yes, she did."

"Well, maybe you could name the building for her."

"Oh, we didn't get it." Claudia dropped the pencil into a rust-colored stoneware mug of other pens and pencils. "We would have had to close yesterday, and without Sylvia's signature we couldn't. The sale fell through."

"You're not going to pursue it?"

She shrugged. "We can't. Without the money she was going to put into it, we can't possibly afford it."

I gazed at Claudia, trying to decide if there was a hint of smug satisfaction in her attitude. Perhaps so, but I didn't think winning an argument, even over a large financial transaction, would be enough reason for her to murder a long-time colleague.

"I don't suppose Donna would give you the money her mother intended to donate," I said slowly.

"I seriously doubt it," Claudia said. "Donna's never been interested in historic preservation. She's always said it was a waste of time and money. A bit of leftover youthful rebellion, I think. Anyway, it's too late. They've probably sold the building to the other bidder by now."

"Do you know who the other bidder was?"

She shook her head. "No idea. We were going through our real estate agent, who was dealing with the seller's agent.

Sylvia might have known, she was good at ferreting out that kind of information. That's one of the things that made the Trust so successful. She always knew when some historic building was about to come on the market. She loved making preemptive acquisitions."

"So what happens to the Trust now?" I asked. "Sylvia was the president, wasn't she?"

Claudia nodded. "I'm the V.P. I'll run things until the board decides on a new president."

"It'll probably be you, won't it?"

"I suppose so." Claudia looked up at me and flashed a smile, the first real smile she'd shown during the conversation. "Unless they find some other sucker."

"You love the work, too, don't you?" I asked.

"Yes, but I'm not Sylvia. I don't think anyone can replace her."

She seemed genuinely sad. If she had wanted control of the Trust, she certainly hid it well. My instinct was to believe that she hadn't. I felt quite sorry for her, almost more so than I'd felt for Donna.

"Could you do me one more favor?" I asked.

"If I'm able."

"I'd like to learn more about Captain Dusenberry. A— visitor told me that he was murdered. In the house."

Silvia's brows rose. "What a horrid coincidence, if it's true. I don't know, but I'll have Shelly pull the file and send you a copy of whatever information we have."

"Thanks. Well, I've taken up enough of your time," I said, gathering my coat and purse. "Thank you for seeing me."

"Thanks for the visit. I needed to come up for air."

I put on my coat and wrapped my scarf around my neck. "Come to our opening tomorrow, if you like. Four o'clock."

She smiled, but it was more polite than enthusiastic. "If I have time. Thanks."

On my way out I asked Shelly for one of the Trust's brochures. I don't know why, but I thought I should look it over. Maybe it would give me some additional insight into Sylvia's way of doing business.

It was getting quite dark now, and the rumble of thunder that greeted me as I stepped out of the building was enough to make me scuttle to my car. I drove to the tearoom and hurried in the back door. Vi was just coming out of the butler's pantry with a cozy-covered teapot on a tray. She smiled.

"Hi, bo—uh, Ellen."

"Hello, Vi. Everything going all right?"

She nodded. "Just one party of two left. They're in Marigold, I thought it would be cozier than the big parlor."

"Fine. I'll be upstairs if you need me."

It was after five, but Kris hadn't left yet. I caught her just as she was leaving her office.

"Do you have a minute?" I asked. "I'd like you to check something for me on the Internet."

Her brows rose, but she flipped the light switch on again. The stained glass chandelier lit with rich jewel tones. Kris went around to her chair and turned on her computer, then looked at me expectantly.

"How easy is it to find out who's selling historic properties in Santa Fe?"

"Hm." She frowned for a moment, then started typing.

I took off my coat and sat down in one of her guest chairs. I can stumble my way around the Internet, but Kris is a whiz. If there was information out there, she'd find it. After a minute her screen lit up brightly, and she started scrolling with her mouse.

"Hm. The National Trust has one listed for sale. Other than that it's a lot of real estate pages. I'd have to look at each one's site to see what they're offering."

"No, no," I said. "I want to know about the owners, not

real estate agents."

"I'll add 'owner' to the search." She clicked away for a minute, then shook her head. "Couple of 'for sale by owner' listings, but not much else. The Santa Fe Preservation Trust's registry page came up."

"I think by the time it's listed for sale it's too late," I said. "Is there a way to find out if an owner is looking for preservation funding?"

"I'll try...no, I get some pages about applying for preservation loans, but that's it. The Trust shows up there, too."

I frowned. I had been the rounds with the sources of preservation loans. It was Sylvia who had helped me find them. She must have connections with all those groups. Maybe that was how she found out who was looking for help with an historic property, or perhaps who wanted to sell one.

"Okay, thanks, Kris," I said, standing up.

She shut down her computer. "Sorry I wasn't more help."

"No, it helped. Thanks."

"You're trying to figure out why that lady was killed."

She said it as a statement, not a question. Her eyes regarded me calmly. Maybe it was her manners or her style of dress, but she seemed older than twenty-three.

"Yes," I said. "Not doing a very good job of it, I'm afraid."

Kris put on her long, black coat. "I'll see what I can dig up."

"Don't spend a lot of your personal time on it."

"I wasn't going to. It'll give me something to do tomorrow if it's quiet. Tonight I'm going clubbing."

A flash of lightning made us both look toward the window. The gauze curtains stirred in the restless air, then the rumble of thunder rattled around the house.

"Stay warm," I said as we both left the office.

She grinned. "I will. Great night to be out."

To each her own. I like thunderstorms—most people who live in New Mexico like rain—but I prefer to enjoy them from the comfort of a fireside chair.

7

I watched Kris down the stairs, then put my coat and purse away before following. It was nearly six, and the last customers were leaving the tearoom. I thanked them for coming and locked the front door behind them.

Dee and Vi were already clearing Marigold, setting it up for the next day. I tossed another log on the fire there, to keep the chimney warm so it would heat my suite, then covered it tight with the screen and went out to the gift shop to close out the cash register and pack the day's dismal receipts into a bank bag for Kris. On my way upstairs I looked in on the kitchen. Mick was just setting the dishwasher to run, and Dee and Vi were putting on their coats.

"Anybody need a ride home?" I asked.

Mick shook his head. He had his own car—an old Mustang that was parked outside the back door. It was a restoration work in progress, currently several shades of paint dominated by primer gray.

"Thanks," Vi said, "but Dee's giving me a ride."

I looked at her closely, seeking signs of stress. She seemed better than she had that morning.

"I started the linens washing," Dee said as the servers headed for the back door.

"Okay, I'll finish them," I said. "Thanks. See you both tomorrow."

Mick stood in the door of the dishwashing room as he removed his apron—a small ritual of his, I assumed part of leaving the work behind—then hung it up and went to fill out his time sheet at the rack on the wall by the fireplace. He wore a slight frown, which prompted me to thank him as he headed for the door.

He nodded. "I might be in a little late tomorrow. Putting in a new muffler. That OK?"

"As long as you're here by three-thirty."

"I will be. Thanks."

I locked the door behind him and watched him head for his car. Alone in the big, old house, I stood looking out the window at the back porch, listening to the rain drum on the roof.

It occurred to me to wonder if the outside doors to the dining parlor were locked. I hadn't thought of it the previous night.

I walked through the side hall, past the butler's pantry and the restroom and out into the main hall, then stood before the closed door into the dining parlor, feeling reluctant to open it. Willow's advice echoed in my mind—best leave the room alone for a while. Wouldn't want Captain Dusenberry to get too stirred up.

That settled it. I opened the parlor door and turned on the light switch. The chandelier threw its warm glow over the table and chairs, the sideboard and the china cupboard, all gleaming with fresh polish. I turned to my right, toward the French doors, just as a flash of lightning sent blue-white light through the back yard.

A man was standing on the porch, silhouetted against the chiffon-curtained glass door. The next second darkness swallowed him.

My reaction was purely instinctive. I ducked out into the hall and flattened myself against the wall, staring at the window lights around the back door, waiting for the sound of the stranger entering the dining parlor. Instead someone tried the back door, then knocked.

Okay, murderous ghosts don't knock. I peeled myself off

the wall and walked to the back door, trying to breathe calmly. I paused to turn on the porch lights and look out the windows.

Mick stood outside, huddled in his light jacket with his ball cap pulled low over his eyes. I unlocked the door and opened it.

"Sorry," he said, stepping in. "Forgot my tunes."

I waited while he fetched his music player and headphones from the kitchen. He stuffed them in his jacket pocket and grinned at me as he went back out.

"Thanks, Ms. R. Night."

"Call me Ellen, Mick. Good night."

Ms. R. Sounded like "bizarre." Better than "boss," I supposed, but only by a little bit.

I locked the door and went back to the dining parlor. Mick's headlights sent another momentary flare of light through the glass door. The car's engine rumbled mightily as he started it, confirming a need for interior as well as exterior work. I watched the headlights fade back and swing away, then turn out into the alley and vanish behind the neighboring building.

"All right, let's try this again."

I returned to the dining parlor and approached the French doors, but hesitated before touching the handles. I didn't remember cleaning them the night before. I bent to peer at them, looking for the black fingerprint dust that the police had gotten all over the room. I saw a grain or two caught in the crevices, but none of the smudges I'd had to clean from the china and glassware and furniture. There were no fingerprints on the door handles.

That was definitely strange. There should have been prints all over them. We had used those doors a lot while we were decorating and setting up the dining parlor.

I left the handles alone and locked the deadbolt with my key. Glancing at the sideboard, I remembered the missing napkin and wondered if someone had used it to wipe the door handles. The killer might have left by those doors, using the napkin to keep from leaving prints and taking it away afterward.

I frowned, then returned to the kitchen and looked out the window. I could see the dining parlor doors if I stood far to the right and leaned forward over the counter, but someone just working at the counter probably wouldn't be able to see anyone leaving by those doors.

So anyone could have left that way undetected. For that matter, anyone could have come in those doors and probably not have been seen except by whoever was in the dining parlor.

I groaned. Instead of narrowing the possibilities down, I had just thrown them wide open. Anyone with a grudge against Sylvia, who had known she was going to be at the tea, could have staked out that back door and come in when they saw their chance.

"Wait a minute," I said aloud. "It was a crime of impulse. Staking out the back door is premeditation."

The killer was someone at the tea. I didn't like that, but I kept coming back to it. I had invited Sylvia's killer into my house, and unwittingly provided the opportunity for the murder.

"Ugh."

I went back to the dining parlor, turned off the chandelier and closed the door. Anxious now to get away from the room, I ran upstairs and put the bank bag on Kris's desk, then went across the hall into my suite. I turned on every light, leaving the hall light on as well. The downstairs lights were on, too. I didn't care; I'd get them later. Right now I wanted light in the house.

I put Chopin's Etudes on my stereo and cranked it up over the pounding of the rain on the roof, then went to work putting my suite back in order. As I picked up the mess Detective Aragón had made, I couldn't help remembering our weird confrontation that afternoon.

He was mad at me, personally. I represented something he hated. It wasn't fair, but fairness didn't enter into it. I remembered his expression—cold eyes, hint of a sneer—as one I'd seen before, on the playground at school, in the high school hallways.

Anglos are a minority in Santa Fe, and growing up you're aware of it. Contempt in the dark eyes turned toward you from clusters of chollos. Groups of mean-eyed girls from the Catholic school controlling the sidewalk as you walked home. All kids have to deal with that stuff, but racial tension adds an edge to it. I had Hispanic friends, plenty of them, but there were some who wanted no friendship.

It didn't matter that my grandmother had been born in Santa Fe. That had just caught Aragón off guard, but it wouldn't change his mind. He wouldn't stop being angry because he'd realized he was wrong. It would probably make him *more* angry. I'd made an enemy, and that was a problem.

"Good thing he's a cop and not in a gang," I muttered as I put fresh sheets on my bed.

Having a cop mad at me was bad. Having him be the lead detective of a murder investigation involving my house was rather more than bad. He could easily continue harassing me, even to the point of filing charges against me. They might not stick, but it would cost me time and effort to fight them, and I needed to put everything I could into the tearoom right now. If the tearoom failed, I'd be in a huge mess.

I stood in the middle of my bedroom and sighed, then closed my eyes. The music had run out, and the rain beating on the metal roof close above filled my head. I let the tension drain out of me and decided to pull a Scarlett O'Hara. I just wouldn't think about it until tomorrow.

Or maybe after tomorrow, because tomorrow was the grand opening. I still had the flowers to do. Dinner first, though. Dinner and a glass of wine.

I went to the little kitchenette in my suite behind the sitting area, just a mini refrigerator/freezer, a two-burner counter-top stove and convection oven combo, and a small microwave. Enough for me to fix meals for myself without having to go downstairs and rattle around in the industrial kitchen. There was also a small sink, a mini dishwasher, and a temperature-controlled wine cooler, just big enough for two dozen bottles.

My father taught me to like good wine and good cheese. In fact I owe most of my expensive tastes to my dad.

I opened a bottle of cabernet franc and put a pot of water on to boil for pasta, then peered in the fridge to see what I had to put on it. Some mushrooms, red bell pepper, and a small zucchini would make a decent primavera. I took them out, along with a leftover half an onion and a couple of cloves of garlic. Sliced those and set them sautéing in olive oil while I cut up the veggies.

The wine and the thrumming rain made me relax, finally. I put the vegetables in with the onions and garlic, which by this time were filling the room with a heavenly smell, and sprinkled in a few herbs. Pasta water was boiling, so I added oil and threw in a cup of penne, then set the timer.

On impulse, I went across the hall to my office and fetched the thank-you tea place cards, then carried them and my wine to my chair by the chimney.

My sitting area is right above Dahlia and Marigold, on the south side of the house. The fire downstairs had warmed up the chimney, so it was quite cozy. I lit a candle on the table beside my chair and snuggled in, tucking my feet under me as I sipped my wine and sifted through the cards, looking at the names, hoping for inspiration.

Claudia Pearson.

My thoughts drifted back to my conversation with her that afternoon. I had gone in half-suspecting her of Sylvia's murder, but after talking to her I felt pretty sure she hadn't done it. What she had told me, though, had raised another possibility. Who stood to gain by Sylvia's death, and was also at the tea?

Donna Carruthers.

I pulled out Donna's place card and gazed at it. I hated to think that a woman would kill her own mother, but the fact was that it sometimes happened. Donna and Sylvia had different ideas about what mattered.

Sylvia had been about to give away a large amount of money. *Any* Santa Fe property was expensive, and historic properties extremely so, especially if they were close to the plaza, like mine.

Was Donna the sort to kill her mother for money? I was assuming she stood to inherit her mother's estate. Would she regard Sylvia's intention of putting a large amount of money into the purchase of an historic property for the Trust as disinheriting her? Did she even know about it? And would that make her angry enough to kill?

I tried to remember if the topic had come up during the thank-you tea.

I wish I could stay, Ellen dear, but we have a meeting at the title company. Thank you for a wonderful afternoon.

I drew in a sharp breath, recalling Sylvia's remark as the guests were leaving. Could that have been enough to spark Donna to murder her?

I couldn't very well ask Donna. What I could do, perhaps without inflicting any further pain on Donna (which I didn't want to do if she was innocent), was try to pinpoint more closely who was in the room right before Sylvia was murdered.

According to Claudia, Donna was last in the room, alone

with Sylvia. To confirm that I could ask Vince, who had stayed talking to Donna after Claudia left the dining parlor. I found Vince's place card and moved it to the top of the stack, to remind me I wanted to talk to him.

The kitchen timer went off. I set the place cards down and went to the stove, stirred the veggies, and dumped the pasta into a colander in the small sink. Glancing at the clock, I saw that it was early yet, but I decided not to call Vince that night. It would be better to talk to him in person. Maybe he would be at the grand opening Friday afternoon.

I topped off my wine glass, stirred a little cream into the sautéed veggies, and cut a chunk of Romano cheese to put into my hand-cranked grater. Dumped the pasta onto a stoneware plate and the sauce over it, and carried it all back to my chair. The rain had slacked off a little, and I put on some soft chamber music while I ate.

I was beginning to feel quite mellow, more than I had in days. I'd spent all my waking hours on the tearoom for so long I'd almost forgotten that there were other things in life, other decor besides Victorian.

In my own suite I'd deliberately gone for a different style, just to make it my special refuge from work. Out in the public rooms everything was Victorian, but in here it was more Renaissance, with heavy green and gold acanthus-leaf brocade and wine-red velvet, gold silk braid and tassels instead of Victorian lace. I had candles all over, and rich hangings on my canopy bed that I had made myself, functional so that I could enclose the bed in velvet curtains all around if I wanted to, as such beds were originally intended.

My parents had bought me the canopy bed when I was ten, after a year of my begging and pleading. The hangings had been all girly then, ruffles and lace, but the bed itself was good solid maple. I had refinished it before moving it into my suite, made the new hangings, and splurged on luxurious sheets and blankets and a velvet comforter. I could hear the bed calling to me, but I had to do the flowers first.

I finished my wine and took care of the dishes, then went downstairs. Lights were blazing everywhere, no doubt racking up an obscene electric bill. I turned them all off except for the butler's pantry and the kitchen.

In the pantry I took the clean linens from the washer and loaded them into the dryer stacked above it. Remembering the missing napkin, I wondered if I should tell Detective Aragón about it. That might serve as a peace offering. He undoubtedly knew the doorknob had been wiped, but maybe he'd like to know how. I had his number, and it probably wasn't too late to call.

"Nope. Scarlett O'Hara," I told myself, and went off to arrange the flowers.

My vases were in the china cupboard in the dining parlor. I turned on the hall light again, unwilling to walk through darkness to open that door. It was silly, but it made me feel better.

I got out every vase I had, plus an old china teapot with violets painted on it. The lid had long since broken but I couldn't bear to part with it, and it did make a nice base for a floral arrangement. I loaded it on a tray with all the vases and carried them to the kitchen, then conscientiously returned and turned out the lights before delving into the big refrigerator for the flowers.

I tuned the radio of Julio's boom box to the classical station. Surrounded with beautiful, fragrant flowers, I felt my mood lifting and was soon humming along with the music as I clipped and arranged the blooms.

The big vases I filled with dramatic sprays of gladiolus and iris. Smaller vases got roses or heavenly-smelling freesias. Nothing seemed quite right for the teapot, though.

I set it on the kitchen counter and stood back, trying to

envision the perfect arrangement for it. I could take apart the centerpiece from the thank-you tea, but that was still pretty fresh and I liked it on the dining table. I glanced up at the window to check again whether I could see the dining parlor's back door from there. I couldn't, but I did see a splash of light falling across the porch from that direction.

At first I thought it was the hall door, but I could see another, fainter band of light just at the bottom edge of the window. Leaning forward, I confirmed that the lower light was coming from the hall door, spillover from the kitchen lights. It was the French doors from the dining parlor that were pouring light onto the porch.

Not wanting to waste power, I went out to the hall and opened the dining parlor door, this time feeling brave enough to leave the hall light off. I shut off the switch and the chandelier went dark. A pale glint trembled along the edge of one crystal. The room seemed to be holding its breath.

"You're imagining things, Rosings," I said aloud, then closed the door and returned to the kitchen.

I kept glancing at the violet teapot while I finished with the rest of the flowers. Finally it occurred to me that lilacs would look perfect spilling out of it. There were purple and white lilac bushes growing between the tearoom and the building to the north. I caught up my clippers, ran some cold water in the teapot, and went out the back door.

The rain had fallen to a light drizzle. I walked north along the porch, then stepped off it onto the grass and into the rain, inhaling deeply. There is nothing quite so wonderful as the smell of rain.

I set the teapot on the grass at the foot of an old lilac bush that was at least ten feet tall and easily as wide. A whole row of them ran along the north side of the house. I clipped several sprays of the beautiful, pale purple blooms, shook the rain off them, and dumped them in the pot. The neighboring bush was white lilacs, and I clipped some of those, too, then carried the pot back to the house.

I was about to step on the porch when I glanced up and froze. Light was pouring out of the dining parlor door again. I was certain I had turned that light off.

Which meant that someone was in the house.

8

I stood frozen, heart pounding, watching all the back doors. I had locked the French doors in the dining parlor. The kitchen and the hall also had doors that opened onto the porch. The hall door was locked, but I'd left the kitchen door open.

Coatless, I was beginning to shiver in the cold. I stepped onto the porch, trying to make no sound as I got under its shelter.

If someone was in the house, they must have gone in the kitchen door and then into the dining parlor, turning on the light. That implied they were searching for something in the dining parlor, but the police had been all over the room. It didn't make sense.

Could they be waiting to ambush me? Why, though? Had the killer found out that I was asking questions? Other than my staff, the only one I'd talked to that day was Claudia.

I waited a long time, but nothing happened. Finally I set the lilacs on a bench on the porch, then slowly approached the French doors. I had my garden snips in hand, not much of a weapon but better than nothing. I paused, listening for any sound of movement from inside.

Nothing. I stepped quickly past the doors and paused again. Still no sound, so I cautiously turned the handle of the kitchen door, trying to be silent as I slipped inside.

I stepped out of my shoes and padded barefoot into the hall to face the dining parlor door. Light showed beneath it.

I put my ear to the door to listen. No sound but the faint music from the radio in the kitchen.

All right. Make it quick. If there's a lunatic in there, slam the door and get out of the house.

I glanced at the side hall. That was my escape route, through the kitchen. I'd run to Katie's and call the police from there if I had to.

Taking a firm grip on my garden snips in my left hand, I put my right on the doorknob, turned it swiftly and pushed the door open, so hard it banged against the wall.

There was no one in the room.

The chandelier was on, and I noticed one of the crystals moving back and forth slightly. Just one.

I glanced up at the ceiling. Kris's office was overhead. Could someone have gone up there? Could Kris have stopped in late after her clubbing?

Or could the murderer be up there, waiting to ambush me? Or Detective Aragón, could he be snooping around?

Or maybe it was Jack the Ripper.

"Stop making up stories, Rosings," I muttered, turning off the chandelier and closing the door.

I put my shoes back on, fetched the lilacs from the porch, then locked the kitchen door. Determined to behave normally, I began trimming and arranging the lilacs in the teapot, though I did turn off the radio.

If the murderer was in the house, I'd hear him or her coming down, because the staircase is old and it creaks. Likewise, if Kris had come in I'd eventually hear her moving around. Or Detective Aragón. Or Jack.

No sound except for a couple of rumbles of distant thunder. By the time I'd finished the lilacs, I was pretty sure I was alone in the house.

I distributed the flowers in the parlors, making sure to put some iris in Iris, roses in Rose, and alstroemerias in Lily. Silly, perhaps, but it made me smile. I put a big vase of gladiolas on the hostess stand and set the lilacs on top of a half-high bookcase on the long wall of Jonquil. I'd have to plant some jonquils and hyacinths in the garden for next spring.

Satisfied that everything was ready for the grand opening, I shut off the parlor lights and returned to the kitchen to clean up the mess from flower arranging. When everything was spotless again and ready for Julio, I turned off the lights and reached for the hall switch to light my way upstairs.

The dining parlor light was on again.

Warm light, golden on the polished hardwood, spilling across the hall floor from beneath the door.

The house was silent. I hadn't heard anyone coming down the stairs, and I was sure there wasn't anyone in any of the downstairs rooms. I'd just been in all of them, even the restroom, distributing flowers.

I hadn't put any in the dining parlor, because there was already an arrangement there. I hadn't gone into that room at all, so I knew that I hadn't turned on the chandelier.

Okay, why? Why would someone keep turning on that light? Just to freak me out, was all I could think of, but I didn't think any of my staff would try to mess with my head like this.

Detective Aragón might, but I'd expect him to be more direct. Maybe it was Willow, trying to convince me of Captain Dusenberry's existence.

Or maybe it was Captain Dusenberry.

I closed my eyes and rubbed my forehead, wondering if I should call Gina and ask her to come over and take me out for a drink. Clearly the stress and the tension were getting to me.

I decided on a hot bath instead. Flipping on the hall light, I strode purposefully toward the dining parlor and opened the door.

It was empty. A single crystal on the chandelier was twisting slowly back and forth. I turned it off, pressing the switch firmly downward as if to keep it from drifting up again, and closed the door.

Going up the stairs I began to feel nervous again, and just to ease my mind I looked into Kris's office and then my own. There was a small stack of message slips on my desk, and I glanced through them to make sure I hadn't missed something important.

One was about a funeral service for Sylvia on Saturday afternoon. I should go to that, I thought. I left the slip on the top of the pile, then went across the hall and checked my cell phone voicemail. Other than a cheery message from Gina informing me that she'd seen me on three of the four news stations, there was nothing.

I locked myself into my suite and did a quick check of all the dark corners. I told myself I was making sure I'd straightened up everything after having the place tossed, but really I was checking for murderous intruders.

I hadn't looked under the bed for monsters since I was about twelve, but I did it now. Fortunately I found nothing scarier than a couple of dust bunnies.

Satisfied that I was safe, I ran a hot bath and lit a bunch of candles, then poured some sandalwood oil into the tub and soaked until the water went tepid. I was sleepy by then, the previous short night having caught up with me. I went to bed with the whisper of rain overhead, and didn't wake until my alarm went off at six.

When I came downstairs Julio was already in the kitchen, with salsa music playing softly on the boom box. His baker's cap and pants were paisley in Mardi Gras colors, purple and green with gold accents. A little wild, but all right. I knew there were much more flamboyant things in his wardrobe. With his white chef's jacket he'd look professional enough for the opening.

"Morning, boss," he said, looking up from the counter where he was mixing the first batch of scones. "Wild and crazy night last night?"

"Ellen, please. Not really. I just did the flowers. Didn't I get it all cleaned up?"

"Yeah, but you left the light on in the dining parlor. Saw it when I came in."

My heart skittered. I stared at him, wondering if he could be playing an elaborate head game with me. He glanced up.

"Don't worry, I turned it off."

"Thanks," I said, and went into the butler's pantry to make the pot of tea I so badly needed.

I took it up to my office. Knowing I should keep out of Julio's way on this busy day, I went over to my suite to make some toast and cut up an orange for breakfast, after which I started going through messages.

I considered ordering flowers for Sylvia's funeral, but I knew she would prefer a donation to the Trust, so I wrote out a check and enclosed it in a note card. I wrote a note to Donna, too, expressing formal condolences, but decided not to tell her about the gift to the Trust.

When Kris arrived she looked in on me and smiled. She was dressed in wispy ivory lace, possibly an antique dress, with a black lace choker at her throat and more black lace in her hair.

"You look lovely, Kris," I told her. "Did you have fun last night?"

"Yeah. We drove down to Albuquerque."

"On a Thursday?"

"That's the night for Euphoria. Best goth scene in the state."

"Oh. Well, I hope the roads weren't too bad."

"Nah. Great storm! Lots of lightning and thunder."

I nodded, wondering if the storm could have affected the electricity in the house. That was a comforting thought, as long as I ignored the fact that the light switch had been physically turned on. Repeatedly.

"Do you hate thunderstorms?" Kris asked.

"Hm? No, I like them."

"'Cause you looked kind of unhappy there for a second."

I picked up the pile of message slips and riffled through them. "Did I? No, I like storms. I used to chase them, back in high school."

She laughed. "Not much to do in Santa Fe if you're a kid."

"Ain't that the truth." I saved out the message about the memorial, then dumped the rest in the wastebasket.

"I'd better start pulling voicemail," Kris said. "Maybe we'll have some reservations. One of my friends said they saw you on the news." She gave me a cryptic smile, then went to her office.

The day swung along pretty well from then on. We did have some new reservations, it turned out. Maybe Gina had been right.

I stayed busy at the hostess station and in the gift shop from the time we opened. It helped that the sun had come out, lighting up the rain-freshened gardens and lawns.

Tourists emerged from their hotels to stroll the streets of Santa Fe, looking at the shops and museums, and some of them stopping in for a spot of tea. My spirits rose and the day went by so quickly I was surprised when Vi tugged my sleeve and told me it was twenty to four.

"You said you wanted to change for the opening," she reminded me.

"I do. Thanks, Vi. Can you hold down the fort?"

"Sure."

I dashed upstairs and put on the dress I'd chosen for the opening, a Victorian-style amber crepe dress with dark cream-colored lace. I put my hair up and touched up my makeup, and arrived back at the hostess station just as Gina showed up at five minutes to four. She had newspapers tucked under one arm and a bouquet of yellow roses in the other, and was wearing a bright purple dress.

"Hey, it's the TV star! Can I have your autograph?" She grinned and handed me the roses, then caught me in a one-armed hug.

"Gina! You already brought me flowers!" I buried my face in the roses, inhaling their lovely scent.

"Those were for the tearoom, these are for you. Oh, and I brought copies of the papers. Figured you wouldn't have time."

"Thanks," I said. "Come back to the pantry and help me decide what to do with these. I've used all the vases."

"Oh, don't worry about them. Just stick them in a jug and deal with them later."

"That's a great idea! I have a pitcher they'd look wonderful in."

We went back to the pantry where I pulled out a large, green-tinted Mexican glass pitcher. With a few inches of water in the bottom, it was perfect for the roses. I played with them a little, spreading them out, picking off a leaf here and there.

"Those would look nice on the mantel in the dining parlor," Gina said.

I shot her a look. By this point I was suspicious of any interest in the dining parlor, beyond the point of reason, I knew.

"I want to talk to you later about the dining parlor," I said. "And right now I want to talk to the staff about it. Could you ask Vi to step back to the pantry for a minute?"

Gina fetched Vi while I gathered the others in the pantry. Julio and Mick joined us, and I rang Kris's phone to ask her to come down. Everyone crowded into the little room, surrounded by pots of fresh-brewed tea keeping hot under velvet cozies and serving trays decked with fresh flowers. Dee looked at me expectantly, Iz fiddled with the flowers on the tea trays, and Mick stared into space, zoned on his tunes. He hastily removed his ear buds as Vi and Gina came in.

"Just a few quick words before the party," I said. "First of all I want to thank all of you for your hard work, and for putting up with the upheaval of the last couple of days. Secondly, for those of you working with the guests, I want to ask you not to show the dining parlor. We're keeping that room closed for today. Better keep them out of the kitchen, too," I added, glancing at Julio. "They're welcome to go into all the tea parlors. Any questions?"

Vi raised a hand. "Who's watching the gift shop?"

"Let's take turns," said Dee. "Half an hour each."

"I'll go first," Iz offered.

Leaving them to work out the schedule, I carried the pitcher of roses to the front of the house and put them on the mantel in the north parlor. The room was filled with flowers now, evoking a conservatory. It smelled heavenly and looked quite lovely.

I had opened the pocket doors to make the front parlor into one large, square room, and with Mick's help had moved aside the screens and pulled the credenzas that normally served as sub-dividers into the center to form a buffet table. It was there that we'd serve the afternoon tea that would demonstrate Julio's talent to our first official guests.

The bells on the front door jingled. I went out to greet the first arrivals for the grand opening, and was soon busy welcoming a steady flow of guests, checking names off the reservation list Kris had printed out. That list was longer than I had expected, I was pleased to see. Many of the names on it were friends, like Katie and Manny Salazar and Aunt Nat, but there were also lots of people I didn't know. As they arrived I noticed that quite a number of them were college age, and a number of those were rather striking in appearance.

One young man was resplendent in a black morning coat and a top hat which he very courteously removed as he came into the tearoom. His straight, dark hair was loose and hung in a shining waterfall down his back, longer than mine, I noted with slight envy. He carried an ivory-headed walking stick to complete the ensemble. I only caught a glimpse of the knob beneath his hand, but thought it looked a little like a skull.

A friend of Kris's? I was too busy to ponder it. The main parlor was beginning to get crowded by now, and Dee and Vi were moving through the room filling teacups.

Leaving Iz in charge at the hostess station, I joined the chattering guests. Kris had come down and was doing her bit, moving from group to group. I saw her cross the room to where three of the college-age guests, all women, were admiring a statuette replica of the Nike of Samothrace that stood on a pedestal in the corner of Lily. Two of them had black hair and the third had vivid henna-red hair that brushed the shoulders of her black lace dress.

"Julio's ready," Dee said in my ear.

"Thanks. He can go ahead and bring out the savories," I told her.

She nodded and hurried out with an empty teapot. I stepped in front of the fireplace and raised my hands, and the chatter died down. Taking a deep breath, I smiled.

"Thank you all for attending our grand opening. I and the staff of the Wisteria Tearoom are delighted to welcome you today."

There was a smattering of applause from the few guests who didn't already have teacups. Gina winked at me, then turned to smile at the gentleman she was talking to, a suntanned, sandy-haired man I didn't recognize.

He was dressed in rancher formal: a brown suede jacket and bolo tie over a white pinstriped western-style shirt and new blue jeans. He, too, had removed his hat (a cowboy model, no doubt, which I presumed was now keeping good company with the topper on the hat rack in the hall). I wondered if Gina had found a new beau.

"To celebrate our opening we're serving a full, three-course afternoon tea," I said, glancing toward the hall where I saw Julio and Dee waiting with platters of food. "The first course of savories will be presented by our chef, Julio Delgado."

Julio came in, proudly bearing a large platter on which toast points, lettuce, cornichons, minced onions, capers, and chopped hard-boiled egg were all artfully arranged around a large tower of molded pâté. He set it on the sideboard with a ceremonial flourish.

Dee's platter of deviled eggs joined it, and Vi followed with plates of tiny cucumber and watercress sandwiches. They all went back to the kitchen and returned with a brie en croûte, a platter of cherry tomatoes stuffed with chive cream cheese mousse, and my parents' giant crystal punch bowl brimming with chilled shrimp and wedges of lemon.

I caught Julio's elbow and brought him forward to take a bow, then let him escape back to the kitchen while the guests fell on the savories with enthusiasm. The servers returned with fresh pots of tea and began making the rounds, filling cups and smiling at the guests, lovely in their lavender dresses and white aprons.

The guests began to disperse through the tearoom, spilling across the hall into the south parlor to find seats while they enjoyed their tea and savories. I walked through the rooms and stopped to chat with each group. I spotted a familiar-looking head of platinum hair, and ducked behind a screen.

It was Willow. I was so not ready to talk to her.

I went out into the hall and saw Claudia Pearson coming in the front doors. She wore a hat and gloves again, this time over a forest green suit. I smiled and went forward to greet her.

"I'm sorry to be late," she said. "Still catching up at the Trust."

"I'm so glad you could come! We're on the first course, so you're really not late. Please help yourself," I said, gesturing toward the main parlor. "Nat and Manny are in Hyacinth if you'd care to join them."

"Thanks, I think I will. My, what a beautiful spread," she added, gazing at the sideboard. "I thought Mr. Ingraham gave you a nice notice in the *New Mexican*, by the way."

"Did he? I haven't seen it."

Keeping an eye out for Willow, I fetched Claudia a cup of tea while she helped herself to the savories, then walked her over to Hyacinth and saw her comfortably settled with my aunt and Manny. It was chickenhearted of me, but I wasn't ready to return to the main parlor. Instead I went back to the pantry, where Vi glanced up at me from making more tea.

"Where are those newspapers Gina brought? I thought I left them in here."

"Dee stuck them up on the shelf," Vi said.

I pulled them down and searched through the *New Mexican* for Mr. Ingraham's food column. I was a bit disappointed to find that the review was for another restaurant, but beneath it under the heading "Eye on the Town" was a single line: "Opening this week is the Wisteria Tearoom, a promising new establishment offering traditional English tea with Victorian ambiance."

Not bad. I folded up the paper and tucked it back up on the shelf, hoping that the nod meant Mr. Ingraham would come back and try the full afternoon tea, and perhaps give us a review.

"There you are," said Julio, looking into the pantry. "Come here a minute."

"What is it?"

I followed him into the kitchen, worrying that the clotted cream hadn't, or something equally disastrous. Instead he took a plate off a shelf and showed it to me. It held a selection of the savories, including a tiny pâté mold in the shape of a star.

"This is yours. I knew you wouldn't have time to eat anything out there."

"Oh, Julio, thank you!" I picked up a deviled egg garnished with capers and hot paprika—there were two of those on the plate, and half a dozen of the shrimp—and bit into it. "Mmm. Divine."

He grinned, then a timer went off. "Scones," he said, and rushed to the oven, leaving the plate in my hands.

I ate a shrimp, then put the rest back on the shelf and braced myself to face my guests. I returned to the main parlor and spotted Willow chatting with Bob Hutchins, Katie's husband. The savories had been pretty thoroughly devoured by now, and Dee was clearing the empty platters while Vi collected dirty plates.

Gina was setting a stack of fresh plates at one end of the sideboard. I hurried over to her.

"You don't have to do that! You're a guest!"

"Just thought I'd help out a bit. You've got a full house, congrats!"

"Thanks. I think Kris stacked the deck a little. Who's your friend, by the way?"

Gina glanced toward Rose, where the rancher-looking gent was sitting with Jody Thompson. "That's Ted. He's in real estate. Thought I'd show him the tearoom. He deals with a lot of out-of-town folks, and they're always asking him to recommend places to eat. He might send a few customers your way."

"Well, thanks!" I glanced at Ted, who looked at ease in a red velvet wing chair with a cup of tea balanced on his denim-clad knee. "I would never have guessed he was a real estate agent."

"He was out showing horse properties to a couple from Connecticut this morning," Gina said.

"Ah."

As soon as the savories were cleared away, Julio and the servers brought in platters of scones and large bowls of clotted cream, blackberry jam, and lemon curd. There were cheddar scones with scallion butter, orange-lavender scones, currant scones, and heaps of cream scones fresh from the oven. Another platter held an array of sliced tea breads and a bowl of creamed butter to spread on them.

I called the guests back to the north parlor to hear Julio describe the scones and breads. They listened appreciatively and attacked the food with less urgency but no less gusto.

Things were a little more relaxed now, and after seeing the second course under way I went to the gift shop to check on Iz. I found her just about to hand the hostess duty over to Vi.

"All present and accounted for," she said, indicating the guest list. "Plus seven walk-ins. We may need some more tea samplers, we're almost sold out. Are there more packaged up?"

"They're in the storage room upstairs," I said. "I'll get them."

"I'll go. You're busy." Iz caught up the large, ribboned wicker basket that held the samplers, took the last three out and left them on the display table, and darted out.

As I stepped into the hall to watch her run upstairs, I met several older ladies meandering there. They all wore nice print dresses, florals or geometrics. One petite, silver-haired lady wearing a beige cashmere cardigan like a cape over the shoulders of her green polka-dot dress came up to me, beaming.

"Ms. Rosings, you have a lovely establishment!" she said.

"Thank you! I'm so glad you like it."

"There's just one thing," the lady continued as her friends clustered around her. "We want to see the murder room."

9

I was nonplussed, but managed to gather my wits. "I'm so sorry," I said, "but that room is being kept closed for now."

"Oh," said the small, elderly lady. She and her friends exchanged disappointed glances.

"Out of respect for the deceased," I added, glancing up the hall toward the front of the house. Several other guests, including a few of the goth-looking ones who were probably Kris's friends, were idling about between the tea parlors.

"I see," said the lady, looking resigned.

One of her companions, a thin, frail-looking woman with her gray hair up in an untidy bun and bright, bird-like eyes, stepped forward. "When do you think it will be open again, so we can see it?" she asked in a booming contralto.

I swallowed. "Well, normally it's available for parties of eight or more—"

"Good! We can get eight together, don't you think, Sarah?"

Sarah tugged at her sweater to straighten it. "I guess so."

"How about next Friday? What do you think, girls?" The other elderly ladies nodded, and the bird lady turned to me, smiling brightly. "We'd like to reserve the murder room for afternoon tea next Friday," she said.

I winced inwardly, wishing she would lower her voice, but smiled and nodded. "All right. Let me make sure the *dining parlor* is available, and we'll put you down for four o'clock next Friday."

They followed me to the hostess station, passing the goths standing in the hallway. One of them—an extremely tall girl in a floor-length burgundy velvet dress with long, pointed

sleeves à la Morticia Adams—gazed at me as she took a
languorous sip from her teacup. I hurried past and marked
down the bird lady's phone number on the reservation sheet at
the hostess station.

"Our business manager will call to confirm your
reservation," I told her, writing out a card with the date and
time and "Dining Parlor" in large letters. I handed it to her,
then went back to the north parlor.

A reservation for eight. I should be jumping for joy, but
between the elderly ladies' yakking about the "murder room"
and Willow wanting to make the tearoom a stop on her ghost
tour, not to mention Kris's picturesque friends, I was worried
we'd get a dark reputation we wouldn't be able to shake. I
supposed I could close the dining parlor permanently, but
something in me rebelled at the thought. I wanted it to be seen
for the charming room that it was, not shut away in shame.

The scones and breads were mostly gone by now, and Iz
and Dee were passing among the guests with fresh pots of tea.
I caught Dee's eye and asked her to start brewing the Wisteria
White tea—my special signature blend—that would be served
with the sweets. As she hurried to the pantry I gathered all the
remaining food onto one platter, then carried the empty
serving plates out on my way to the kitchen.

A small cluster of goths was still in the hall. As I passed,
the one in burgundy velvet caught my eye.

"I just wanted to tell you I thought that was really tacky,"
she said.

I stopped. "Beg pardon?"

"Those old ladies, asking to see the Room," she said,
lowering her voice on the last word in a reverent tone. "I
mean, how gauche can you be?"

I managed a weak smile. "Oh. Yes. Thank you."

She smiled back, and I escaped to the kitchen where I
handed the platters over to Mick. Julio was in the middle of

the room, humming, surrounded by cream puffs, almond macarons, tea cookies, chocolate truffles, and cascades of petits fours decorated with buttercream wisteria blossoms.

On the center island stood the largest of our three-tiered tea trays, on which Julio was arranging dainty puffs of meringue topped with fans of fresh, sliced strawberries standing up in stiff dabs of pink whipped cream. He looked up at me and grinned.

"Is this the special dessert?" I asked.

"Yep. Try one."

I did, biting it in half. The crunch of the meringue and creamy sweet-tart strawberry filling was augmented by a breath of alcohol. I closed my eyes, trying to identify the flavor.

"Brandy?" I guessed.

"Close. A little orange liqueur, stirred into strawberry jam. Just a thin layer underneath the strawberry cream."

"It's heavenly, Julio!"

"Thanks." He grinned, then went back to loading the tray with the strawberry treats. "I'm just about ready."

"I'll send the girls back," I said.

I met Iz in the hall, carrying the last platter, which had only a couple of scones left. "Your aunt's looking for you," she said.

"Thanks. Julio's ready to serve the sweets."

"Okay," she called over her shoulder.

As I reached the parlor I saw Nat hovering by the door, watching for me. She caught my arm and spoke in a low, worried voice.

"Oh, good! I don't know if it's a problem, but I thought you should know about it."

"Know about what?" I asked as she dragged me across the room toward Jonquil. For answer she just nodded her head toward Claudia Pearson, who stood talking with Gina's rancher-type real estate friend, Ted.

"My client wasn't happy about having to settle for a lower offer," Ted was saying, a hard edge to his voice.

Claudia frowned slightly. "Well, it was unfortunate, but it couldn't be helped. We weren't able to close without Mrs. Carruthers's participation."

"Mrs. Carruthers!" said a loud voice behind me. "That's the lady who was murdered!"

I turned to see the bird lady looking at us, eyes bright with curiosity. Her friends were ranged behind her, and beyond them every other guest in the room stood staring. Some looked shocked, some amused, and a couple surprised.

The awkward silence stretched out. I glanced toward the door and was grateful to see Dee and Iz waiting to bring in the sweets.

I stepped to the center of the room. "And now it's time for our third course of afternoon tea, the sweets. Chef Julio will present his pièce de résistance, and our staff will pour our specialty house tea, Wisteria White. I hope you enjoy it."

All eyes turned toward the doorway, and a round of "oohs" and "ahs" went up as the sweets were carried in and arranged on the sideboard. I stepped back and let Julio take center stage, then turned around.

"Mrs. Pearson," I said in a low voice, catching Claudia's arm. "Just the person I needed to talk to! Will you excuse us?"

I smiled sweetly at Ted and half-dragged Claudia out of the room, past a few stragglers coming in for the third course. I didn't stop until we were through the gift shop and into Hyacinth, where I let Claudia go. She gave me a skeptical look.

"Sorry," I said. "I just thought maybe you needed a little breathing room."

She laughed. "Actually, yes. Thank you."

"I take it he's the agent for the historic property owner."

"Yes. Not too pleased about the deal falling through."

"No. Well, that's understandable."

"It's just as well you pulled me out of there," she said. "I ought to be leaving anyway. I'm meeting my husband for dinner."

"Oh—you'll miss the sweets!"

She smiled. "I've tried some of them, and I can always come another day."

"Let me at least get you some of the strawberry puffs. I'll put them in a box for you to share with your husband."

"That's kind of you. Thanks."

I fetched a carry-out box from behind the hostess station and darted across the hall to the main parlor. The sweets were disappearing fast, but I managed to nab a couple of the strawberry puffs for Claudia. She met me in the hall, having donned her gloves again.

"Thanks for another lovely afternoon," she said.

I opened the door for her. "Thank you for coming."

"See you tomorrow at the service?"

She was referring to Sylvia's funeral. Appreciative of her tact, I nodded and smiled. "Yes."

I saw her out, then returned to the parlor. The servers were going around with teapots, and I anxiously watched the guests sample the final tea.

Wisteria White was my big finale, a delicate blend of white Darjeeling and white rose petals that I had created myself. I had spent the last week tinkering with the recipe, serving tastes of it to Julio and the girls and Gina and anyone else who got within reach, until I felt pretty confident that it would please my guests, but now I was nervous.

No one looked disgusted or set aside their cups. They sipped the tea and nibbled sweets and chatted happily. I took a cup for myself, and inhaled the fragrant steam, catching the whisper of white rose petals and the underlying hint of currant, all within the light, flowery fragrance of the white

Darjeeling. Ghost flavors, barely there. Meant to catch the imagination as much as the palate.

I saw Julio talking with a tall, sleek-looking blond man about his own age, both holding strawberry puffs which they turned this way and that. They seemed deep in serious discussion, and I realized the blond guy must be Julio's roommate. Silently wishing Julio victory in the dessert competition, I moved on, chatting with the guests.

Gina caught my eye from across the room and beckoned to me. She was standing with Ted the real estate guy. I made my way over to her.

"Ellen, I'd like you to meet Ted Newbury. Ted, this is my dearest friend, Ellen Rosings."

I offered my hand, hoping he wasn't still annoyed. Apparently Claudia's departure had lightened his mood, because he gave me a charming smile and shook hands.

"Nice to meet you. Gina's been telling me all week how wonderful your tearoom is, and I see that she's right."

"Thank you. I hope you enjoyed the tea."

"I'm a bourbon man myself, but the food's all been great."

I smiled. "It's nice of you to give us a try."

"Oh, I'm glad to know about your place. Some of my clients will just go crazy for this sort of thing. Do you have some business cards I could give out?"

"I do indeed. I'll get you some."

I started toward the door and was blinded by a sudden flash of light. When I could see again I found a young woman blocking the doorway, wearing jeans and a red sweater and holding a camera with a gigantic lens. Annoyed, I advanced on her.

"May I help you?"

"I'm from the *Journal*," she said, taking a step backward into the hall. "Dave Krips sent me to get some photos to go with a follow-up story he's writing."

"I see. Well, that's fine, but I'd rather you didn't disturb my guests."

"Yeah, okay. Can I get a shot of the room where the murder happened?"

I was tempted to say yes just to get rid of her, but I knew that if I did, the bird lady would magically appear and start talking about the murder room at the top of her lungs. I shook my head.

"Sorry, that room is not open to the public. There's really nothing to see in there, anyway."

"How about a picture of you, then?"

"Yes, all right."

I stepped into the gift shop, hoping to get her away from the guests. The bird lady and her friends were milling around in the shop, looking over the merchandise. Dee was at the hostess station, ringing up a purchase for one of them. I stood at the other end of the counter next to a vase of gladiolas and iris.

"Is this all right?" I asked the photographer.

"Yeah. Can you be holding a teapot?"

I fetched a chintz teapot from one of the display tables and held it in front of me. "How's this?"

"Great. Hold that."

She took a dozen photos at least. Finally she went outside to take some pictures of the house, and I returned the teapot to its display and fetched a handful of business cards for Ted. I found him and Gina by the fireplace, talking with Kris.

"Great," Ted said, accepting the cards. "Thanks."

"Thank *you*," I told him. "Let me know if you need more."

"Will do." He tucked the cards in his coat pocket and turned to Gina. "Gotta roll along. See you tomorrow night."

"Okay," Gina said, presenting her cheek to be kissed. Ted obliged, then turned to me.

"Nice meeting you, Ellen. Good luck with this." He made a

vague gesture at his surroundings, gave me a quick smile, then left, just hastily enough that I had the impression he was relieved to be going.

I looked at Gina. "New beau?"

"Oh, we've just gone out a couple of times. I'm still evaluating."

"He seems nice, for an all-American dude." Kris said.

I glanced at her, amused and wondering if she intended to damn with faint praise.

Gina gazed after Ted. "Yeah, I think so. He's got some depth. Tomorrow's the big test. We're going to dinner and a concert."

"Rock and roll?" I asked.

"Chamber music, at the Lensic."

"He doesn't look like the chamber music type," Kris observed.

"I know, that's why I picked it."

I laughed. Gina grinned, then slid her hand into my elbow. "Tonight, though, I'm all yours," she said. "Shall we paint the town?"

"I think painting my nails is about all I'll be up for."

"Oh, good, we can have a girl party!"

Kris smiled and moved away. The guests were starting to disperse, and I left Gina sitting by the fireplace nibbling a strawberry puff while I stood in the hall saying goodbye.

"Congratulations, Ms. Rosings," said a voice that made the muscles between my shoulders tense.

I summoned a smile as I turned. "Thank you, Willow. How nice of you to come to the opening! I hope you enjoyed it."

"Oh, yes. Some very interesting people here. I predict great success for you."

"Well, I hope your prediction comes true."

She gave a knowing smile. "It will."

The last to depart were the goths. Half a dozen of them

stopped to compliment me on the tearoom, including the young man with the skull-headed cane and the Amazon in burgundy velvet.

"We'll be back," she said in a voice so sober it almost sounded like a threat. The impression was reinforced by her smiling down at me; she must have been over six feet tall.

I thanked her and saw them all out, then put up the "Closed" sign in the window by the front door. Dee looked at me from the hostess station and grinned.

"Good day," she said.

"Yes, thank heavens! Did we book many reservations?"

She showed me a list half a page long. "I'll give it to Kris. Did she go upstairs?"

"Not yet," Kris said, coming out of the south parlor and taking the page from Dee. "Thanks! I'll get these into the computer."

"You could do it tomorrow," I said. "You've already stayed late."

"That's okay. I was having fun, that doesn't count as work." She went out into the hall. I followed.

"Thanks for asking your friends to come," I said, walking with her to the foot of the stairs.

"I knew they would like it. We might want to schedule a private party some time. Would you mind?"

"Of course not."

She gave me a cautious look. "They'll want the dining parlor."

"At least they were polite enough not to demand to see it today."

She smiled and hurried up the stairs. Returning to the main parlor, I found Vi and Iz collecting plates and teacups. The sideboard was already cleared.

"Has Julio left?" I asked Vi as we passed in the doorway.

"Uh-huh. He went home with his roommate. Mick's

waiting to help move the furniture."

"We'd better vacuum first."

"I've got it," said Dee, coming in with the vacuum cleaner.

Gina got up from her chair and caught my arm. "Come on, let's get out of the way."

I let her pull me into the hall, but balked at the stairs. "Let me get something to eat. Julio made me a plate. Do you want anything?"

"Yes, five hundred more of those strawberry things."

I grinned as we started toward the kitchen. "Aren't they great?"

"Inexpressibly fabulous."

I glanced at the dining parlor door and saw light underneath. Stopped and frowned.

"What?" Gina said.

"Tell you later. Just let me turn out this light."

I opened the door and nearly jumped out of my skin when I realized the room wasn't empty. Katie Hutchins was in there, on her hands and knees on the floor.

10

Katie! What are you doing?"

Katie looked up at me, eyes wide and face flushed, and backed away from the table. I went to help her up, taking her arm. She was just a little plump—not a bad thing for an innkeeper—and older than me by a decade or so. She was a long-time Santa Fe resident, with golden hair starting to go to silver, set off by a cream-colored silk blouse and turquoise slacks.

"I l-lost an earring the other day," she said, still peering under the dining table as she leaned back on her heels. "I was just looking for it."

"The police searched this room pretty thoroughly. If your earring was in here, they probably took it away."

"Oh. Yes, I suppose you're right." She sounded forlorn, but allowed me to help her to her feet, brushing at the knees of her slacks.

"Shall I find Bob for you?"

"He went home to check on our guests."

"Let me walk you over there, then."

"No, no." She seemed to gather herself, straightening her blouse and glancing at me with an embarrassed smile. "Thank you, but I think I can make it across the street by myself."

I went out into the hall, got a skeptical look from Gina, and held the door open for Katie. She gave the dining parlor a last, worried look, then came out. I turned off the chandelier and closed the door.

"It was a lovely party," Katie said as we walked to the front door, Gina a few steps behind.

"Thank you, Katie. Thanks for coming. Would you like

some scones for your guests?"

She smiled and seemed to relax. "That's sweet of you. Thank you."

"I'll get them," Gina offered, and strode off toward the kitchen.

Katie and I stood in the hall in awkward silence. I wondered why she'd slipped into the dining parlor instead of asking me about her earring.

"I hope the earring wasn't irreplaceable," I said.

She brushed her hair back from her face. "Oh, well. It was my mother's, that's all. Not terribly valuable, but I'd like to have it back."

I nodded. "I'll keep an eye out for it, and ask the servers to do the same."

Gina returned with two carry-out boxes, which she handed to Katie. She gave me a curious glance.

"Thank you, Ellen," Katie said. "I do wish you the best with the tearoom. This week has been—difficult."

Gina let out a crack of laughter. "You can say that again!"

I shot Gina a quelling look as I unlocked the front door for Katie. We said goodbye and I watched through the side lights as Katie went down the path to the street, then crossed and went into the B&B.

"Lost an earring, huh?" Gina said as I turned away from the door.

"Maybe she really did."

"Yeah, right. I think she was looking for something incriminating."

"What would that be? We know what the murder weapon was."

"I don't know! A blackmail letter?"

It was my turn to look skeptical. "I'm sure the police collected all the blackmail letters when they went over the room."

Gina shrugged. "What were you going to tell me about that room, anyway? Other than the fact that it induces bizarre behavior in anyone who goes near it?"

"Let's get some tea and go upstairs. It's sort of a long story."

We brewed a pot of Wisteria White and took it up to my suite along with the savories Julio had saved for me and a plate piled with petits fours and strawberry puffs. Kris came out of her office with her coat over her arm just as we reached the top of the stairs.

"Got the reservations entered," she said. "I'm heading home."

"Okay, thanks for your help."

"No problem. Here's some scoop I found. Didn't have time for a lot today, but it's a start."

She handed me a printed page of notes under a heading of "SYLVIA CARRUTHERS." I glanced up at her, surprised.

"Thanks! This is excellent."

"I can do more tomorrow. See you in the morning."

"What's that about?" Gina asked as we went into my suite.

"Oh, she offered to find me some information about Sylvia Carruthers. I wanted to know if she had interests beside historic preservation."

"What?" Gina said in mock indignation. "Are you implying she would spend an instant on anything other than The Cause?"

"I just wondered."

We made ourselves comfortable in my suite with the food and the teapot on the little table between two overstuffed chairs. I poured myself a cup of tea and sighed after taking a sip. I was coming down from the high of the successful opening, and despite Willow's prediction, I still had plenty of doubts about the long term.

Food was a good cure for depression. I picked up a dainty

watercress sandwich and bit into it without the least bit of daintiness.

"This isn't your dinner, is it?" Gina asked, watching me over her own teacup.

"Um—no, it's lunch. I guess I'll get to dinner around ten, if at all."

Gina put down her cup. "That does it. I'm taking you out. You need a break from this place."

I finished the sandwich and reached for a cracker spread with gooey brie. "Not tonight, Gina. I'm really beat."

"When's the last time you left this house?" she demanded.

"I went out yesterday afternoon."

"Oh."

Her stern expression relaxed a little. I wasn't about to tell her I'd only gone out to talk to Claudia.

"So what were you going to tell me about the dining parlor?" she asked.

I picked up a knife and cut into the pâté, choosing my words as I spread some on a toast point. I decided on simplicity.

"I think it might be haunted."

Gina gave me a pitiful look. "You *have* been stuck here too long. Come on, we're going to the Ore House for a drink."

"No, I'm enjoying this. I hadn't tasted the pâté before. Did you try it?"

"It's fantastic. So are the shrimp. Don't change the subject."

"I'm not. I think the dining parlor is haunted, and here's why."

I told her about my adventures with the light in the dining parlor, including Mick's impersonation of the ghost and my excursion to the lilac bushes. Gina listened, shaking her head now and then.

"The fact is, I can't explain the light being turned on again and again. I'm positive I was the only one in the house. It must have been Captain Dusenberry's ghost."

"Or Sylvia's?"

I looked at Gina. "I hadn't thought of that."

She rolled her eyes. "Get a grip, Ellen. Obviously, someone snuck into the house while you were cutting the lilacs, turned on the light to freak you out, and then hid."

"I don't think so. Not unless they spent the entire night hiding and then snuck out past Julio and me in the morning. Why would anyone bother?"

"Maybe it was Katie. Doesn't she serve tea, too?"

"For her guests. She doesn't have a lot of room."

"But maybe she's trying to eliminate the competition."

I shook my head and took a sip of tea. "Our businesses are complementary. Besides, she's established, she doesn't need to worry about me and she's certainly too busy for such shenanigans."

"What was she doing in there today, then?"

I sighed. "I don't know. Looking for an earring?"

"I don't buy it. She's up to something."

I ate a deviled egg, refusing to be drawn into speculation about Katie. Gina picked up a shrimp, dangling it by the tail as she frowned in thought.

"This business with the light hasn't happened before, right? It started yesterday?"

"I don't remember it happening before, but maybe it did and I just didn't notice. Or maybe the murder and all the cops got the captain stirred up."

"You've been listening to that ghost tour lady. Mm, good shrimp. What does he do to it to make it so wonderful? It's just a shrimp."

"He makes his own shrimp boil. Secret recipe."

Gina gave a blissful sigh. "Too bad he's so young, or I'd marry him."

"Don't you dare!"

"Don't worry, I'm not a cradle robber." She held out her empty teacup.

"You're not an old maid, either," I said as I filled it, then topped off my own cup. "I've seen happy couples with a wider age gap. That's not permission to steal my chef, by the way."

"Understood. And I wouldn't, anyway."

"Yes, you would. You'd whisk him away to the Bahamas or someplace."

Gina laughed, the throaty laugh that made her such fun company. "Only for the honeymoon! No, I'm working on Ted at the moment. Don't have time for another project."

I gave her a skeptical look. "One at a time, eh?"

"I'm a serial monogamist."

I looked over the wreckage of the savories, decided I'd had sufficient protein, and reached for a strawberry puff. Gina picked one up as well.

"Been waiting for you to do that," she said.

"You didn't have to wait."

"Yes, I did! Miss Manners said."

I smiled, shaking my head. "This is hardly a formal dinner."

"Yes, but you're my hostess and my dear friend and besides, if I don't have the willpower to resist gobbling these sweets on sight after stuffing my face with them downstairs all afternoon, then I'm a pretty sorry case."

She grinned and popped the entire strawberry puff into her mouth. I laughed and did the same.

"Mm. Oh, Julio!" I lay back limply in my chair.

"If only he could see you," Gina said. "*You'd* be the one going off to the Bahamas with him!"

"No, no. I don't mix business with romance."

"*I* do."

"Well, you can get away with it. You've always got more

new clients. Has Ted told you much about his work?"

She shrugged. "Dinner conversation, yeah. He just sold a place near you, I think."

I perked up at that. "The historic property?"

"Hm. Maybe. I don't really remember. Do you want me to ask?"

"Maybe not flat-out ask, but if you can get him to talk about it I'd be interested to know. Especially who bought it."

"Okay." She leaned forward, resting her forearms on her knee. "Is there a purpose to this snooping and pooping?"

"Well, yes. Sylvia was involved in an attempt to purchase a property for the Trust, and I think Ted might have been the seller's agent."

"Oho!"

"The deal fell through when she died."

I went on to describe the bidding war Claudia had mentioned, and how Sylvia's death had prevented the Trust's expensive acquisition. Gina listened, her eyebrows climbing higher.

"Did Donna know about all this?" she asked when I'd finished.

"I don't know. If she did..."

"I'd call it a pretty damn good motive for murder! Her mother about to spend half her inheritance on some old house that she wouldn't even own?"

I shrugged, feeling uncomfortable. "I don't want to make assumptions."

"Hmph. What about our charming detective? Does he know?"

I made a face. "Detective Arrogant? I haven't the slightest. Let's not talk about him."

"Don't you like him?" Gina cocked her head. "I thought he was kind of cute."

"Yeah, but he's—don't get me started." I snarfed a petit

four, then picked up the page Kris had given me. "Let's see what we've got here. Besides the Trust, Sylvia was a member of the Arts Council and the Historical Society. She was on the School Board from 1995 to 1999."

"When Donna was in school," Gina said.

"Yes, probably."

"I bet she was on the board before that, it just wasn't on the web."

"Maybe. Other than that, this all looks like Trust stuff. She's been in the papers a few times."

Gina took the page out of my hand and glanced over it. "She sure kept busy."

"She was a mover and a shaker." I frowned, thinking. "Claudia Pearson said she knew about historic properties before they came up for sale. I wonder if the Arts Council and Historical Society were avenues of information."

"Listen to you," Gina laughed. "Ellen Rosings, Investigator Extraordinaire! I've created a monster."

"Well, I'm just trying to puzzle it out. I mean, the sooner this murder is solved, the sooner I can get on with my life, with the tearoom."

Gina put the notes down and reached over to clasp my hand. In the soft, jeweled light of the stained-glass table lamp, her dark eyes gleamed. "This has been tough on you."

"Yeah, well. What's life without a challenge, right?"

I smiled at her, but in fact I was feeling a little low. Maybe it was just let down after the excitement of the grand opening. It had gone well. Now only time would tell if the tearoom was destined to survive.

"You know," I said, "I think I'll take you up on that drink after all."

We stuffed the leftovers into my mini-fridge and went downstairs. The staff had left, and the house was quiet. I waited for Gina to fetch her coat, then started toward the back door.

The light in the dining parlor was on.

I stopped and pointed to it, giving Gina a significant look. She shrugged. I opened the door, half expecting to find someone looking around in there, but the parlor was empty. Turned off the light and closed the door.

"Shall we walk?" I asked, opening the back door.

"Sure. I could use a stretch."

The evening was brisk, but it was nice walking through downtown Santa Fe. The chill had kept most of the tourists inside, though there were a couple wandering around the plaza gawking at the empty gazebo and looking in the store windows.

Gina and I hurried across to the Ore House on the plaza's southwest corner. Not haute cuisine but it had a nice bar, served good margaritas, and had been around forever. We verified that the quality of the drinks was still up to par and stayed chatting over a second round.

Gina kept me laughing with stories of an obnoxious but high-paying client at work, and never once mentioned ghosts or cops or dead bodies, or even tea. I began to feel almost normal.

Finally we called it a night. Gina walked back with me to the tearoom, and we walked around to the rear of the house again, where she had parked her car.

"Well, goodnight, girlfriend," she said by the door of her Miata. "See you soon."

"OK. Have a great time with Ted tomorrow night."

"Oh, I sure will. We'll see how great a time he has."

I grinned, gave her a hug, then turned to go into the house. I didn't get two steps.

"Gina."

"Hm?" She looked up from unlocking her car.

"Look at the dining parlor doors."

A warm glow of light came through the gauze-curtained glass. I heard the hiss of Gina's sudden inhalation.

"Shit," she said. "It's haunted."

11

Who else has a key?" Gina asked, coming up to stand beside me on the porch. We both stood staring at the light in the dining parlor.

"Only Julio," I said. "He wouldn't mess with me."

"Maybe he forgot something and came back to get it."

I gave her a skeptical look. "In the dining parlor?"

"Okay, no. Are you sure no one else has a key?"

"Positive. I changed the locks when I bought the house." I took out my keys. "Well, thanks for corroborating. It's nice to know I'm not nuts."

"You're not nuts, and I'm coming in with you."

"Thanks, hon, but you don't have to," I said, unlocking the hall door.

"Yes, I do." Gina's face was set in a look of grim determination.

"What are you going to do?" I asked. "Stand guard over me all night? Stay in the dining parlor and turn off the light whenever it comes on?"

"I'm going to walk through the house with you and make sure it's empty."

I gave in, feeling comforted by her concern even though I thought there was nothing she could do. I held the door for her, then locked it behind us. Gina nodded toward the dining parlor door. I opened it.

No one in the room. I walked over to the outside door and verified that the deadbolt was thrown.

"Look," Gina said, pointing at the chandelier.

One of the crystals was swinging back and forth. "Yeah, it

does that," I said.

"That is creepy!"

"It's probably just a vibration. Maybe when I opened the door it jostled the ceiling."

"But wouldn't they all be wiggling, not just one?"

I glanced at the chandelier again. Just the one crystal moving, all the rest were still. The skin on my neck began to crawl.

"Thanks, Gina. That'll really help me sleep tonight."

I turned off the light switch and stepped out into the hall, pulling the door closed behind me. Gina shrugged.

"Sorry. I just call 'em like I see 'em."

We went through the house, turning on lights and carefully turning them off behind us. The staff had restored the north parlor to its usual configuration, with the pocket doors pulled mostly closed and the credenzas and screens dividing the alcoves. All the tables were set with fresh linens and clean china for the next day.

The fresh flowers filled the rooms with cheerful color, and I found myself drawing deep breaths, trying to catch a whiff of scent. My tearoom was a beautiful place, I reminded myself. A place to be proud of. Destined for success.

I tried to believe that as I collected the pitcher of roses from the mantel in the north parlor. Gina came with me up to my suite. I set the roses on my bedside table.

"Willow was at the party today," I said, following her as she looked in the offices, mirroring what I had done the previous night. Just as I had found then, there were no intruders.

"Maybe she's the one turning on the lights!"

"To convince me there's a ghost?" I considered it, then shook my head. "She'd have to have some kind of remote control, or she'd have been seen. And she hasn't had access to install something like that."

Gina looked disappointed. "We didn't check the kitchen."

"I'll come down with you and look."

We started down the stairs, the ancient boards creaking beneath our feet. Gina glanced back at me.

"Want to spend the night at my place?"

I gave her a weary smile. "Thanks, but you know, that's not going to solve anything in the long run. Whatever's going on in this house, I'm going to have to live with it."

"Somehow that doesn't sound very cheery. Oh, crapola!" she added as she reached the hall and turned toward the back door.

"Light on again?" I asked, looking over her shoulder.

"Uh-huh."

There it was, the familiar splash of light across the floor of the darkened hall. I sighed, then strode toward the dining parlor, flipping on the hall light switch as I went.

This time when I opened the door, I saw four of the chandelier crystals moving. One crystal in the precise center of each side of the chandelier, lined up with the walls. That was pretty undeniably weird, I thought as my stomach did a slow flip.

"Okay," I said to the room. "I get that you're here, but could you please not keep turning on the light? It wastes electricity."

"Sylvia wouldn't waste electricity," Gina whispered in my ear.

"Captain Dusenberry probably never worried about conservation," I whispered back.

"Yeah, he probably used oil lanterns anyway," Gina agreed.

"Why are we whispering?"

We looked at each other. Gina reached out and turned off the light switch, and I pulled the door shut.

"Still want to look in the kitchen?" I asked.

Gina shot a resentful glance at the dining parlor door, then went into the kitchen and pantry entrance across the hall. "Might as well. You got any booze in there?"

I turned on lights as we passed the pantry and entered the kitchen. "Just the stuff Julio uses for cooking. If you want a drink we can go back upstairs."

"Nah."

Gina stood by the center island, gazing around the empty kitchen. She frowned at the narrow stairs that led up to the small attic, which we used for storage.

"It's locked," I said. "Julio and I have the only keys."

"OK. And that cubby under the stairs?"

We went over and checked it. The entrance to the cubby space, also storage, had no door and was covered by a calico curtain. Gina pulled it aside, revealing nothing scarier than sacks of sugar and flour. She let it fall again.

"I guess I'd better get home. You sure you'll be all right?"

I shrugged and smiled as best I could. "I was all right last night."

She grabbed me in a big bear hug. "Maybe it's a friendly ghost."

"Hasn't throttled anyone that I know of."

Gina pulled back and stared at me, wide-eyed. She didn't say a word, but her appalled expression told me she was thinking of Sylvia.

"Gina," I said firmly, "Sylvia Carruthers was not killed by a ghost."

"Right. Sure you don't want to come home with me?"

"Thanks, but no. Now go get your beauty sleep. You have to look gorgeous for Ted tomorrow."

I opened the kitchen's outside door for Gina. She glanced across the porch toward the dining parlor door. It was dark.

"Call me if you need anything," she said. "Anytime. I mean it. Call me if you have a bad dream."

"I will." I smiled, trying to look more brave than I felt. "Now stop fretting. I'll be fine."

She gave me a worried smile back and went to her car and got in. I waved and closed the kitchen door, locking it. I watched out the window as she drove away, then I left the kitchen, turning the light out behind me.

The hall was dark. The only light was a dim glow of the city coming through the lights around the front and back doors. I stood for a moment, listening to the house, the small settling sounds of an older building. Beyond that were the city sounds: distant music, voices of passing tourists or kids out on the town, the occasional rush of a passing car. All normal sounds.

I looked at the dining parlor door. The space beneath it was dark.

"Thank you," I said, and went upstairs to go to bed.

The next morning was quiet. The dining parlor light remained off, for which I was silently grateful. I spent the early morning doing the receipts from the previous night, and took them to Kris just before ten thirty.

"Thanks," she said. "I found some more stuff about Sylvia for you."

"Would you leave it on my desk? I'm going to the funeral service."

"Ah, that's why the sober look today."

She nodded toward the plain navy dress I was wearing. She was back in black—a chiffon dress with long, floaty sleeves.

"I should be back in a couple of hours," I told her.

"I won't say have fun." She gave me a deadpan look, then picked up the bank bag.

I went downstairs to wait for Aunt Nat, who had offered me a ride. Checking the reservation list I saw that we had only two groups at eleven, so I sat in Jonquil, where I could watch for Nat out of a front window. Dee brought me a cup of Darjeeling.

"That was really fun yesterday," she said.

"I'm glad you thought so. Thanks for all your hard work."

"Is every Friday going to be like that?"

"Not that elaborate, no. We'll serve a full afternoon tea, but we won't rearrange the furniture."

"Oh, good!" she grinned. "That was the least fun part."

"Amen to that," I said.

I drank my tea, gazing out at the wisterias on the porch, thinking of all the plans I had made. When the weather got warmer I intended to put patio tables out on the *portal* for additional seating. If the tearoom lasted that long.

Nat's car pulled up outside just as I finished my tea. I went out to the hall and put on my hat and coat, and was met at the door by Manny Salazar, wearing a dark suit and a gray overcoat.

"I offered to drive," he explained as we walked out to the car. "She's kind of down this morning."

"Oh? I hope she's all right."

"Just feeling her years, I think. You know we're not spring chickens any more."

Nat waved at me through the car window as Manny opened the back door. I slid into the seat and clasped the hand Nat reached back to me.

"Thanks for picking me up," I said.

"I'm glad you're coming with us," she said, turning her head to look back at me. "Nice to have younger people around. This is the third funeral I've attended this year."

I squeezed her hand, then sat back as Manny drove the short distance to Rosario Cemetery on the north side of town. The oldest cemetery in Santa Fe, it was still active. Having a plot there was a mark of some prestige, and usually indicated a long-time Santa Fe family.

My own family was not Catholic, so my parents were buried in Memorial Gardens on the south side of town, but Sylvia's family was here. I glanced away from the open grave draped with artificial turf as Manny dropped us at the door of the chapel and went away to park the car. Nat took my arm and we walked together into the old, adobe chapel.

This was actually the second chapel, built in the early nineteenth century after the first had collapsed. The original chapel had been built by De Vargas, who had pledged to carry his statue of the Virgin Mary there every year in thanks for the successful return of the Spanish to Santa Fe after the Pueblo Rebellion. The statue, now known as "La Conquistadora," was kept in the much more elaborate and famous San Francisco Basilica near the Plaza, but once every year she was carried with great ceremony to Rosario Chapel in fulfillment of De Vargas's promise. Her passage, now a full-blown parade, was the basis of Santa Fe's annual Fiesta.

The small chapel was almost filled. Sylvia had many friends, it appeared. As Nat and I took the last spots in a pew near the middle of the building, I thought about the irony of this place of peace being the result of the conflict between the Pueblo Indians and the Spanish colonists.

The structure was simple but lovely, its high adobe walls soft and thick, with stained glass windows glowing like jewels against the whitewash. This chapel felt peaceful, despite its history.

The soft strains of Barber's "Adagio for Strings" played in the background. Sylvia's casket lay elevated at the front of the chapel, a spray of white flowers on top of it and a large photo of Sylvia on a stand beside it. Seeing her face for the first time since her death gave me an unexpected pang of sadness. I hadn't known her very long or very well, but I had reason to be grateful to her and to regret the community's loss.

Donna was sitting in the front pew, her hair looking

reddish beneath a small, modern black hat. Her dress was black also, but with white polka dots. Two other women sat with her, neither of whom I recognized.

As the music built to a shimmering crescendo, I saw Claudia come in carrying a folded sheet of paper. She gave me a fleeting smile as she continued to the front and sat across the aisle from Donna. Wondering what had become of Manny, I looked around toward the door and saw Detective Aragón standing against the wall at the back of the chapel, wearing a dark suit and black raincoat instead of his motorcycle leathers.

My heart gave an unpleasant lurch and I quickly faced forward again. A moment later Manny squeezed into the pew beside us, and shortly the mass began.

What was Aragón doing there? I wondered. Cops on television attended funerals to observe suspicious behavior, but maybe he was merely paying respect to Sylvia.

I frowned and tried to put him out of my mind. I didn't like the thought of him behind me, watching everyone in the chapel, taking note of which suspects were present. I couldn't help thinking his eyes were on me.

The service was simple, delivered by Sylvia's priest who had known her for decades and could actually talk about her life with understanding and intelligence. He spoke of her charity and her devotion to Santa Fe's history, then invited Claudia Pearson to give the eulogy. Claudia came forward and unfolded her page of notes, from which she read a short speech about Sylvia's work with the Santa Fe Preservation Trust.

Donna had not felt up to giving the eulogy, then. I wasn't surprised. Whatever her relationship with her mother, she must be upset by Sylvia's death, especially the manner of it. I remembered how hard I had found it to give the eulogy at my own mother's funeral, and when Dad had died so soon afterward I'd been so crushed I was unable to say anything at all, and had left the task to my brother.

Claudia finished speaking and returned to her seat, and the priest went on with the mass. When the time came for communion, Manny went forward while I sat listening to the music with Nat clinging to my hand.

I glanced back at Detective Aragón, curious whether he intended to take communion. Apparently not, for he hadn't moved from his place against the wall. He looked my way and I faced forward again, trying to pretend he wasn't there.

When the mass ended Donna stood up and walked out at once, looking composed if slightly pale, with her friends close behind. The pall bearers carried out the casket and the congregation began to disperse, spilling out of the chapel into the chilly sunshine of a spring afternoon. Manny, Nat, and I didn't go to the graveside, choosing instead to remain in front of the chapel. A small cluster of people gathered around the grave. I could see Donna's polka-dot dress.

Beyond them a fence marked the division between Rosario Cemetery and the much larger National Cemetery. Rows of military markers curved across the rising slope in the distance, bright white against the green grass. Nearer by, in the oldest part of the cemetery, the gravestones were less regular and showed evidence of age. Mature cottonwood trees, just now leafing out, cast restless dappled shadows over the markers.

I remembered Willow's suggestion that I visit Captain Dusenberry's grave if I wanted to make peace. That advice seemed a little less ludicrous now.

Katie and Bob Hutchins made their way over to us. Katie looked sad and a little tired, but gave me a small smile.

"Wasn't that a lovely service?" she said.

Nat nodded. "I like that photo of Sylvia they had on display. I hadn't seen it before. Maybe Donna would lend it to me so I could get it copied."

We stood chatting for a few minutes, Nat and Katie

exchanging reminiscences. I glimpsed Detective Aragón hovering nearby and ignored him. Finally Donna and her friends climbed into a limousine and were driven away.

Manny went off to fetch his car while Nat and I said goodbye to the Hutchinses. As Katie shook my hand she leaned close and hissed in my ear.

"What's that man doing here?"

I knew who she meant without having to follow her glance. "Paying his respects, I guess."

"Rather unfeeling of him to intrude! What must poor Donna have thought?"

Having no idea what she thought, I just shrugged. Katie went off with Bob, and Nat and I walked forward to meet Manny, who had joined the line of cars picking up passengers in front of the chapel. I opened the front door for Nat and helped her in, then stepped to the back door. Before I could open it a man's hand reached for the handle, blocking my way.

I looked up in surprise and found Detective Aragón gazing back at me. A rush of resentment made me say the first thought in my head.

"I'm surprised to see you here, Detective."

"I could say the same to you. Thought you didn't know Mrs. Carruthers that well."

"I didn't, but she was a friend of my aunt's," I said, nodding toward the front seat of the car. "And in any case, I have good reason to be here. Without Mrs. Carruthers's help I wouldn't have been able to open the tearoom."

He stood still, slightly frowning as he appraised me with his dark gaze, then at last opened the car door. I got in, maintaining my dignity with an attitude of cold formality.

"Thank you," I said, then used fastening my seat belt as an excuse to turn away.

Detective Aragón closed the door and stood watching as Manny drove us away. Not until the car pulled out onto Paseo de Peralta did I relax. I only half heard Nat's repeated thanks to me for coming with them.

"Do you have to get back to the tearoom right away," she said, "or can you come to Donna's with us? We're only planning to stay a little while."

"Sure, I'll come with you."

I was curious to see more of Donna, and to see her home. So much of one's personality is expressed in one's residence. I also admitted to myself that I wanted to observe her behavior. As bad as Detective Arrogant, I told myself.

Donna lived in Colinas Verdes, one of several developments on the northwest side of town, out of the city proper. As Manny drove through the countryside, over and between hills dotted with piñon and juniper trees, I marveled at how many new and expensive-looking houses had been built in the area. Santa Fe attracts money, and a lot of it was out here, where the lots were anywhere from two to twenty acres in size and offered sweeping vistas.

Donna's home was very modern, with lots of steel and huge windows, perched on top of a hill. Cars jammed the gravel driveway and spilled out onto the street. Manny parked, and the three of us walked together up the steep drive.

Inside, the house was just as angular and modern as it appeared from outside. The front door opened onto a small entryway, which in turn led to a large, high-ceilinged living room filled with chattering people, most of whom I didn't know.

Donna seemed to favor chrome and glass, and her decorating was austere. The only color was on the white walls, in the form of vivid abstract paintings. She had a lot of them, along with the occasional piece of abstract sculpture.

Donna stood near a gas fireplace whose artificial logs were cold and dark. A largish group of people surrounded her, having what appeared to be an animated discussion. Deciding to wait a little for a better opportunity to pay my respects, I offered to fetch Nat a drink and found my way into the kitchen.

It was huge, almost as large as the tearoom's commercial kitchen, and almost everything in it was brushed steel. People were chatting in here, too, though in a more relaxed way as they grazed from plates of elegant finger food on a long, granite-topped counter.

The food caught my eye—professional interest—and I was intrigued. It looked rather like abstract sculpture, so ornate that it must have been catered. I wished Julio could see it, not because I wanted such food in the tearoom but because I thought it would amuse him.

I took a celery stick filled with a piped squiggle of pimiento cream cheese from a silver Nambé ware platter on which identical-length sticks were arranged with military precision. I half expected a waiter to rush to replace my celery and repair the design.

I did spy a young woman a little older than my servers, in black slacks and formal white shirt with her hair pulled back into a businesslike ponytail, collecting abandoned wine glasses from the windowsills of the adjacent dining nook. I nodded when she glanced up at me; she gave me a brief smile in return. I poured cups of soda for myself and Nat and wandered back out to the living room.

Donna had taken a seat on a white leather sofa. I gave Nat her drink and strolled toward Donna, hoping to get a moment to say hello. Seated beside her was a painfully thin redheaded woman in a fuchsia dress, talking a mile a minute.

"—really a shame you missed it! The First Lady was there and everyone thought the Frankenthaler was fabulous! Come by the gallery before Friday and you'll see what I mean, though of course all the best pieces have sold but you might find something you like. It's an outstanding show, really!"

The woman paused to take a breath and I stepped forward, smiling at Donna. "I just wanted to tell you how sorry I am."

Donna looked up with a slight frown. "Oh, thank you. Thank you for coming, Ms..."

"Rosings. Ellen Rosings."

"Right, from the tearoom."

The woman in fuchsia stared at me as if Donna had announced I was from the moon. I acknowledged her presence with a fleeting smile, then turned my attention back to Donna.

"Your mother helped me accomplish my goals. I really wouldn't have succeeded without her. I want you to know that I'll always remember her generosity."

Donna pressed her lips together in a thin smile. Her gaze shifted to Nat and Manny, who had come up beside me. Nat reached out a hand toward Donna, who took it briefly.

"Donna, dear, I'm so sorry," Nat said, shaking her head. "Sylvia was a good woman."

"Thank you," Donna said.

"Did she live here with you?" Manny asked.

"Oh, no. She had an old ramshackle place on Otero Street. It belongs to the Trust now."

"She left her house to the Preservation Trust?" I asked.

Donna turned a flat gaze on me. "Actually she gave it to them years ago, after my father died. She kept living there, but she signed the house over to the Trust. I guess she was afraid I'd try to update the plumbing or put in double-pane windows, God forbid."

"She did care passionately about historic buildings," Nat said.

"Yes."

The silence stretched for an awkward moment. The roomful of strangers stared at me and my aunt, and Donna's hard gaze dared Nat to say more.

At last a young man in a black suit with a shock of blond

hair hanging over one eye came up and, as though we weren't there, started chatting to Donna about a movie he'd seen at the local art theater. Donna looked at him and nodded, the tension gone from her face. Nat and I moved away, and Manny drifted after us.

"Did you want to talk to anyone else?" I asked Nat.

She looked around the room. Most of the guests were closer to my age than to hers.

"I guess not. I don't see any of Sylvia's friends here."

"Maybe they knew—" I caught myself about to say that Sylvia and Donna didn't get along.

"What?" Nat asked.

"Nothing. I'm ready to go whenever you are."

Nat looked at Manny. "Let's go, then. I could use some lunch in a quiet place. Do you have time to join us?" she asked, turning to me.

"Um, not today if you don't mind. I have a couple of things I need to get done."

I didn't tell her that they involved trying to figure out who had killed Sylvia, and why. Seeing Donna had reminded me that I wanted to find out what she and Sylvia had been talking about before Donna left the tearoom on Wednesday. I'd been meaning to ask Vince Margolan about it, but he hadn't come to the grand opening or to Sylvia's funeral. I'd half expected to see him at the funeral or at Donna's. I decided to drop by his gallery and say hello, and see what he could tell me.

A breeze stirred the wisterias as I hurried up the path and stepped onto the tearoom's front porch after Manny and Nat dropped me off. I turned to wave goodbye, then went in to check on things before walking over to Vince's.

All was quiet at the hostess stand. One customer was browsing in the gift shop, there were a couple of parties in the main parlor, and Dee told me three groups were coming in at four.

"Julio's saying he might go home early," she added.

"Okay, thanks."

I went back to the kitchen to see Julio, who was sitting at the break table by the fireplace, poring over a cookbook. He looked up as I came in.

"How was the funeral?"

"Quite nice, as funerals go. I hear you'd like to leave early."

"Yeah, if you don't mind. Andre wants me to come to the Bistro and try his dessert."

"I don't mind at all. You did a great job yesterday, and I know you worked extra hard. The strawberry puffs were a huge hit, by the way."

He grinned and closed his cookbook, tucking it away on a shelf with dozens of others. "Thanks. See you Tuesday morning."

"Right. Have a great weekend."

He tossed a smile at me over his shoulder as he hung up his chef's jacket. I locked the kitchen door behind him then went back out into the hall, glancing at the dining parlor door as I passed. No light beneath it, I was pleased to see.

"I'm going out for a few minutes," I told Dee, as I tucked a couple of scones into a box. "Just across the street."

"OK. To the B and B?"

"No, to Mr. Margolan's gallery. It's in that little brick house, catty-corner to the north."

The house was a pleasant one, with the rambling construction of a building that has grown as its residents prospered. No Victorian lines here, though it was made of brick, an indication of the wealth of its builder, and that it was probably built after the railroad had come through in the 1880's. Brick would have been too expensive to import before then, which was why my house, though Victorian in design, was built of adobe.

The windows were covered with white paper. I stepped

onto the small porch and knocked at the front door. Vince Margolan opened it, wearing a black turtleneck and jeans.

He was about forty with medium-length blond hair and a sleek, tailored New York look. Just then the hair was a little disarrayed, which made him seem rakish and rather appealing. When he saw me he gave a self-conscious start.

"Good afternoon," I said, smiling. "I'm sorry to interrupt. I wondered if you might have a few minutes to chat?"

He glanced over his shoulder toward a table spread with large blueprint pages in the middle of the room. Another man stood there, slender with salt-and-pepper hair and beard, wearing glasses, a plaid shirt, and jeans.

"If this is a bad time I can come back," I added.

"No, no—ah. No. Come on in. Gene was just leaving." Vince strode to the table and rolled up the sheets, handing them to the other man. "This all looks fine. We'll go over the details later."

"I'll go ahead and start getting the materials, then," said Gene.

"Yeah, fine. Call me."

Gene gave me a nod as he left, and Vince beckoned me in. The front room of the house was wide and low-ceilinged, with white-painted walls and a weather-beaten hardwood floor. Just now the room looked bare and stark. Loose ends of wires stuck out in places from the walls and ceiling. No furniture except the table and a standing lamp. Its bright fluorescent bulb cast harsh shadows of the work table across the floor, reminding me of Donna Carruthers's abstract art.

"Sorry I don't have any chairs in here or I'd offer you one," Vince said.

"That's okay," I said. "Looks like you're remodeling."

He nodded. "Hoping to get the gallery opened in a couple months. What can I do for you—Ellen, right?"

I nodded. "I brought you some scones. I guess you were

busy yesterday."

"Yeah. Very busy." He accepted the box of scones and put it on the work table, then shifted some tools that lay there, straightening them into a line.

"I just wanted to ask you about Wednesday, if you don't mind," I said. "I think you were one of the last people who talked to Sylvia."

"Oh." He frowned a bit, possibly in distaste.

"Sorry to bring up an awkward subject," I added, "but I've been trying to puzzle out what happened, hoping it'll bring me some peace of mind."

"Well, I'll tell you what I can. The cops didn't think I helped much."

"I was wondering if you knew what Donna and Sylvia Carruthers were talking about. I think you were in the room with them when everyone was leaving?"

"Um, yeah. I was telling Donna about the Fanshawe Gallery's opening. She was real interested, but she didn't show up for it last night."

I gave a small smile. "She was probably getting ready for the funeral this afternoon."

"Oh, was it today? Oh."

Vince glanced toward the bare work table, then back at me. He ran a hand through his hair, making me think that was how it had gotten ruffled.

"Well, I'm not sure what they were talking about," he said. "Sylvia said something to Donna about, 'Are you doing something Friday?' and then I left the room."

"Did you see anyone else go in?"

He shook his head, blinking. "No, I didn't notice anyone."

"I see. Well, thanks," I said, taking a last look around at the bare walls. "Good luck with the remodeling. It isn't easy working within the historic building preservation guidelines."

He laughed as he walked with me to the door. "Yeah, I bet

you know about that."

"Oh, yes! It's worth it, though. This is a great part of town. I hope you'll enjoy being here."

"Thanks." He opened the door and leaned against it, a slight frown hovering on his brow. "Say, Ellen?"

"Yes?"

I paused on the doorstep. Vince hesitated, and I put my hands in my coat pockets against the chill breeze.

"I'm sorry about—about missing your opening," Vince said. "I hope it went all right."

"It did, thanks."

He was quite close, and almost seemed to be leaning toward me. Then he flashed a sudden smile.

"Thanks for stopping by. I'm a little shy about getting to know the neighbors."

I smiled back. "Well, don't be. Come in for tea some time. Neighbors are always welcome."

"I will."

I left and crossed the street, hurrying back to the tearoom. As I closed the gate of the tearoom's white picket fence behind me I glanced toward Vince's gallery. He was still in the doorway, watching me. I waved, then hurried inside, ready for a hot cuppa.

It was just before four, and a trio of women were talking with Dee at the hostess station as I came in. I slipped past, intending to go to the butler's pantry and make a pot of Darjeeling. Dee caught my eye.

"Ms. Rosings? There's someone here to see you."

Her voice sounded a little worried. I gave her an inquiring look.

She glanced at the customers, then added, "He came while you were across the street. I put him in Marigold."

"All right. Thank you, Dee."

I took off my coat and hat and hung them in the hall

between a fur-collared camel hair coat and a black raincoat. I stepped into the restroom to smooth my dress and my hair, then went through the gift shop and into the back part of the south parlor to Marigold, the most remote of the alcoves.

The chair by the window was empty, so I had to step past the screen and credenza in order to see my visitor. I did so, and I'm afraid I stopped and stared in surprise.

Seated in a rust-colored wing chair, staring moodily into the fire, was Detective Aragón.

12

W hat are you doing here?" I said, and was immediately sorry for it. Not only was it rude, it made me seem hostile, which was the last thing I needed. For all I knew I was Detective Aragón's prime suspect.

He grimaced but didn't shoot back the sarcastic comment I was expecting. He was still wearing the suit he'd had on at the funeral, and now he shifted in his chair as if uncomfortable.

"I want to talk to you," he began, then paused as Dee entered the room behind me.

"Can I bring you anything?" she asked, giving me a worried glance.

I looked at Aragón. "Would you like some coffee?"

He fidgeted again. "How about tea?"

There was a pause, then Dee asked, "What kind?"

"Lapsang Souchong," I said in a burst of pique.

Dee's eyes went wide and her lips twitched as she no doubt imagined the detective's reaction to the strong, smoky tea. For most it was an acquired taste.

I relented. "On second thought, make it Ceylon. Thank you, Dee."

I sat in the chair by the window, trying to settle my feelings. Perhaps it was just that the day had been a bit emotional for me, with the funeral and all. I wasn't ready for another round of sniping with Detective Arrogant. I took a deep breath, imagining Miss Manners's mantle of civility settling on my shoulders.

"What may I do for you, Detective?"

He gazed at me, a tiny frown creasing his brow, then he

swallowed and looked away toward the fire. He leaned forward with his elbows on his knees and his hands laced between them.

"I want to offer you an apology." He cleared his throat, then faced me again, his jaw muscles tight. "I'm proud of my work. I'm good at it. But the last time I was here I behaved unprofessionally toward you. I'm sorry."

I took a breath, relieved and rather surprised. "Accepted."

"Thanks."

He leaned back in the wing chair, gingerly as though worried he would break it, and looked around the room as if surprised to find himself there. I remembered what Julio said about his family's lack of money.

"Since you're here," I said, "I have a question or two, if you don't mind."

He shrugged. "I don't promise to answer them, but you can ask."

"I was wondering if you had found an earring when you searched the dining parlor."

His gaze snapped to my face, suddenly sharp. "What kind of earring?"

I blinked. "Well, I don't know what it looks like. Katie Hutchins said she'd lost one at the tea that day."

Detective Aragón's eyes narrowed and he continued to stare, but didn't say anything. I leaned back in my chair, returning his gaze.

"So you did find it," I said.

He pressed his lips together. "We found an earring, yes."

"Good. Katie will be glad to hear it."

"She can't have it back. It's evidence."

"Well, I'm sure she'll understand that," I said slowly. "Once you have the case settled she can request to get it back, can't she?"

He continued watching me, frowning slightly. The mantel

clock chimed the half hour, its tones gradually fading to silence.

"I'd appreciate it if you didn't say anything to her about it," he said.

"All right."

I felt a pang of foreboding on Katie's behalf. She couldn't have killed Sylvia, could she? Though it had been odd to find her searching the dining parlor. I brushed the thought aside, not wanting to think ill of Katie, who was a good neighbor.

"Speaking of getting things back," I said, "I assume I'll eventually get my dress back?"

Aragón shrugged. "Can't promise."

"Yes, I know. Evidence. I'm sure you found fibers from it on Mrs. Carruthers's dress. I'm more interested to know what kind of fibers you found on her back. She must have been strangled from behind."

He frowned and opened his mouth to say something, but then Dee came in with the tea, and for a couple of minutes we were busy with cups and saucers. She had brought some scones as well, and put them on the low table between us along with lemon curd and clotted cream. As she straightened, she cast me an anxious glance. I smiled to reassure her, and thanked her as she left. Detective Aragón and I settled back with our teacups.

"Would you like milk or sugar in your tea?" I asked, indicating the selection on the tea tray. "Or we can have lemon if you like."

"Uh, no thanks," said Aragón, lifting his cup.

I watched him take a sip, his thumb and forefinger pinching the small handle of the china cup as if he was afraid it would shatter if he lost control of it. He set it down in the saucer with a small clatter.

"What kind of tea did you say this was?"

"Ceylon. It's from Sri Lanka. It's just a nice, mellow black tea, the sort of thing you find in most tea bags, only this is a higher quality."

His lip curved up in a lopsided smile. "Nothing but the best, eh?"

"Well, yes. Treat your customers well and they'll come back. That's the theory, anyway." I took a sip of tea, found he was still watching me, and added, "I'm proud of my work, too."

He nodded, then gave a soft laugh. "You know, I assumed it was just a hobby for you. Guess I was wrong about that."

"Yes, you were," I said, bristling slightly.

"Sorry."

He smiled, and somehow that made me appreciate this apology more than the first. I smiled back, then glanced down at the cup in my hand. It was a Haviland Limoges cup with a spray of tiny roses beneath an ornate gold border, matching the cup Detective Aragón had balanced on his knee. In that pattern I owned only the two cups and saucers, two tea plates and the matching teapot; they had been in my collection before Nat had suggested I open the tearoom, and were among my best pieces.

"I put everything I have into this tearoom," I said. "If it fails..."

I couldn't finish that sentence, couldn't face the possibility of failure. The tearoom had pulled me out of depression, and I was terribly afraid that losing it would send me spiraling down again.

"That took a lot of courage," Aragón said. "I guess having a murder here your opening week hasn't helped much."

I gave a small shrug and took a sip of tea. "Too soon to tell. My friend Gina thinks the publicity may actually be good for us, though I'm sorry to think that could be true. Or it may have killed us."

"I hope not," he said.

I met his gaze and was surprised to see a soft expression on his face. Maybe the fierce detective had a hint of kindness in him.

"Thank you."

He smiled, and I found myself thinking that he really was attractive. Quite gentlemanly, in fact, in his suit and tie. He cleaned up nicely.

"Would you like a scone?" I said, putting down my cup and picking up the small plate of scones from the tea tray.

"Is that what they're called? They look like little biscuits."

"They're like a biscuit, yes. A little sweeter, and more moist. They're from England, and over there 'biscuit' means a cookie."

"You have these sent from England?" he said, looking incredulous.

"No, no," I laughed. "Our chef makes them. I meant they originated in England. Or some say in Scotland."

"Okay, I'll try one."

He set aside his teacup and accepted a scone, carefully putting it on his tea plate. Following my lead, he pulled it open.

"This is clotted cream and this is lemon curd," I said, offering the twin condiment dish. "I like scones with both."

His brows rose. "Clotted cream? Sounds gross."

"It's just cooked down really slowly, so it's very thick. Try a little."

I spread lemon curd on half a scone and put a dollop of clotted cream on top. He followed suit, watching me to make sure he was doing it right, like a kid at his first grown-up dinner party. I took a bite and he did the same. His scone crumbled a little and he hastily dropped the rest on his plate.

"They do fall apart sometimes," I said. "They're so tender."

"Mm," he said. "Good. Wow, that cream stuff is really...creamy."

I smiled. "I first tasted clotted cream in England. I think that was what made me fall in love with English tea."

"So you brought it back to Santa Fe." He picked up his teacup and sipped. Looked a little more comfortable this time.

"I've tried to," I said. "It isn't easy to make here—my chef —well, you wouldn't be interested in the details."

Feeling shy all of a sudden, I finished the tea in my cup and picked up the teapot, offering to refill the detective's cup. He nodded, ate the rest of his scone, and reached for another.

"Oh, by the way," I said as I poured for him and then myself, "I thought you might like to know that we're missing a napkin from the linens we used on Wednesday."

"Why would I like to know that?"

"Well, I think the killer probably used it to wipe the back door handles in the dining parlor. I suppose they took it with them and dumped it in the trash somewhere. I looked around out back but didn't find it."

He was frowning now. "How did you know the door handles had been wiped?"

I put the teapot down and covered it with the cozy, then picked up my cup and took a sip. "When I cleaned the room I found that black fingerprint dust all over the china and the furniture, but there wasn't any on the door handles. I assumed that was because they had been wiped, so there were no prints for the powder to stick to."

Detective Aragón nodded slowly. "You're pretty observant."

"I think that's a compliment, so I'll say thanks."

He gave a half smile. "It was a compliment. You want to be careful, though. Take too much interest in an investigation and cops get suspicious."

"I can't help wanting to figure out what happened in my own home."

He shrugged and nodded acknowledgment. I ate the rest

of my scone, realizing with slight surprise that I felt more relaxed and comfortable than I had all day. Detective Aragón was turning out to be pleasant company, when he wasn't in cop mode.

"Did Claudia Pearson tell you about Mrs. Carruthers's intention of donating money to buy a property for the Trust?" I asked.

"Yeah, she mentioned it."

"I'm wondering if Donna Carruthers knew about it. Assuming she's the heir, she might have objected."

Detective Aragón leaned back in his chair and gave me a long look, which would have intimidated me had the corner of his mouth not turned up in a slow smile. "She knew," he said. "She told me about it. She was pi—I mean, she was annoyed about it."

"I thought she must be. I know she and her mother didn't see eye to eye. There was a little tension between them at the tea, now that I think of it."

He tilted his head. "Do you remember over what?"

"I'm afraid not. I just remember being worried they'd get into an argument, so I changed the subject."

"So you think Donna Carruthers is a suspect."

"We're all suspects, aren't we? Everyone who was at the tea?"

A grin crinkled the skin at the corners of Aragón's eyes. "Yeah."

I swallowed, looking down at my cup. I'd wanted him to deny it. I swirled the tea, gazing through it at the flowers painted in the bottom of the cup.

"Although Mr. Ingraham and Mr. Salazar and my aunt all left while Mrs. Carruthers was still alive," I said. "I assume you collected that information."

"Yes."

I looked up. "You're laughing at me."

"No," he said, chuckling. "I think it's cute."

"Cute?"

I gave him an indignant look. He shifted in his chair, lounging comfortably now.

"Yeah, I mean—you're doing pretty good for not having access to all the evidence."

I took a deep swallow of tea, then set the cup aside, stifling a sigh. "I hope you don't mind my talking it through. It makes me feel less...helpless."

"I don't mind." His face went serious, though not the harsh seriousness of the investigator. "I can't tell you what we're doing, though."

"I know."

We fell silent, but it was a comfortable silence, softened by the gentle crackling of the fire. Detective Aragón wasn't the only one who had made false assumptions. I had assumed he would remain bullheaded and generally intolerable, but today he had shown me a different side.

"Where did you go to high school?" he asked suddenly.

"Santa Fe High."

"Oh. I went to Capital."

I nodded. Capital High was out in the southwest part of town near the municipal airport, a newer school.

"I thought maybe you went to Prep," he added.

"No, my folks weren't that rich."

The moment I said it I felt a shift, a return of constraint. Julio must have been right; money was a touchy subject for Detective Aragón. I felt regret that the pleasant mood had been spoiled.

"Well, I'd better be going," he said, standing up. "Lots of work to do. Thanks for the tea and the—scones?"

"Scones, yes. You're welcome."

I stood up, too, wanting to say more but not really knowing what. I followed him out into the hall where he donned his black raincoat.

"Come by any time," I told him. "Next Friday at four we'll be serving a full afternoon tea."

He looked at me with the flat cop stare I remembered. Then he gave an exasperated sigh.

"What does that mean?"

"It means more food," I said. "Sandwiches and salty things as well as scones and sweets. It's a meal, really. Come try it."

"Maybe."

His face was a mixture of lost boy and tough cop, a shifting shadow in a gentleman's clothes, as if he couldn't make up his mind what to be. He dug his hands into the pockets of his raincoat and hunched his shoulders, and the cop took over.

"Stay out of trouble, Ms. Rosings," he said, turning toward the front door.

"You, too, Detective," I said quietly.

He didn't turn around, but raised a hand and waggled it in farewell, then stuffed it back in his pocket. I watched him go, my feelings a bit confused. I was relieved that he apparently wasn't angry with me any more, and glad that he didn't seem to mind my making my own inquiries about the murder. On the other hand I felt rather unsettled by the knowledge that my understanding of his character was much poorer than I had thought.

Detective Arrogant. I blushed a little for having thought of him that way.

Dee came out of the north parlor with an empty teapot. She paused and glanced toward the front door.

"Is he gone?"

"Yes. Thanks for adding the scones."

She dimpled. "I thought maybe it would sweeten him up a little."

I chuckled as we both headed for the butler's pantry. "I think it was an adventure for him."

"Did he ask you more questions?"

"No, apparently this is his day off."

"Cops are never off duty," she said with conviction. "Never completely."

"Mm. How are the customers doing?"

"Jonquil's done, Lily's almost done. Iris wants more tea."

"Go ahead and make it for them, then you can go home. I'll close up."

She glanced at me. "You sure?"

"Positive. You've all done a great job this week."

I fetched a tray from the pantry, which I took to Marigold to clear away the dishes from the tea Detective Aragón and I had shared. By the time I was done, some of the customers were ready to leave, and I followed them into the gift shop. Iz glanced up from the hostess station.

"You can go, Iz. I'll finish up."

She bobbed her head with a shy little smile. "Thanks, Ms. Rosings. See you Tuesday."

As the staff departed and I helped the last few customers settle their bills, a quiet peacefulness settled over the tearoom. The gentle music of a Mozart concerto for flute and harp set a relaxing background, and I took pleasure in the simple tasks of helping my customers. At six, I locked up and began clearing the last of the dishes. Mick got them washed, then went home as well, leaving me alone.

I tidied the parlors, not setting out fresh china as we would be closed Sunday and Monday and I didn't want the settings to get dusty. The staff would be gone—going about their lives for our "weekend." It felt strange knowing that for the first time in months, I would have the house to myself for two whole days.

Of course, there were plenty of things that needed to be done around the tearoom. I would keep busy enough, but I had been working so hard every day for so long that the lack of pressure and the prospect of actually having a little free time seemed alien.

I turned off the lights in the parlors, shut off the stereo, then closed out the cash register and took the bank bag up to Kris's office, locking it in the top drawer of her desk. Going into my own office, I found several paperclipped pages of printout on my desk, with a sticky note from Kris saying this was all she could find on the Internet. I sat down to look them over.

An old newspaper article about School Board politics mentioned Sylvia's name, but only in passing as a member of the Board. There were a couple of mentions in fluffy articles about events around town, one of them when Sylvia's husband had still been alive. I realized I didn't know much about Donna's father. Maybe Kris could find out some stuff about him.

That was getting a bit far afield, but you never knew what might be interesting, and besides, I was starting to enjoy digging around for information. It was a little like treasure hunting.

I turned the page and found that Kris was there ahead of me. Roger Carruthers had been a well-known businessman in Santa Fe for four decades before his death in 1997. He had owned a chain of office supply stores, which Sylvia had helped to manage and had sold after his death. Ever since then she had devoted herself to charitable work, most notably with the Santa Fe Preservation Trust.

Donna had graduated from Santa Fe Prep in 1999, and a clipping from that spring showed her as Prom Queen. She had dropped out of sight until 2006, when she appeared listed as a Gold Circle patron on the website of a modern dance company that performed in both Santa Fe and Scottsdale.

I laid the pages down and gazed out my window at the twilit evening sky. If Donna was playing patron of the arts, she had to have a fair amount of money. I was no judge of modern art, but I'd have been willing to bet that the pieces on display in her home had cost a pretty penny.

It appeared that Roger Carruthers had left both his widow and his daughter comfortably well off. Either that or Donna had found some other source of income, but she wasn't married, had no career of which I was aware, and I hadn't noticed any men around her exuding the possessive air of someone who spends a lot of money on his significant other.

So Donna was financially independent. That fit with her rather blasé description of her mother's gift of her house to the Trust, and pretty much shot a hole in my suspicion that Donna might have killed Sylvia because of the money she was going to sink into the Trust.

Of course, greed knows no limits for some people. She could have been angry about the money even though she didn't need it. Or she could have killed her mother out of spite. There was no lack of that between mother and daughter, but it was not as easy to credit as a motive for murder.

I found myself wondering what Detective Aragón would think of my theories. I was tempted to fax him the information Kris had gathered, but quickly talked myself out of it. He had a whole team of investigators looking for this sort of thing. He would probably think my fax was cute.

I left the papers on my desk, giving up for the moment. It was getting on toward seven-thirty, and I hadn't had lunch except for a couple of scones and one artistic celery stick. I was decidedly peckish.

I went across the hall to my suite and threw a frozen pot-pie in the oven. Not a commercial pot-pie, but one Julio had made as a possible lunch time offering, along the line of British meat pies. I had fond memories of lunches in crowded tearooms in England, seated at tiny tables elbow to elbow with other patrons, wolfing down hot casserole lunches like steak and kidney pie washed down with pots of tea.

Julio had come up with a couple of versions, a turkey pot pie and a sort of beef bourguignon pie, and had frozen them to test how well they would stand up to being stored that way. If they worked out, the servers would be able to heat them up quickly at lunch time, preserving our aim of keeping the food prep time to a minimum during most of our business hours.

The present exception to that rule was the full afternoon tea on Fridays, with hot savories and sandwiches that had to be made fresh. If afternoon tea became popular, as I hoped it would, we would add it on more days.

At the moment we only served cream tea and light tea during the rest of the week. For that, the petits fours and other sweets could be made ahead and needed little or no prep right before serving. The exception was the scones, which had to be baked fresh, but they could be made ahead and frozen.

The savory smell of the pot pie began to fill my suite, making my mouth water. I made a salad while I waited, and poured myself a glass of wine. I was just beginning to think about putting on some music when I realized I was already hearing music. Harp and flute music. The stereo downstairs was on.

"Oh, no," I said, and closed my eyes for a moment, then took a big swallow of wine and went downstairs.

The doors were locked. Julio hadn't come in, and no forced entry had occurred. Even the light in the dining parlor was off, but the stereo was cranking out Mozart.

I stood in the hall staring at the dining parlor door. "Like music, do you?" I said softly, then went into the butler's pantry and took the Mozart disc out of the stereo.

"We already listened to this today," I said, feeling foolish that I was explaining my actions to a ghost.

I pulled out a disc of Chopin's Ballades, which were rather too exuberant for business hours, and put them on. Piano music filled the house. I turned it up a bit louder so I'd be able to hear it upstairs. Felt a little silly doing that, too, but I shrugged it off and went back up to rescue my pot pie, which was just shy of starting to burn.

The pastry was crispy gold and steaming. Gravy had burbled out of the slits in the top crust and browned, making a tantalizing caramelized smell. I slid the pie onto a plate, heaped salad beside it, and sat down to enjoy my dinner with a good book for company.

An hour later I was sated and yawning. The music downstairs had progressed to the next disc in the changer, Handel's "Water Music." I took a bubble bath, then threw on my robe and slippers and padded downstairs to turn off the stereo.

"I'm going to sleep now," I announced in the hall, hoping to fend off any midnight musicales.

If Captain Dusenberry got into the habit of playing the stereo at all hours, I could be in trouble. Maybe I should have left well enough alone. At least the light in the dining parlor couldn't keep me awake.

I went to bed, but despite being tired and relaxed I couldn't get to sleep right away. I lay staring at the brocade canopy overhead, my brain refusing to shut down. Part of it was me waiting for the stereo to come on, but I also found myself thinking through the day.

The funeral, and Donna's house, and the unexpected visit from Detective Aragón all flitted through my mind. I wondered if I was being too obsessive about the murder, then decided that no, it was healthy to want to work through it. Much healthier than denying the seriousness of the situation.

I was a suspect in a murder case. I hadn't really acknowledged that square-on before, I'd just sort of been looking at it from the corner of my mind's eye. Detective Aragón had confirmed it that afternoon, though.

Worst case, I could go to jail. Lose the tearoom, not to mention my freedom for the rest of my life, possibly.

That was why I was trying to solve the murder, I acknowledged to the canopy. It wasn't just for my own peace of mind. It was self-defense.

In that light, it seemed I had made pretty poor progress in four days. I hadn't eliminated any suspects but my staff, Gina, Manny, Nat, and Mr. Ingraham, and it could be argued that any of the latter three could have slipped back to the tearoom and come in the dining parlor's back door.

I threw back the covers and got up, walking around the chimney to my sitting area. Flopping into a chair, I picked up the stack of place cards and sorted through them.

Vince Margolan. Too busy remodeling to care about my opening or Sylvia's funeral. Never met her before the thank-you tea.

Claudia Pearson. Pretty much the opposite; she had made time for the tearoom's opening and plainly cared enough to deliver Sylvia's eulogy, though she hadn't been at Donna's that I'd seen.

Katie Hutchins. Sweet and obsessed about her earring.

Mr. Ingraham, also unacquainted with Sylvia before the tea. Left early, probably innocent. Ditto for Nat, Gina, and Manny.

Me. Not guilty.

Sylvia. I paused, biting my lip as I looked at her name.

"Why did you die?" I whispered. "I wish you could tell me."

I moved her card to the bottom of the stack, leaving Donna's on top.

Donna a killer. I wasn't happy with that. She had a reasonably strong motive, but she wasn't stupid. If she had wanted her mother dead, she would have had plenty of time to plan a safer, less public murder. Sylvia's killer had taken an extreme risk of being discovered, and I still felt strongly that the murder had been an act of impulse, a crime of opportunity.

I was missing something. I wanted to call Detective Aragón and talk over the list of suspects with him. That was nuts; I knew he couldn't discuss the case with me. Annoyed with myself, I went back to bed, rolled over a few dozen times, and finally managed to go to sleep.

The next morning dawned cloudy again. I went downstairs and made myself an omelet, enjoying the luxury of having the huge old kitchen to myself. After carefully cleaning up the dishes and wiping the stove and counter tops (to avoid the wrath of Julio), I called Nat.

"I'm inviting myself to dinner," I told her.

"Finally! Yes, do come. Cocktails at six, dinner whenever Manny gets the grill going."

"Sounds great. What can I bring?"

"Nothing, darling. We've got it all under control. We'll have a few other guests."

"Oh—should I pick another night?"

"No, no! It's no one alarming, I promise."

I laughed. "I just don't want to be a burden."

"You're never a burden, Ellen. We'd love to have you."

"Okay. See you at six, then."

I hung up, wondering what to take as a hostess gift. Not wine; Nat's wine cellar was better stocked than mine. Flowers?

Musing on this comfortable question, I went out to my car and drove to the Unitarian Church, where I'd attended services off and on since coming home from college. I'm not deeply religious, but I do believe in the power of prayer. I had a lot at stake just then, so I thought I should apply for whatever divine assistance might be available.

I arrived in time for the late service. My thoughts tended to drift, but I figured I could be forgiven for that. I sent up a silent prayer for the success of the tearoom. I also put in a word for Donna Carruthers, and one for poor Sylvia. Then I tossed in the names of everyone at the thank-you tea, and all my staff, and Detective Aragón. Might as well cover all bases.

After the service I went out into the parking lot and saw that the cloud cover was breaking up. A brisk breeze sent torn shreds of gray and white flying across a brilliant blue sky. It was good to be out and about, and despite the coolness of the day I kept my window down as I drove home. Remembering Gina's concern that I should get out of the tearoom, I parked my car behind the kitchen and took a walk, heading down Palace Avenue to the Santa Fe plaza.

The breeze stirred the new leaves budding out on the cottonwoods. Indian jewelry vendors were already doing business beneath the long *portal* of the Palace of the Governors, their handmade wares laid out on colorful blankets. Silver sandcast bracelets, pendants and bolo ties and squash blossom necklaces sporting huge chunks of turquoise, traditional and more modern styles of jewelry all looked inviting. I strolled along behind the tourists who were doing the serious shopping, and paused at a blanket covered with heishi necklaces.

The strands of tiny beads—coral, silver, turquoise, and a rainbow of other stones I couldn't identify—lay there mocking me. Figure it out, they seemed to say. I saw no lemon agate among them.

Turning away, I crossed the plaza to La Fonda, the historic hotel on the plaza's southeast corner. La Fonda's been a magnet for celebrities and Santa Fe socialites not just for decades but for centuries. It's where the President stays when he's in town. Everybody who's anybody goes there, as well as a lot of us who aren't anybody in particular. I decided to stroll through the old hotel and then stop at the French Pastry Shop for a cappuccino and something sweet and sinful.

La Fonda is a fabulous, jumbled pile of brown stucco,

renovated in the early twentieth century by architect John Gaw Meem, one of the creators of Pueblo Revival style. Meem's hallmarks are seen throughout the building in the heavy, carved beams and zapatas, Mexican tile ornamentation and punched tin light fixtures, and many other details that made La Fonda one of the defining places of what is known as Santa Fe Style.

I went in the front entrance and up a half dozen steps to the lobby. The dark flagstones of the steps and the floor are polished smooth with the wear of countless feet. Shop display cases take up a lot of the lobby walls now, but there's still some art on display, including classic Santa Fe Opera posters, Fiesta posters, and the famous paintings of dancers—matachines, the Buffalo Dancer, the Shalako and the Spanish dancer—and other images by early 20th century Santa Fe artist Gerald Cassidy.

I wandered down the hallway that ran along one side of La Plazuela restaurant, which had been an actual open-air *plazuela* before I was born but was now enclosed. The restaurant is still a gathering place for Santa Feans as well as visitors. The food's excellent, though they serve what we call "gringo chile," suitable for the tourist palate but lacking the heat most locals prefer.

A long, glass wall had been added between the hall where I was walking (which had once been an outdoor *portal*) and the restaurant. French doors in places along it gave a clear view into the restaurant, but the panes of glass all around them were painted with bright Mexican-folk style designs, birds and flowers and animals and geometrics in vivid, chaotic colors.

As my gaze wandered over the pictures, I glimpsed a familiar face through the one of the doors. I stepped back and paused, my heart jumping with alarm as I put a red, yellow and green rooster between me and the restaurant. Cautiously I peeped around the edge of the painted pane. Donna

Carruthers was sitting in the restaurant.

She looked very different than she had at the funeral. Today she was wearing a dress made up of large, rectangular panels of lime green and turquoise, her hair was pulled into a stylish French twist, and her face was shining with laughter. She sat at a large round table having lunch with several others, a couple of whom I'd seen at her house the day before.

There was one other face I knew at the table. Seated next to Donna, wearing a black sport coat over a gold turtleneck and black jeans, was Vince Margolan.

13

I drew back, though it was pretty unlikely that Donna or Vince had seen me. I frowned at them around the edge of the painted rooster, wondering if they knew each other better than I'd realized.

Vince hadn't been at the funeral or the reception at Donna's house, but here he was today, looking awfully chummy with Donna. Maybe they moved in the same circles. They were both interested in art, so it wasn't a stretch.

I didn't know what kind of art Vince would be showing in his gallery. I had assumed that since it was in an historic house it would be a kind of classic, Santa Fe gallery with sweeping landscapes, cowboy art, traditional Southwestern stuff. But maybe not.

I stepped a little closer to the windows again, shamelessly spying on Donna and Vince. The conversation at the table appeared to be lively. I saw Vince lean toward Donna to say something to her. She laughed and touched his wrist.

"Pretty, aren't they?" said a man's voice behind me.

I jumped and turned, then managed a smile. It was a stranger, probably a tourist, an older man in a polo shirt and, oh dear, plaid slacks.

"Um, yes," I said, realizing he meant the painted windows. I pointed to the pane next to the rooster, which bore an agave plant rendered in shocking green. "I was just trying to figure out what this one is."

"I think that's a yucca," said the helpful stranger.

"Oh. Thanks."

He showed no sign of going away, just stayed standing

next to me, gazing at the windows. I stepped away, bypassing the shops in the hallway to wander deeper into the hotel, past a couple of meeting rooms and a bank of elevators. Here I paused. Before me, embedded in the wall, was a large image of La Guadalupana on painted tiles.

La Guadalupana is another Virgin Mary, very different from La Conquistadora. Guadalupana is surrounded in a full-body halo of radiant light, and stands on a crescent supported by a cherub. She wears a blue mantle spangled with stars, and often has roses at her feet. She's the patroness of New Mexico—of all the New World, really—and one of my favorite cultural images. She can be seen everywhere, and many a rose-scented candle bearing her image has been lit in New Mexico churches and chapels, shrines, and in private homes. I've lit more than a few myself, and I'm not even Catholic.

I touched the tiles, cool and smooth beneath my fingers. La Guadalupana always has a calming effect on me. I realized it was foolish of me to act guilty for watching Donna and Vince. I had seen two people I knew through the window, no crime in that. My feelings were too easily ruffled lately. I decided it was definitely time for the French Pastry Shop, and retraced my steps.

The tourist gent had gone, but I didn't dawdle in the hall of windows. I couldn't help glancing through them at Donna and Vince's table of artsy people, though. They were still there, still chatting over their lunch. I continued to the lobby and crossed it to the Pastry Shop's inside door.

The smell of French onion soup welcomed me, and I succumbed to temptation and ordered a bowl of it along with my cappuccino and one of the shop's decadent Napoleons. I sat at a table by the window and watched the people walking up and down San Francisco street. I could see the cathedral— now a basilica—Bishop Lamy's pet project, rising in imposing grandeur at the east end of the street.

My cell phone rang. I dug it out of my purse, checked the caller ID and saw that it was Gina, so I answered, speaking quietly so as not to disturb the other patrons. Ordinarily I would have stepped outside, but I didn't want to abandon my lunch.

"Hi, dearie! Happy first day off," Gina said in a cheery voice. "Want to meet for lunch?"

"Actually, I'm already having lunch. I'm at the French Pastry Shop. Care to join me?"

"Be there in a flash," she said. "Boy, have I got news for you!"

"What is it?" I asked.

"No, you have to buy me a gooey dessert first!"

"Tease."

She hung up and I went back to savoring my soup, chopping with my spoon at the crouton and the wonderful, stringy cheese. I was just finishing the last salty spoonful when Gina came in the shop's street-side door. She was wearing a knee-length cable-knit cardigan over a splashy floral sun dress, and carrying a manila envelope. She grinned at me as she came over to my table.

"Chilly out there! What are you having, French onion? That sounds perfect." She sat down and handed me the envelope.

"What's this?" I asked.

"Clippings of all the news stories about the tearoom. I knew you wouldn't have time."

"Oh. Thanks." I gazed doubtfully at the envelope. No doubt the clippings had pictures of crime tape and other things of which I didn't want to be reminded.

"Save them for later. I just thought you should have a record."

"My dear, efficient friend." I tucked the envelope beside my purse, then squeezed her hand. "Thanks."

A waitress wandered over to take Gina's order. Gina asked for soup and a bottle of mineral water.

"What do you want for your gooey dessert?" I asked.

"That looks fine," she said, pointing to my Napoleon.

I looked at the waitress. "Another of these, and I'll have another cappuccino, please."

"Oh, yum!," Gina said. "Me too!"

"You know," I said after the waitress had left, "maybe French onion soup would be a good lunchtime thing for the tearoom."

Gina bugged out her eyes at me. "What? The tearoom serving conventional lunch? You're selling out already?"

"No, no. Lots of British tearooms serve lunch. Meat pies and stuff like that—casserole lunches. Julio and I have been talking about adding a few choices like that. It would bring in a lunch crowd."

"Oh. Well, that's okay, then. How about green chile stew?"

I shook my head. "Sorry, no green chile in Great Britain."

"Rats. You make such good chile stew, too."

"I'll make some just for us."

The waitress returned with Gina's soup and dessert and our drinks. I sipped my cappuccino.

"The tea lady drinking coffee," Gina said, grinning at me over her soup. "Don't let the press get hold of that."

"I'm off duty."

I took another sip, licked foamed milk off my upper lip, then started in on my Napoleon. Flakes of puff pastry scattered under my fork. I took a bite, then looked at Gina.

"So, how was the big date?"

"Fabulous! Ted actually *liked* the chamber music, even though he'd never heard it before. He wants to go to the symphony concert next week."

"Wow! Sounds like you found a keeper."

"He's definitely got potential. And, my dear, I got him

talking about his work, and he told me all about the building he sold in your neighborhood. Apparently the transaction was a big hassle and he was more than happy to complain to me about it, so I got all the juicy details."

"Do tell!"

She took a bite of soup. "Well, first of all, you were right about it being historic. It's right on your street."

"I wondered."

"Second, you'll never guess who bought it!"

"Shirley MacLaine."

"No, silly, she likes out in the country! Ted showed her a ranch once, but the views weren't good enough for her."

"I give up," I said.

"Vince Margolan! The gallery guy who was at your thank-you tea!"

"Vince," I said, feeling stupid.

"Yeah! Small world, huh?"

I frowned. "But he's just remodeling his gallery."

Gina nodded. "That's the place he bought."

"I thought he already owned it."

"No, he was leasing. The owner decided to sell, and was going to offer it to Vince, but then the Trust approached him and made a preemptive offer. Ted smelled a bidding war and he was right. He talked to Vince, and Vince came back with a higher offer."

"Whoa, this is weird." I gave a nervous glance over my shoulder. "Vince Margolan and Donna Carruthers are over in La Plazuela having lunch right this minute."

"Wow, really?" Gina looked up from her soup, grinning. "Let's go spy on them!"

"Gina!" I lowered my voice to a whisper. "No!"

"Why not? We might figure out what they're up to!"

"They're up to having lunch with some friends. Speaking of which..."

I took a bite of my Napoleon. Gina pushed aside her empty soup bowl and picked up her fork, attacking her pastry.

"If we hurry we could catch them. Maybe Donna put Vince up to it!"

"Shhh!"

She switched to a whisper. "Donna's got a lot of money, right? And Vince is probably spending a lot on his gallery. Maybe she paid him."

I frowned. "That sounds kind of convoluted. I need to think about this."

I glanced at the door to the lobby, puzzling over Vince and Donna and the property sale. I felt like I was trying to push my way through fog.

"Oh, by the way, I have another little tidbit from Ted," Gina said.

"Hm?"

"Our friend, Detective Arrogant?"

I took a sip of coffee. "What about him?"

"He's famous for hating real estate people."

"How odd. Any idea why?"

"No clue. Ted said he won't talk to them. If he's working a case and a real estate agent is involved, he always sends some other cop to interview them."

"Oh."

Maybe it was because he didn't have the bucks to shop for fancy real estate. That didn't seem enough to cause such an extreme response, but I'd had a taste of Aragón's capacity for irrational reaction. I wouldn't put it past him to be touchy about anyone who dealt with large amounts of money.

I didn't mention this to Gina. After the detective's apology, it didn't seem fair to rip him up. He must have had his reasons for feeling as he did.

Gina dropped her fork onto her empty plate and raised her hands in the air. "Done! Let's go."

She snatched up both our tickets and hurried to the cash register. Resigned, I ate the last couple of bites of my pastry. By the time I finished she was back, standing by my chair and practically vibrating with excitement.

I got up, slung my purse over my shoulder, and tucked the envelope of clippings under my arm. Gina was already heading for the door into the hotel. I followed, wondering what Miss Manners would recommend as the perfect response if one was caught spying on acquaintances.

Gina crossed the lobby to the restaurant's entrance, standing just off to one side as she peered in. She hadn't spotted Vince and Donna yet, but I could see that they were getting up and saying goodbye to their friends.

Adrenaline surging, I caught up to Gina, slid my hand through her elbow, and pulled her on past the open doorway.

"They're coming," I whispered.

I dragged her around the corner where we could peer through the painted panes of glass. Farewells took a couple of minutes.

"Who are the others?" Gina asked.

"I don't know. I saw the redhead at Donna's after the funeral. We weren't introduced."

The party broke up, Donna leading the way out of the restaurant with Vince on her heels. I ducked further back behind the glass wall, pulling Gina with me and hoping Donna wasn't planning on visiting the shops behind us.

Fortunately, she and her friends all headed for the parking garage. Gina tugged at my arm. I resisted until the last of the party was across the lobby and heading out of sight into the hallway, then let Gina drag me after them.

"This is a bad idea," I said, sotto voce.

"We might learn something important!"

Gina's heels clacked on the tile floor, making me wince. As we entered the hall I could see Donna's friends strolling along ahead of us.

"Slow down, Gina!"

She slowed to a brisk walk, but we were still catching up to them. I stopped in front of a display window and pretended to admire its contents while I counted to ten. At five, Gina took off without me.

At eight, I caved and followed her. Donna's party had gone through the door to the garage, and Gina was blasting through after them. I hurried to catch up and found myself outside, next to Gina, with the noise of traffic from San Francisco street surrounding me.

The redhead and a man I didn't recognize were nearby, waiting for the elevator to upper levels. I glanced away and saw Donna and Vince walking up the aisle between rows of parked cars together. Gina took off after them, and I hurried to catch up.

Could Donna and Vince be an item? I had assumed they hadn't met before my tea, but maybe that was wrong. Both art people. Maybe they'd met at some gallery.

Donna and Vince stopped beside a silver Mercedes. Gina stopped short in front of me and I nearly crashed into her. She caught my hand and pulled me behind an SUV, peering through its smoked windows at our quarry.

They stood talking by the car while I shifted from foot to foot, wishing I was somewhere else. "This is stupid," I whispered to Gina. "Let's go."

"Wait."

Smiling, Donna got into the Mercedes. Vince closed the door, waving as he stepped back. I ducked, hoping he wouldn't notice us behind the SUV, and that it wasn't his car. He walked on up the aisle while the Mercedes pulled out and drove away.

"Huh," Gina said, clearly disappointed. "No kiss."

Vince got into a black BMW. The brake lights came on and

the engine started. The car sat thrumming for a couple of seconds, then backed out and headed for the exit.

"Can we go now?" I asked.

Gina sighed. "I guess. You're a little edgy today. The ghost hasn't been keeping you up, has he?"

"No. Well, he did turn on the stereo last night."

"Oh, Christ on a crutch!"

"Only once. I think I'm working things out with him."

"Jeez, will you listen to yourself?"

"Hey, you saw the light in the dining parlor! I thought you were behind me on this."

"Yeah, but—but you don't want to get chummy with this ghost guy! And especially you don't want to talk about him in front of other people," she added, her voice dropping to a whisper as an older couple made their way past where we stood.

I stepped out, heading for the street. "Gina, I think Captain Dusenberry's the least of my problems."

"Yeah. Let's go to a movie or something. Take your mind off all this morbid stuff."

"Good idea."

We got in Gina's car, drove to the multiplex at De Vargas mall, and found a silly movie, which did take my mind off things for a couple of hours. As we came back out to the parking lot my gaze fell on Rosario Cemetery across the street, and the ranks of white military markers marching up the hill beyond it in the National Cemetery.

"Gina, are you in a hurry to get anywhere?"

"Nope."

"Then do you mind if I go to the grocery store?"

"That depends. Are we shopping for the tearoom?"

"No, no. I just thought of something I'd like to pick up."

We went into the supermarket nearby, where I bought an inexpensive bouquet of flowers. Gina gave me a curious look, but didn't ask why. As we got back to her car I explained.

"I'd like to take these over to the cemetery."

"Oh, uh-huh. For Sylvia?"

"No, for Captain Dusenberry."

"Aw, no! I thought we were getting away from that stuff!"

"Willow told me his grave is over there. I just want to make a gesture, all right? It'll make *me* feel better."

She sighed. "Okay, but after this no more ghost or murder stuff today, all right?"

"Deal."

She drove up the street to the National Cemetery's entrance, then wound back down to the very back near Rosario, to where the earliest military graves were located. The National Cemetery had first been created to receive Civil War casualties, and some of the markers in that section were pretty weathered.

"Where is it?" Gina said as she parked the car.

"I don't know. I guess we should have checked the list up by the gate."

"Want to go back?"

"No, let's just walk through and see if we can find it. It should be in the oldest part here."

I got out of the car and held the flowers to my face for a minute, smelling spicy-sweet carnations. Gina joined me and we took off tramping across the damp, green grass, heading for the corner of the fence that separated the National Cemetery from Rosario.

"Great," Gina said. "Just how I wanted to spend my Sunday afternoon."

"Cemeteries are interesting," I said. "Haven't you ever visited Arlington?"

"Sure, but there's a house and stuff there, and lots of cool statuary. Here the markers aren't even interesting, they're all the same."

I strode along the first row of markers, looking for Captain Dusenberry's name. "Well, yes, because they're military. But the names are interesting––and look at that, there's a different cross on this one."

Gina glanced at it. "Means he was a Confederate. They all have that."

I grinned. "Thought you weren't interested in cemeteries."

"Yeah, but my dad dragged me to Gettysburg when I was a kid. We have a great-great-umpty-great uncle there."

We came to the end of one row and started down the next. The day had warmed up a bit, enough that the breeze was pleasant instead of chilly and made the shadows of new leaves dance over the grass.

We paused to read the text of a large, imposing monument that turned out to be the remains of a group of Confederate soldiers who had been found buried together in Glorieta Pass, east of town. Moving moved on, we noted the time frames of various markers and the ethnicities of the names.

"Here he is," Gina called out.

We stood before the marker and I read it aloud. "Captain Samuel Dusenberry, died April 5, 1855. I guess that's him. I should have checked his name."

"How many Captain Dusenberrys do you think there are out here?"

"Good point."

I slid the flowers from their plastic cover and laid them at the bottom of the grave marker, then stood silently thinking about Captain Dusenberry. Maybe I ought to try to find out more about him. Willow probably knew everything there was to know, but I was a little hesitant to talk to her about my unorthodox house guest.

Or was I his guest? He might see it that way, having been the original owner of the house.

Don't go there, Rosings, I told myself. That way lies

madness.

I gazed at Captain Dusenberry's name, said, "I wish you peace," then turned away.

Gina put an arm around me and we walked back to the car, no longer looking at the names on the markers. I glanced back when we reached Gina's Miata, and spotted my flowers peeking out a little from behind the gravestone. I noted which row it was in, and saw a gnarled cottonwood nearby that would help me remember its location. I didn't plan on making this a pilgrimage, but I might want to stop by again.

"Now," Gina said as she drove back toward the gate, "what are you doing for dinner tonight? And don't say you're going to stay home."

"Actually, I'm going to Nat's. She's been bugging me to come over."

"Good. Have a fabulous time. Tomorrow night I'll take you out."

I gazed across at her and smiled. "Darling Gina, you spoil me."

She grinned and brushed a dark lock of hair back from her face. "That's what friends are for! You'd do the same for me if someone had been murdered in my house."

"Two someones. Captain Dusenberry was killed there too."

She raised a warning finger. "Ah-ah! No murder or ghost stuff!"

"Hey, you brought it up!"

"My bad. Let's go shopping."

The rest of the day passed quickly. I followed Dr. Gina's orders and kept busy with fun stuff, easy because Dr. Gina came along as enforcer. We went back to De Vargas and cruised the stores, then drove out to Santa Fe Place and rode the carousel. After strolling through our favorite shops there we hit the nearby outlet mall for good measure, and Gina dropped me at home with a handful of shopping bags. I didn't go hog-wild, but I did splurge a little, for the first time in months.

Glancing at the clock in the kitchen as I came in, I saw that it was almost five-thirty. I had just enough time to change and drive over to Nat's place. I hurried upstairs and jumped into a rose and cream flowered broomstick skirt and an oversized sage green sweater, combed my hair loose and put on some dangly earrings.

Before leaving I checked the front door, just to make sure it was locked and there were no tell-tale notes or dead bodies on the front porch. The sun was starting to set, and the wisterias stirred in a light breeze. They were beginning to leaf out, I saw; tiny pale green fronds sprouting along the smooth gray vines. Soon the leaves would dominate and the clusters of purple flowers would fade, the vines putting out occasional blooms through the summer but not the spectacular lavender cascades that marked spring.

I had the sense that time was flying, that I was missing out on the pleasures of springtime (all too fleeting in New Mexico) because of being so busy. I resolved to take more time for stopping and smelling the roses, or the wisterias, or whatever happened to be blooming.

Deciding to start now, I unlocked the front door and stepped out onto the porch. The breeze that made the wisteria blooms tremble was cool, a warning that the evening would be chilly. I caught a spray of flowers in my hands and buried my face in them, taking in their scent.

Heady, sweet but not a simple sweetness; a fragrance with the sort of depth and complexity one might expect of the bouquet of a good wine. I had always marveled at the scent of wisterias, as well as their stunning beauty. A miracle flower.

These flowers had drawn me to them, to this house. These old vines had seen a lot of people come and go. Maybe Mrs.

Dusenberry had planted them, if there was a Mrs. Dusenberry.

No ghost stuff!

I smiled, then locked up and went through the hall to the back door. Dining parlor light off, stereo quiet. I let myself out and hopped into my car, enjoying the sunset as I drove out to Tano Road.

Similar to Donna's neighborhood but much older, Tano Road is close to Opera Hill, where the Santa Fe Opera juts its dramatic silhouette into the sky northwest of town. The road runs west, more or less, and as I drove along it I enjoyed what was shaping up to be a spectacular sunset, with light spinning golden along the edges of towering clouds.

I turned down Nat's dirt driveway to twine my way up a piñon-dotted hill to her house, a half-bermed wonder of mixed flagstone and adobe, part Chacoan, part Pueblo Revival, part Santa Fe sixties. It was a comfy old jumble, facing north with views of the Jemez Mountains to the west and the Sangre de Cristos to the east.

Nat greeted me at the door, wearing a green and gold tropical print dress that reminded me of Julio, though it was more subdued than most of his outfits. She caught me in a hug.

"Thanks for coming, Ellen."

"Thanks for letting me barge in. If I'd known you were having company I wouldn't have asked. Here, these are for you," I said, handing her a jar of chocolate-covered bing cherries, part of my spoils from the afternoon's shopping.

"Thank you, darling! And you know I've been trying to get you for dinner for days. Come on in and say hello to the others."

The others turned out to be Deb and Alan Carter who had been friends of my parents, Suzanne Marks who was a buddy of Nat's from the Opera Guild, and Thomas Ingraham. Manny stood out on the patio at the grill, frowning in concentration at whatever was sizzling there. He waved at me through the glass door.

"I'll fetch you a drink, dear," said Nat, and bustled off to the kitchen. I turned to Mr. Ingraham, who looked more casual today than he had at the thank-you tea, wearing slacks and a herringbone jacket over a silk shirt.

"It's good to see you again, Mr. Ingraham."

"Thomas, please," he said, smiling at me over a tumbler of what looked like gin and tonic.

"Then call me Ellen. Thank you again for coming over on Wednesday, and thanks especially for mentioning the tearoom in your column. That was kind of you."

"Well, considering the fuss the news-hounds were making over the unfortunate fate of Sylvia Carruthers, I thought you deserved a little positive press, just for the sake of balance. Next time you'll get the full going-over, though," he warned. "No quarter."

"I should hope not," I said, smiling. "We'll be on our toes."

Nat came out of the kitchen with a tray of tumblers. I accepted one and sipped. It was indeed gin and tonic. I took the lime slice off the rim of the glass and squeezed it over my drink, then dropped it in.

"Speaking of the chaos last week," I said, "I hope the aftermath didn't trouble you too much."

Thomas's brows rose slightly. "You mean the police? They grilled me for half an hour and decided I was harmless. Haven't heard a peep since."

"Oh, good."

"Fortunately I went to the paper's office immediately after I left your tearoom, and they were able to confirm that I was there by five-fifty."

"Five-fifty?"

"Yes, the police were very nitpicky about the exact time of my arrival. My luck that the paper's receptionist answered a phone call just as I came in, and logged the time."

I took another sip of my drink, mulling that over. Maybe I should try to reconstruct the time sequence of Wednesday's events. I glanced up and saw Thomas watching me.

"You hadn't met Sylvia before Wednesday, right?" I asked.

"Not formally. I saw her around town. You know she was quite a gadabout—in all the historic groups, and several of the art groups. Definitely a force of nature. I've seen her brangle on more than one occasion."

"Are you in all the same groups with her?"

"Oh, a few." He smiled, swirling the ice in his glass. "Music is my passion, you know. I'm a member of several 'friends of' organizations."

"I thought food was your passion."

"Food is my job. I'm passionate about it, but in a different way. Thank God for people like your aunt," he added, glancing toward Nat, who was passing drinks around to the other guests.

"I agree with the sentiment, but why do you mention it?" I asked.

"Because she's one of the few people in town who's not afraid to ask a food critic over for dinner." He looked at me with a wry smile. "I don't get many private invitations. People are worried I won't like their cooking. As if I'd publish a column about their dinner party."

"That's terrible!" I said.

He shrugged. "Occupational hazard."

"Well, I promise to invite you over for dinner, and not worry about your critique. Oh—but it would be in the same room we were in on Wednesday, I'm afraid! Maybe you'd prefer not to come back."

"Nonsense, I'm not so dainty. Can't afford to be, for the reason I've just given you. And for the same reason, I'll shamelessly accept your invitation in advance." He smiled, then tipped up his glass to get the last swallow of his drink. "Think I'll track down Natasha and get another of these. May I get you one?"

"Oh, no thanks. Still working on this."

He strolled away and I joined the Carters and Suzanne. Alan Carter had worked with my father, and was now retired. He and his wife were both lean and sun-bronzed, with round faces creased by smile lines. In the manner of long-term couples, they had grown to look similar. Now they both welcomed me with wide, warm smiles, and gave me their congratulations on the tearoom's opening and condolences on the murder.

"Your folks would have been proud," Alan said. "You just stand your ground, and you'll come through all right."

"Have they figured out who did it?" Deb asked.

I shrugged. "If they have, they haven't told me."

"You poor thing," said Suzanne Marks, lazily stirring her drink. "It must have been just dreadful for you."

This wasn't exactly comforting, but I smiled and thanked her. I didn't know Suzanne well, but I knew she was a good friend of Nat's. She was wearing a black velour pant and sweater set with a fuzzy fuchsia scarf, and had her auburn hair styled in a chic bob. Large chunks of turquoise were evident in all of her jewelry, though it was more modern in style than traditional.

Nat returned from a consultation with Manny to announce that dinner was served, and we all wandered into her dining room, which was filled with golden-red light from the last of the sunset. A west-facing picture window gave us a glimpse of a sky splattered with gray clouds edged in crimson.

Candles on the table lent a warm glow to the room, and we all sat down to salad, rice pilaf, and salmon steaks expertly grilled by Manny. A nice chardonnay from Gruet, a New Mexico winery, accompanied the meal. As the odd wheel, I sat between the Carters and Manny, across from Thomas Ingraham.

"Try this sauce on the salmon," Thomas said, passing me a gravy boat brimming with a creamy sauce. "Natasha's outdone herself."

"Salmon's pretty good without it," I said, glancing at Manny.

He grinned. "Thanks, but it's even better with. That's Nat's special dill sauce. Pass it over here when you're done."

I poured a dollop of the sauce beside my salmon and handed the boat over to Manny. One taste of the sauce and I was in heaven. It was delicate and rich at the same time, the perfect complement to the grilled salmon.

"Mmm! Oh, Nat!" I moaned. "Do you share recipes?"

"Only with family," she said, grinning.

The meal progressed at a relaxed pace. Pleasant conversation with good company, not to mention a bit of tipsiness from the cocktails, made the evening a delightful break for me.

Gina was right. I really had needed some time away from the tearoom. I needed to be with people—friends, not just customers and staff.

Lemon sorbet and crisp little rolled cookies topped off the meal, after which we moved back to the living room for coffee and more conversation. The party broke up around ten. I hung around as the other guests were leaving, intending to help with the clean-up, but Nat wouldn't let me.

"You have enough of that to deal with every day," she said, shooing me away from the kitchen. "You go on home and get a good night's sleep."

"Okay. Well, thanks for giving me the chance to drive out here. I see there are some places for sale in the neighborhood."

Nat sighed. "More and more. The taxes are obscene. I've thought about selling, myself."

"Nat! Sell your wonderful house, that you've been living in for forty years?"

"Well, with Hal and the kids gone it's really too big for just me. It's a lot of work to keep up, you know." She glanced over her shoulder toward the kitchen, where Manny was banging around cleaning up. "I haven't decided," she added.

I didn't want to pry. She and Manny had been seeing each other off and on for years, but lately it seemed things were starting to get more serious. Serious enough for Manny to run tame in her house for a dinner party. If he wound up proposing and she gave up her house to join him in his place in town, I could hardly blame her.

Nat saw me out, fielding my repeated thanks for the lovely evening. The clouds had cleared off and a thousand stars were glimmering overhead in the cold spring sky. I paused to inhale the scent of the piñon forest, then climbed into my car and drove back into town.

As I came in the tearoom's back door I had an unpleasant sense of deja vu. Blue and red lights were flashing through the hallway from the window lights around the front door.

I hurried down the hall to look out the lights, and was just in time to see a police car pull away from in front of the Territorial B&B across the street. Wondering if something had happened there, I let myself out the front door of the tearoom and hurried over.

I knocked on the front door, quietly so as not to disturb Katie and Bob's guests. After a minute Bob opened the door, a worried frown on his lean face.

"Sorry to bother you this late," I said. "I just saw the squad car leave, and I thought I should come over to make sure everything's all right."

Bob's mouth turned downward and he shook his head. "No, it isn't," he said in a broken voice. "They just took Katie away."

14

What?" I said, "at ten-thirty on a Sunday night?"

Bob just stood there nodding his head and looking miserable. I realized he was in a state of shock, so I stepped into the hall and closed the door behind me, muting the sound of late-night traffic.

The hall was gently lit by punched-tin sconces that cast patterns of light against the white walls. The dining room and living room of the B&B were dark. All the guests must be in their rooms. I drew Bob a little way into the living room, where comfy over-stuffed couches and sofas invited guests to lounge.

"Tell me what happened," I asked in a quiet voice.

"Two cops just showed up and said they wanted Katie to go to the station with them and make a statement," Bob said, rubbing his long-fingered hands together. "I couldn't go with her—we have guests, someone has to be here."

"Do you want me to go down there and be with her?" I offered. "Maybe I can find out what's going on."

Bob's eyes flickered with hope, and a small smile softened his face, then vanished again. "What if they put her in jail? We have to get breakfast in the morning—"

"I can help with breakfast if you need it. I'm closed tomorrow. But you won't," I added, speaking my hopes aloud. "If all they want is for her to make a statement it won't take long. I'll go check it out, and give Katie a ride home."

"That's awfully good of you, Ellen. I hate to trouble you."

His shoulders slumped, making him look more than usual like a gangly scientist. His tall, lean frame always looked borderline geekish to me, though in fact he was a versatile handyman, better with carpenter's tools than computers.

"No trouble," I said. "I owe you for all the help you gave me setting up the tearoom. I'll give you a call from the station if there's anything you should know."

I hurried back across the street, not bothering to go inside since I still had my purse slung over my shoulder. I walked around to the back of the tearoom, hopped in my car, and drove to the police station.

I was worried because of the thing with Katie's earring. I remembered how Detective Aragón had reacted when I asked about it, and how he had asked me not to mention it to her. Apparently the earring was a bigger deal than I had thought.

There was not much activity in the police station late on a Sunday night. A young man in handcuffs with a shaved head and tattoos was being escorted down a hallway as I came in. The duty cop, a guy about my age, pudgy with a military buzz, looked up from the front desk.

"I'm a friend of Katie Hutchins. I understand she's here making a statement."

The cop shrugged. I bit down on rising anger, knowing it would do me no good to bristle at this guy.

"Is Detective Aragón here?" I asked. "I have some information for him about the Carruthers case. Would you please let him know I'm here? Ellen Rosings," I added as he reached for a pad of sticky notes.

He scribbled on the top page, then pulled it off. "Ronnie," he called over his shoulder.

A tall, slim cop with body armor making odd, angular bulges in his uniform sauntered over to the desk. The pudgy cop handed him the sticky note.

"Give this to Tony."

The slim guy glanced at the note, then at me, then shrugged and strolled away down a corridor. I sat on one of three institutional metal chairs against the wall. The cop at the desk paid me no further heed, and I was left to fret on my own. After half an hour I stood up, which drew the suspicious gaze of the desk cop.

"Could you direct me to the restroom, please?" I asked.

"Down that hall on the right," he said, pointing toward a hallway that looked like offices.

"Thanks."

I went down the hall, glancing at each door I passed. Some were closed. One on the left was open and proved to be a break room, emitting an odor of stale bread and burned coffee. A cop glanced up at me from pouring a cup of sludge. I flashed a smile and went on.

I found the ladies' room and went in, encountering a female cop on her way out. She gave me a swift, appraising glance, then ignored me. I began to wonder if every non-cop who entered police station was automatically suspected of ill intent.

My intent wasn't ill, though it might well be unwelcome. I was tired of waiting around. If I couldn't find Katie, at least maybe I could find out what was going on with her.

I stepped out of the restroom back into the empty hallway. To my left the cop at the front desk was talking on the phone. I turned right, trying to look like I knew where I was going. I passed a few more closed doors, then the hall I was in dead-ended in a "T" with another hallway. I turned right again, now officially lost in the bowels of the station.

This hallway was a little less presentable. Bookshelves full of binders narrowed the passage, and I felt a little claustrophobic. I continued to the end of the hall, which was blocked by a door marked "Evidence."

Turning back, I tried the other half of the hallway. A man in a neat, dark suit came out of a doorway and looked at me in surprise. He was about forty, with pale hair receding from a high brow.

"Can I help you?" he said.

"I'm looking for the interview rooms," I said. "I'm here to pick up a friend."

"All the way down," he said, nodding to me to continue down the hall. "Left and then right."

"Thank you," I said.

"What was your name, Miss?"

"Rosings. Ellen Rosings."

He frowned. "Sounds familiar. Are you with County?"

"No. I'm the owner of the Wisteria Tearoom."

His face brightened. "That's right! I saw you on the news. Not my case, but everyone's following it, you know. Not your everyday homicide. I guess the vic was pretty well known in the community."

"I believe she was."

"Pretty spectacular job. Strangled with her own necklace, right in public."

Having nothing to say in response, I gave him a polite smile and started forward again. He came with me.

"I hear Tony just got a breakthrough tonight."

"Did he?" I asked.

"Yeah—the lab results came through."

He stopped talking abruptly, as if he'd realized he shouldn't be discussing the case with me. I tried to look disinterested, though I was burning to know what the lab results could be. We turned a corner and the man pointed to another hallway.

"Down there and to the right," he said.

"Thank you very much."

I straightened the shoulder strap of my purse and surged ahead, hoping I had a chance of finding Detective Aragón. As it happened he found me.

"What the hell are you doing here?"

I turned. Tony Aragón had just come out of a door I had

passed. He was wearing a sweatshirt and jeans and smelled of cigarettes.

"Good evening to you as well, Detective," I said, trying to keep my voice pleasant. "I heard Katie Hutchins was here giving a statement. I came to offer her a ride home."

His dark eyes narrowed as he gave me a measuring look. "Yeah? Well, you're going to have a long wait. She's not going home any time soon."

I felt dismayed, but managed to keep calm. "Oh? Has she been arrested?"

"Why would I want to arrest a sweet old lady like her?"

His tone was sarcastic, but his gaze never wavered. I felt like he was some hunting animal measuring its prey, deciding whether to attack or leave me alone. I fell back on courtesy, my favorite defense.

"I don't know," I replied pleasantly. "I rather think that would be up to you to explain."

He gave me the silent stare with which I was becoming familiar. I gazed back, rather proud of myself for not flinching or starting to fidget.

"You can wait in the break room," he said finally.

"Actually, I have a new piece of information to share with you, when you have a moment."

"Oh yeah?"

He stared at me, then seemed to become aware that we weren't alone in the hallway. A couple of uniformed cops, coffee mugs in their hands, were watching with interest on one side, and my helpful blond friend on the other. Aragón glanced at all of them, then pushed open a nearby door.

"In here."

I followed him into a small, barren room lit by utilitarian fluorescent lights. It contained a table and two chairs, all rather weatherbeaten. Nothing on the walls. Aragón sat on the table.

"Okay, what've you got?"

"Donna Carruthers and Vince Margolan are seeing each other socially," I said.

He let out a crack of laughter. "This is a murder investigation, not *One Life to Live*."

I bit back a sarcastic reply. That was his game, and I didn't intend to play.

"Vince is the one who purchased the property Sylvia Carruthers was trying to obtain for the Preservation Trust," I said. "He was having a bidding war with the Trust, driving up the price. Donna might have hired him to do it."

Aragón grinned. "So you sniffed out the sale, eh?"

"I suppose you already knew about it."

"Yeah. And unless Donna and Vince are the best actors I've ever run into, they didn't conspire to murder Sylvia Carruthers."

I gripped the back of a nearby chair, starting to feel frustrated. "They were the last two people in the room with her."

"Yes, they were. And your dishwasher saw Vince in the hall after that, alone. Or didn't you ask him?"

I didn't answer. A slow grin spread over Aragón's intolerable face.

"Thoroughness, Detective," he said. "Got to interview every witnesss."

"All right, all right," I said, annoyed with myself. "You're the professional. I just thought maybe you hadn't heard about the real estate sale."

"I'm glad you brought it up. We like helpful witnesses, we really do. Call if you think of anything else," he said, standing up from the table and ushering me toward the door.

"You're laughing at me again."

"Nah," he said, his mouth twisting up in a grin.

"What about Katie?" I said, stopping in front of the door.

His face went hard. "She's here for questioning."

"Why? Didn't you already interview her?"

"There've been some new developments."

I nodded. "You got some lab results back. I'm guessing they were on the fibers found on Sylvia's clothing."

He didn't say anything. Taking silence for assent I went on, feeling like I was fighting for Katie's reputation, if not her freedom.

"I'm guessing you found fibers from Katie's clothing on Sylvia's left side, especially the sleeve."

Detective Aragón's frown deepened. "Why are you guessing that?"

"Because Katie was seated on Sylvia's left at the tea. They probably brushed against each other as they were passing things at the table."

He didn't answer, just stood there looking disconcerted. I returned his gaze, peripherally aware of the rise and fall of his breathing. A stillness fell over us in the small room, and I found I was holding my breath, waiting for I didn't know what.

"There's more to it than that," Aragón said finally.

"Katie didn't do it."

"I can only think of one reason you'd know that for certain."

I waved that aside impatiently. "Come on, Detective. I'd be pretty stupid to make a show of investigating a crime I'd committed myself."

His mouth twitched. "Yes, you would."

"Why did you drag her in here at ten on a Sunday night? It can't have been just the fibers."

"No, it wasn't just that."

"The earring, then. But why?"

He leaned toward me, his voice a quiet hiss. "Because it was found in Sylvia Carruthers's hand, all right?"

I gaped at him. At first I felt horrified that it could be true, that Katie actually might have lost the earring in a struggle with Sylvia. Then I began to question that assumption.

"That and the fiber evidence were enough to bring her in," he added.

"Which hand?" I demanded.

"Huh?"

"Which hand of Sylvia's was holding the earring? And which ear did Katie lose it from, did you ask that?"

He frowned. "Not yet."

"Well, it matters!"

"The right hand."

"Okay, then it would have to be the right earring, because Sylvia was strangled from behind. If she reached up and caught hold of an earring with her right hand, it would be the right earring."

"Could be the left," he said, looking annoyed.

"Not very likely. If someone's strangling you, you go like this," I said, reaching up my hands to either side of my neck to grab a phantom strangler. "You don't reach across your throat."

He gave a grudging nod. I was feeling more confident now, and enjoying thinking through what had happened.

"Having the earring pulled out could have damaged Katie's ear, too," I said. "What kind of fastening was it, a hook or a post?"

"Does it matter?"

"Yes, because a hook might tear the ear if the earring was suddenly pulled downward, but a post would be more likely to pop off without damage."

He blinked. "It was a hook."

"Ah. Then I'd check Katie's right ear for damage. I bet you won't find any. Sylvia probably spotted the earring after Katie left, and bent down to pick it up. Did you find fibers from

Katie's dress on Sylvia's back?"

"That's enough," Aragón said, reaching past me for the doorknob.

I didn't step out of his way. Instead I put my hands on his chest. Just resisting, not pushing.

"Wait," I said quietly. "Please. I'm just trying to help, and trying to understand what happened. Were there fibers from Katie's dress on Sylvia's back, or just on her left side?"

He grimaced. "Definitely on the side. The back is inconclusive."

He took a step back, and I let my hands fall. His face had gone flat, eyes the blank stare that he used to discomfit people he was questioning.

"You did find fibers on her back, didn't you?" I said.

He frowned. "We haven't matched them yet. Now come on, let's go."

"But you collected everyone's clothing—"

He stepped around me and put his hand on the doorknob. "Come on, Nancy Drew, I've got work to do."

"Don't you dare patronize me, Tony Aragón!"

His head snapped back and he turned to face me. The surprise on his face was no more than I felt. I had spoken without thinking, and now my heart was suddenly pounding.

I stood his gaze, which was about all I could manage. After a moment his eyelids drooped, hiding his eyes.

"Time to go," he said softly as he turned the doorknob and pulled the door open.

"What about Katie?"

"She can't leave yet."

"I'll wait," I said, rather defiantly.

"Suit yourself."

We stepped out into the hallway, where the uniformed cops were still hanging around chatting. They glanced up as we emerged, and I wondered if they'd overheard us.

"The lounge is that way," Aragón said gesturing down the hall.

"I can find it."

"Don't go poking around."

I shot him a resentful glance. "I won't."

His lips twitched, almost smiling. He got them under control, but relented a little.

"I'll let you know if it's going to be a long time."

"Thanks."

Gathering my dignity, I turned and walked away down the hall. When I got to the intersection with the next hallway I glanced back and saw Detective Aragón watching me. I turned the corner and made my way back to the employee lounge I had seen.

The room had the basic necessities of a staff break room, but no luxuries. A counter with a sink full of dirty mugs. Beside it a dish rack crammed with more mugs and a couple of plastic food containers. Coffee maker, microwave, cupboards, refrigerator. Two vending machines full of junk food. A table and eight mismatched chairs, at which the female cop I'd seen earlier was sitting reading a magazine. She glanced up as I sat down across the table.

"Hi," I said, trying to be friendly.

She looked back at her magazine. I glanced around the room, hoping to find another magazine or something else I could read, but was reduced to admiring the posters on the walls. These consisted of mandatory worker's rights posters, a bulletin board in desperate need of being weeded, and police recruitment posters, which seemed rather after the fact in this room but were better than bare walls.

I got up to look at the bulletin board, mainly to admire several cartoons stuck up amid the welter of memos, announcements for events long past, and stapled articles tacked to the board. After a moment I sensed I was being watched, and turned around to see the cop staring at me.

I smiled and pointed to one of the cartoons. "Funny."

She looked back at her magazine. Having the impression she didn't like me looking at the bulletin board, I glanced toward the workers' compensation poster, decided I wasn't that desperate, and sat down again. After a minute I started cleaning out my purse. I had just finished counting the dollar sixty-seven in change that had been floating around in the bottom when Detective Aragón came into the room.

"Ms. Rosings?"

I hastily scooped my things back into my purse, stood up, and followed his gesture beckoning me into the hallway. Katie Hutchins was there, looking a little dazed. I felt a surge of relief and had to resist the urge to hug her.

"Hi, Katie," I said, trying for a normal tone. "I came to see if you'd like a ride home."

She gave a wavery smile. "That's so sweet of you, Ellen! Thank you."

I took her by the arm and started toward the exit, mouthing a silent "thank you" to Detective Aragón over my shoulder. He didn't respond, just stood watching us go, looking somewhat disgusted.

We didn't talk until we got into my car and were on the way home. I glanced over at Katie, who was still looking shell-shocked.

"Pretty rude of them to drag you out this late," I said. "I thought only TV cops did that sort of thing."

"Oh!" Katie said with a rush of pent-up feeling. "They just kept going on and on about my earring like it was a matter of national security! I couldn't believe it! You know I told you I'd lost an earring on Wednesday."

"Yes, I remember."

"Well, they wanted to know exactly how I'd lost it. They kept asking me again and again. Can you imagine? If I knew how it fell out of my ear, I wouldn't have lost it, would I?"

"No, probably not."

I couldn't watch her face while I was driving, but I could hear the frustration in her voice. She sounded sincere. I found myself wishing I had waited to talk about it until I could sit down with her and watch her reactions, then chided myself. I had just spent over an hour working to get her released. Hardly the time to start doubting her.

"And then that Detective Aragón came in and wanted to know which earring it was, right or left. So I told him it was the left, and he demanded to look at both my ears!"

I turned onto Paseo de Peralta and cruised along behind a low-rider. "He's just trying to be thorough, Katie."

"What on earth does it matter what my ears look like?"

So he hadn't told her where her earring was found. That made sense, I supposed. He probably shouldn't have told me.

"I don't know," I said, "but the police have to check everything. Maybe they were just making sure your earring didn't have anything to do with the murder."

"And they *still* haven't given it back to me!"

I listened while she continued to vent her indignation. She was recovering her spirits, which made me feel relieved. I'd rather listen to her rant than have her sitting crushed and silent, as she'd looked at first.

"And poor Bob! They wouldn't even let me call him. I thought you were supposed to get a phone call."

"That's if you're arrested."

"Oh."

"Katie, if they do this again, just tell them you want to talk to your lawyer. That'll get them off your back."

"I didn't think of that. Hmph."

I turned onto our street and pulled over in front of the B&B. The porch light gleamed a welcome, and I saw Bob looking anxiously out the front window.

"Thank you for the ride, Ellen," Katie said. "You're a gem."

"You're welcome. Good night."

I watched her into the house, then drove around the corner and up the alley to the back of the tearoom. It was getting close to midnight, and I was definitely ready to crash.

I let myself in and stood listening to the house for a moment. No stereo tonight, and no light under the dining parlor door. Maybe Sunday was a day of rest for ghosts as well. Christian ghosts, anyway. Captain Dusenberry probably fit the bill.

I went up and started getting ready for bed, thinking over the police station escapade as I brushed my teeth. I had taken a bit of a risk speculating about Katie's earring, I realized. If she had been guilty, my guesswork might have led to her arrest. Which would have been the right thing to happen, but I'd have felt awful about it.

Maybe I was going too far, meddling in people's fate. It was my fate, too, though. I wanted to get this murder resolved so I could move on and make a go of the tearoom. I had lots of plans, but they were all on hold.

I had donned my satin pajamas and was just about to climb into bed when my cell phone went off, muffled Mozart trying to fight its way out of my purse. I fetched the phone and crawled into bed before looking at the caller ID. It showed "Unavailable." I was tempted to leave the anonymous caller to the appropriate fate, i.e. voicemail, but on the third ring I relented and flipped the phone open.

"Hello?"

"Hi," said a male voice, as if expecting to be recognized. I frowned, trying to place it.

"Yes?" I prompted.

"It's me. Tony Aragón."

"Oh," I said, glancing at my bedside clock. Ten to midnight.

"Sorry to call this late. I figured you'd still be up."

"Just barely," I said, wondering if this was a prelude to the arrival of another squad car. I eyed my wardrobe and the dresser that held my t-shirts and jeans. If I was going to be hauled into the police station, I wanted to get into some comfortable clothes.

"Oh. Well, sorry. I just...maybe I should call back."

"No, it's okay," I said, plumping my pillows. "You've got me, you might as well tell me what you need."

"Um."

I waited, leaning back against my pillows and stifling a yawn. I wasn't going to be much good for problem-solving this late at night.

He cleared his throat. "I was just wondering if you'd like to have lunch with me."

15

I was suddenly wide awake, and suddenly conscious of having a conversation with Detective Aragón while lying in bed. I sat up, feeling a blush creep up my face.

"Lunch?" I said. "Oh. Ah—sure, I guess. When?"

"Would tomorrow be good?"

"Yes, actually, because we're closed Mondays. Where?"

I sounded like a prosecutor, snapping off questions. I couldn't help it. I was nervous.

"You like the Shed?" he asked.

"Love it."

"I can give you a ride, if you don't mind motorcycles."

I detested motorcycles. "Actually, I think I'll walk, if that's okay with you. I could use the exercise."

"Okay," he said. "Meet you at the Shed at eleven-thirty."

"Sounds good," I said.

He hung up. I listened to the nothing of the airwaves for a moment, then closed my phone.

"Bye," I said softly, wondering what the heck he meant by calling at midnight to ask for a date and then not even saying goodbye.

Not a date, I told myself as I got up to put away the phone. Lunch. Lunch is not a date. Dinner and the symphony is a date.

My mind leapt forward to picture me and Tony Aragón double-dating with Gina and Ted. I guffawed. That would be the day!

No, he probably just wanted to talk over something about the murder case. I slid back into bed and lay there wondering what it could be until I finally dozed off.

In the morning I got up and busied myself with chores around the tearoom. With Bach merrily pouring from the stereo I spent a pleasant couple of hours finishing some bits of decorating that hadn't quite been done the previous week, watering all the flowers and removing the faded blooms, and restocking items in the gift shop. The servers had put together more tea samplers on Saturday, so I put price tags on them and refilled the big basket display.

By then it was ten-thirty, time to get ready to meet Detective Aragón. I went upstairs to change.

The dress I'd been thinking about wearing, a pretty, springtime floral, wouldn't work with any of my shoes that were comfortable enough for walking to the Shed, about half a mile away. In fact, my walking shoes were all pretty rustic— more sturdy than lovely.

Well, why was I worrying so much about it? I was having lunch with a cop. Big deal. He'd be wearing his motorcycle duds.

I glanced down at the jeans and green velour sweater I was wearing, decided they were good enough, and kicked off my flats so I could put on walking shoes. Brushed my hair, touch of makeup, and a pair of gold hoop earrings and I was ready.

The day was sunny, so I put on a big straw sun hat and sunglasses before heading toward the Plaza. Tourist season was getting into gear, and the vendors at the Palace of the Governors were so thronged I had to walk down the street instead of the crowded *portal*. That was fine because the street was blocked off along the Plaza. Palace Avenue is closed to cars at the Plaza a lot of the year now. Too many tourists getting run over by impatient drivers. I crossed Washington Avenue and continued east to the Shed.

A wonderful little restaurant at the back of an old *plazuela*, the Shed has been around for decades and is a local favorite.

Purple paint on the door heralds the splashes of color inside. Giant flowers and vines twine around windows and doorways on the thick adobe walls in purple, turquoise, pink, and green with metallic gold embellishments. The designs are reminiscent of the sixties, which was about when the Shed moved to this location.

I was early, so I sat in the sunny *plazuela*, basking in the warmth of a mild morning. Tourists meandered in and out of the shops on either side of the little courtyard, or poked their heads in from the passage to the street and stared at the restaurant, debating whether to try it. I took out my phone to make some notes on menu ideas. I definitely wanted to talk to Julio about French onion soup. Welsh rarebit might have possibilities, too, if it could be made unmessy enough to be eaten like cheese toast, and easy to prep.

"Wow, I almost didn't recognize you."

I looked up at Detective Aragón, standing before me in his leather motorcycle jacket and black jeans, black shades. He grinned.

"Didn't know a fancy tea lady was allowed to wear jeans."

I put away my phone. "What is it with everyone? Yes, I wear jeans, yes, I drink coffee. Give me credit for a little dimension."

He laughed as I stood up, then gestured for me to precede him through the Shed's very narrow door. Despite the crowds of tourists, we were early enough to get a table right away, a tiny one beside a window looking out on the *plazuela*.

He took off his jacket and hung it on the back of his chair, revealing a long-sleeved, red and gray striped shirt with a bosun neckline. I propped my hat and purse on the windowsill. The window was open a crack, letting in the cool breeze and a murmur of voices from the tourists milling around outside.

A waiter appeared, a young man dressed all in black,

which made me look twice. I thought he might be one of Kris's crowd, but there was really no way to tell. He didn't look extraordinarily gothy, though he did have a silver cross dangling from one ear.

I ordered my usual, the number four enchilada plate, with iced tea. Detective Aragón ordered a number five, same dish but with beans and posole on the side. The waiter bustled off, leaving us gazing at each other in a momentary awkward silence. For my part, I was wondering what kind of lunch this would be—business (i.e. discussing the murder case), social, or a little of both.

Aragón cleared his throat. "Nice earrings."

"Thanks."

Miss Manners recommends asking questions to smooth over awkward social moments. I couldn't for the life of me think of one, other than "Why did you invite me to lunch?" which I was able to refrain from blurting.

"Um," he said, "I wanted to thank you for pointing out that stuff about the earring."

"Oh. Sure. Glad to help."

"I was mad about it at first."

"Because you wanted Katie to be guilty?"

He looked at me and brushed a hand over his hair, a gesture I'd seen before. "Not that, exactly. We want to make an arrest, but not if it's the wrong person."

I nodded. I could certainly understand the frustration of not being able to pinpoint the killer.

"Anyway, we're kind of stumped on this case for the moment. I've got three other cases working and right now there's not a lot more I can do on this one."

"You're not dropping it?" I sounded more dismayed than I intended.

"No, no. But it's starting to go cold, I'm afraid." He cleared his throat again. "I wanted to ask you if you remember anyone else being at your tearoom that day who was wearing white."

"White?"

"Yeah. Some of the fibers we can't identify are white."

"There's white all over the tearoom! The servers' aprons are white, and Julio's chef's jacket—"

He shook his head. "No, we checked what all of them were wearing. Doesn't match."

Our lunch arrived, putting a temporary end to the discussion. The waiter carefully set hot plates before us, blue corn enchiladas swimming in the Shed's hot red chile sauce, with a basket of garlic bread on the side for mopping up. I took a bite of enchilada and let the spice explode inside my head, then cooled off with a sip of tea.

"Our linens are white, and there's that missing napkin." I frowned, trying to think why the killer would have a napkin in hand, but Detective Aragón scotched that line of thinking.

"Your napkins and stuff are all cotton, right?"

"Some of it's real linen. That's flax."

"But it's not wool." He cut off a forkful of his enchilada and glanced at me before eating it. "The fibers we want are wool."

"Oh." I took another bite of my lunch, musing. "White wool."

I tried to think of anyone I'd seen wearing white wool that day. Not Claudia's gloves, which were white but undoubtedly cotton. Mick had worn a white t-shirt, also cotton. The other customers, ladies, mostly, were a blur of pastel color as far as I could recall.

Donna had worn a beige sleeveless dress. I had a flash of memory—her graceful movements as she removed a white coat and hung it in the hall.

"Donna had a white coat—"

"We're pretty sure it's not Donna."

"Oh!"

I gazed at him, waiting, but he didn't offer any details. Remembering my own conclusion that Donna would have planned more carefully, I nodded.

"It was a crime of impulse."

"Exactly." He looked disappointed.

I bit my lip, then shook my head. "I can't think of anyone in white wool."

"Okay. If something occurs to you, give me a call."

"I will."

A breeze gusted in the window beside us, carrying the smell of cigarettes. Aragón grimaced and pushed the window shut.

"Damn smokers," he said. "Ban them from the restaurants, and they blow it in from outside."

"You don't smoke?" I asked.

"No." He glanced at me and a slow grin crawled onto his face. "Not all cops smoke. Give me credit for some dimension."

I laughed, then sipped my tea, gazing at him in speculation. I could let it drop, but I decided not to.

"It's just that last night at the station I thought you smelled of cigarettes," I said.

"Oh. Yeah, I was visiting my grandmother when I got the call about the lab results. She's ninety-two and smokes like a chimney."

"Wow. Her doctors don't object?"

"Sure they do, but she's ninety-two, for chrissakes. It's one of the few things she enjoys any more."

"Oh, I see." I sipped my tea again. "Do you visit her often?"

He shrugged, looking a little self-conscious. "I go once a week. I always feel like I should go through decon afterward."

I laughed. "Such sacrifice! You must really be fond of her."

He smiled, then grabbed a piece of garlic bread and started

swabbing chile sauce from his plate. I took a piece too and broke it in half.

"Does she live in a retirement place?" I asked.

His eyes snapped to mine, suddenly angry. "No, she lives in a crummy apartment off Cerrillos Road, all right?"

"Sorry! Just making conversation."

He blinked a couple of times, then took a long pull at his water glass. "I'm sorry. I overreacted. It's just...we can't afford one of those places. And she wouldn't go, anyway. My sister takes care of her."

"Oh," I said. I tried to think of something else to say, another question that wouldn't be dangerous. "Has she lived there a long time?"

His mouth curved down in a frown, but he didn't explode again. "Yeah. She and my grandfather moved there in the seventies after they lost their house." His voice was low and angry, but the anger wasn't directed at me.

"Lost their house?" I said softly. "That's terrible."

His eyes got a faraway look, as if he was gazing into memory. "Abuelito's house, actually—my great grandfather. They lived with him there, out on East Alameda. A big old rambling adobe."

"Sounds like a nice place."

He nodded. "It had been in the family forever. When the galleries started moving in and the taxes went sky-high, it started getting tough to pay the bills. Then Abuelito died, and Grandma and Grandpa couldn't afford to pay the estate taxes. They had to sell the house."

I remembered my dad talking about the shift in the seventies, when Santa Fe suddenly became trendy and went from a sleepy, dusty town to a gallery-ridden Destination. He called it the Aspenization of Santa Fe. Quite a few unfortunate families had lost their ancestral homes for the very reason Tony Aragón was describing.

"They sold it to a real estate shark," he said bitterly. "Guy turned around and sold it to some rich New Yorker for twice the price."

"Oh. I'm so sorry."

"Yeah. Well. Shit happens."

He took another long swig at his water, and I got the impression the subject was closed. I pulled a piece off my garlic bread, swabbed up the last of my chile sauce, and ate it, trying to think of some happier subject.

"I wonder whose house your fancy tearoom used to be," Aragón said in a low voice with a nasty edge to it.

I met his gaze, but refused to go for the bait. He felt cheated. He was venting. It wasn't personal, and I wouldn't let it become personal. Instead I gave him a smile.

"Captain Dusenberry's."

He frowned. "A cop?"

"No, a soldier."

"What, did he lose his pension?"

I chuckled. "No, he was the original owner. Occupant, I should say—the army built it. He died in 1855. I bought the house from a law firm," I added.

"Oh." He stared at his empty plate, which he'd already wiped clean.

"I think he might still be around," I said casually.

"What?"

"Captain Dusenberry. Have you met Willow, the lady who does the ghost tours?"

He shook his head.

"Well, she assures me that there is a presence in the house."

Aragón made a face of disgust. "Yeah, I'll bet."

"She even suggested a ghost might materialize to commit a murder. I should have mentioned it before; you probably want to add the captain to your list of suspects."

"Only if he's wearing a white wool shroud."

I laughed. He glanced up at me, and his sullen expression faded into a reluctant grin.

The waiter came by to pick up our plates. "Care for any dessert?"

"Not for me," I said, regretfully. The Shed's desserts were wonderful, but after Julio's sweets at the opening I needed to behave myself.

Aragón shook his head, and the waiter took a black folder from his waistband and set it on the table. I reached for my purse.

"I'll get it," Aragón said sharply.

I looked at him. The frown was back.

"Working lunch," I said. "Thought it might be Dutch treat."

His face softened. "No, I invited you."

"Okay. Thanks."

He looked at the ticket, pulled a couple of bills out of his wallet and tucked them in the folder, then flipped it shut. He glanced up and saw me watching him, held my gaze for a moment, then looked out the window.

"In high school I would never have asked a girl like you out."

"Why not?" I asked softly.

"Because girls like you would never look at guys like me."

"I don't know. You seem worth looking at."

A swallow moved his throat. I felt myself starting to blush, and reached for my water glass.

"High school's crazy," I said. "Everyone's scared or angry or both."

"Yeah."

He glanced back at me, and for an instant he was the lost boy again. Then his face went blank, back to the cop mask.

"Let's get out of here," he said.

We worked our way through the now-crowded lobby and the almost-as-crowded *plazuela*. Lunch was in full swing and the tourists didn't mind waiting an hour or more for a taste of Santa Fe's history. We went through the deep *zaguan*, a passageway wide enough for a wagon, that led to the street and stepped out onto the long *portal* that fronts the whole block. Across the street to the south and east the cathedral was bustling, too, a tour group listening raptly to its guide in front of the huge wood-and-bronze doors.

"Can I give you a ride home?"

"Oh, uh..." I turned to him and saw that his eyes had gone half-anxious, half-sullen, as if he expected rejection. "Sure," I said with a helpless shrug. The smile he gave me went a long way toward making up for the torture I'd just agreed to.

I really, really dislike motorcycles. They're noisy and obnoxious, and so are a lot of the people who ride them. They disobey traffic rules and endanger pedestrians and I just don't like them. It's a failing of mine, a prejudice. Sorry, Miss Manners, but some things just can't be helped.

Tony Aragón led me to the next *plazuela*, a much bigger one called Sena Plaza. It had been built and for a long time inhabited by the Sena family, an important and wealthy family in Santa Fe's history. Now it was all shops and the Casa Sena Restaurant, a fancy expensive place with nouveau southwestern cuisine. They were serving lunch in their *plazuela* on this pleasant day, with spring flowers making a show in the garden.

We crossed the *plazuela* and went out through a passage on the north side into the parking lot behind the building. Aragón's motorcycle was parked there, all gleaming black and chrome. He lifted the helmet and handed it to me.

"You get to wear this."

"Thanks," I said doubtfully. I took off my hat and put on the helmet, fastening the strap beneath my chin. I slung my purse across my chest. The hat I'd just have to hold.

He had already thrown his leg over the bike, and sat there with his hands on the handlebars, grinning at me. "You look scared."

"I'm not scared. I've just never ridden a motorcycle." The second part was true.

"Never ever?"

"No."

"Well, don't worry. I'll take it nice and easy. Climb on."

I slid uneasily onto the seat behind him, clutching my hat with one hand. I didn't know what to do with the other. I tried gripping the little seat back behind me, but that was awkward.

"Put your arm around my waist and hold on," he said over his shoulder.

I did so, reluctantly and feeling very conscious of the warmth of his back through his leather jacket. He started the motor, gunned it a little, then backed gently and turned around to leave the dirt parking lot.

"Mind if we take a slight detour?" he said over his shoulder, raising his voice over the sound of the engine. "I want to show you something. It won't take long."

"Okay," I called back.

I leaned forward and clung to him like a limpet, which was no doubt what he'd had in mind. Cheeky bastard.

The ride couldn't have lasted more than a few minutes, but my sense of time was distorted and made it seem a lot longer. I was getting overloaded with confusing sensations. I still definitely did not like motorcycles, but I did seem to enjoy touching Tony Aragón, though in a way that was scarier than the bike.

I found myself wondering what he'd been like in high school, wishing I'd known him then, wondering if he'd gone to college or straight into the police academy. Probably the latter, if his family was strapped for cash.

He cruised east to Paseo de Peralta, then turned south. Cars whooshed by at what seemed to me to be reckless speed. I tried hard not to wince as each one passed.

He turned east again, and cruised along the street for a couple of blocks, then coasted to a stop at the curb and touched his foot to the pavement. A park ran the length of the street on the south side. He turned his head north to gaze at a large, sprawling adobe house across the street. A sign out front proclaimed it the "Sagebrush Bed & Breakfast" in elegant, scrolling letters.

"That's it," he said over the subdued idle of the motorcycle engine. "Abuelito's house."

I stared at it, feeling a mixture of pity and embarrassment. No wonder he was angry about losing it. It was a classic old Santa Fe house, from the blue paint on the door and window frames to the stair-stepped adobe wall around a burgeoning garden. He might have inherited it, though from its size and location I suspected it would take more than a cop's salary to pay the taxes.

"Nice place," I said, unable to think of a better comment.

"Yeah. Well, thanks for indulging me. I'll get you home now."

He didn't say anything more until he pulled up in front of the tearoom. The bike tilted a little as he leaned it on the kickstand and I clutched at him, caught off guard.

"Easy there," he said. "You okay?"

"Fine," I said, climbing off the bike and trying to recover my dignity. I took off the helmet and handed it to him. "Thanks for the ride."

"Any time."

He sat there gazing at me. I couldn't quite read his face, amusement or speculation or something else.

"Would you mind if I came inside for a minute?" he asked. "I just want to look at the room again."

"Of course," I said, taking my keys out of my purse.

We went through the gate and down the path to the house. Sunshine had wakened the earthy smells of the garden, making me want to dig in the dirt. I'd plant gladiolas soon, I thought, looking at the new red leaves coming out on the rosebushes I had put in.

The scent of wisteria enveloped us as we stepped onto the porch. Tony Aragón stood gazing at the purple blossoms as if he'd never seen them before. I unlocked the front door and my heart sank a little as strains of Bach wafted out from the stereo I was certain I had turned off.

Just ignore it, I decided. I smiled at Detective Aragón, who was still staring at the wisterias.

"Amazing flowers," he said, then sneezed.

"Bless you. They've been here a long time. Sylvia Carruthers thinks they—*thought*—they might be as old as the house."

He gave me the flat stare for a moment. "Yeah? She knew a lot about stuff like that."

"Yes, she did."

I looked at the wisterias and the view they framed of the Territorial B&B across the street and the corner of Vince's gallery to one side. Nice, historic houses on all sides. A pretty neighborhood. I felt a rush of gratitude all at once, that I was here in this beautiful place, despite the trouble of the past week.

"Well, come in," I said, leading the way.

He followed me down the hall to the dining parlor. I frowned at the spill of light from under the door, then opened it and with a gesture invited the detective to go in.

The chandelier cast a cheery glow over the gleaming polished wood of the dining table. I watched Tony Aragón slowly pace through the room. He paused to stare at the outside door, then looked up at the chandelier. I followed his gaze and stifled a sigh when I saw one of the crystals swaying back and forth.

"Is there someone upstairs?" he asked.

"No."

"You sure?"

"My chef has the only other key, and he's off today."

Aragón's eyes narrowed as he watched the moving crystal. "Maybe I ought to go up and check it out." He glanced at me. "With your permission," he added.

I felt an irrational urge to refuse. The last time he'd been upstairs it had been expressly against my wishes, and I was still a little annoyed about that. There was no need to show him my suite, though. The room above the dining parlor was Kris's office.

"If you insist, but you won't find anyone," I said.

"I don't insist," he said quickly.

I shrugged. He gazed at me, brows drawn together. He glanced at the chandelier, then back at me.

"You've seen this before."

I nodded. "Old houses settle."

"Wooden houses. This is adobe."

"Yes, well." I sighed. "I meant it when I said I thought Captain Dusenberry was still around."

His eyes widened. "You're shi—you're kidding me!"

I raised my hand to the light switch. "The chandelier was off when I left this morning. He turns it on. This is the room where he was murdered."

Aragón's eyebrows went up and his gaze went to the chandelier again. "Room's going to get a reputation."

"It already has. I have goths and a bunch of morbid old ladies who want to have tea in here, not to mention Willow wanting to make it a stop on her ghost tour."

"Oh, man. Yeah, I can just see a bunch of punked-out goths sitting around this table drinking tea."

"Actually, it's the old ladies who creep me out."

He paced around the room again, keeping an eye on the chandelier as if he expected it to hop down and start dancing on the table. I waited, relieved that he hadn't accused me of being a nut case. Maybe he was thinking it, but he was polite enough not to say it.

"Haunted dining room," he said finally, cocking an eyebrow at me. "Might be a good marketing angle."

"You sound like my friend Gina." I noticed a faded lisianthus bloom that had fallen onto the dining table from the centerpiece, and stepped over to pick it up. "Actually, Captain Dusenberry's all right. It's kind of nice to have a man around the place," I said, trying for wry humor.

Aragón didn't laugh. "Does he do anything else?"

"He turns the stereo on," I said, nodding my head toward the butler's pantry across the hall. "I think he likes music."

Aragón closed his eyes briefly and shook his head. "You sure no one could be getting in here and doing this stuff?"

"Pretty sure. Why would they?"

"To scare you."

"It's weird, but it's not really scary."

He frowned. "Listen, if anything else strange happens, you let me know."

"Okay. Going into ghost busting?"

"I sure hope not." He glanced around the dining room once more, then shoved his hands in his pockets. "Guess I'm through here. Thanks."

"Sure."

I turned off the light and pulled the door shut as we stepped into the hall. "Thanks for the lunch, Detective—"

"Call me Tony." He looked at me, then hunched a shoulder in a shrug. "The only people who call me Detective Aragón are reporters and the top brass."

"Okay, Tony," I said. "Then I'm Ellen."

We started down the hall toward the front door. "There was a girl named Ellen in my fifth grade class," he said. "She was a total snob."

"How unfortunate," I said in my best Miss Manners voice.

He glanced at me sidelong and laughed. "Ah, don't get in a huff. She wasn't pretty, either."

"This is supposed to reassure me?"

"Yeah, cause she wasn't anything like you."

"Well, thanks, I think."

We stopped at the front door. He turned to face me.

"I'm not great at compliments, I guess," he said.

"Maybe you just need more practice."

"Maybe."

He continued to gaze at me, dark Spanish eyes under slightly drooping lids. I felt my pulse increase slightly. He opened his mouth to say something, then his cell phone went off. Muttering a curse, he pulled it off his belt and glanced at it.

"Gotta go," he said, reaching for the door.

"Okay. Thanks again."

"No, thank *you*," he said, pointing the cell phone at me. It rang again and he brought it to his face as he stepped out the door. "Yeah, what is it?"

I watched him stride down the path, aware that my heart was still beating faster than it should.

Miss Manners is opposed to cell phones on the principle that they interfere with normal social interaction. I felt inclined to agree, but it wasn't until after Tony Aragón's motorcycle had disappeared down the street that I let myself wonder what would have happened if his phone hadn't rung.

16

I spent the afternoon puttering around the tearoom, trying to remember white wool and thinking over the murder case in general. Tony had seemed discouraged about it, and it was hard not to pick up the feeling.

The fact that the police lab hadn't been able to match the fibers to any of the clothing they'd collected brought back the possibility that anyone could have snuck into the dining parlor through the outside door. There would have been a slight risk of being seen from the kitchen window, but it was feasible.

At around four I went to the butler's pantry to make myself a pot of tea, and while I waited for the kettle to boil I tried to imagine myself a cold-hearted killer bent on taking down Sylvia Carruthers. I spied on Sylvia to find out where she would be and when, and chose the tearoom as the best place to kill her.

Why the tearoom and not somewhere else? Because I knew when she'd be there, and I knew I could sneak in the back door. How did I know what room she'd be in? Well, I didn't. I just took a chance (reasonable) that the hostess was having her party in the dining parlor. How did I know I'd be able to catch Sylvia alone? I didn't, but trusting in my own luck and ingenuity, I donned my white wool coat (not very inconspicuous, but oh well), and crept up to the back of the tearoom an hour and a half after the party began, to await my opportunity to strike.

With no weapon. I knew she liked big fancy necklaces, so I planned in advance to use whatever one she was wearing to strangle her.

As a logical scenario it pretty well stank. Maybe I wasn't cut out for this kind of speculation.

The kettle boiled. I emptied the warm water from my favorite hydrangea chintz teapot, put in tea leaves and poured hot water over them, the fragrant, flowery scent of Darjeeling rising with the steam. While it steeped I made myself a sandwich, shamelessly raiding Julio's refrigerator for bread, lettuce, and the last little bit of leftover pâté.

I glanced at the kitchen window a few times while I moved around in there, confirming that one mostly couldn't see the porch and the dining parlor door. Someone crossing the backyard and the little parking area would be taking a greater risk of being seen. Maybe the killer had come around the north side of the house, near the lilacs, and slipped onto the porch from there.

I took my tea and sandwich, plus a couple of leftover petits fours and a small bunch of grapes, upstairs to the sitting area by the window at the front of the house. I had put some of my favorite ornaments from my parents' house around the area— southwestern stuff that didn't fit with the Victoriana downstairs—things I loved and remembered from childhood, like an old mudhead kachina and a pottery frog we had picked up on a trip down to Mexico.

The frog had a big, gaping mouth that glowed mysteriously when lit by a candle inside. I remembered being entranced by it at evening patio parties as a little girl, a magical arch of flickering golden candlelight, the frog itself invisible in the darkness.

Now, afternoon sunlight streamed in the window and the frog sat dark, hiding in the shadow behind the drapes. I left the gauze curtains closed to soften the light a bit, and was still able to bask in the radiant warmth while I relaxed with my tea.

It had now been five days since Sylvia's murder. I mulled over my previous speculations. I still kept coming back to

Donna, or Donna with Vince's help, as the most likely killer. Donna seemed to have the best motivation for the crime. Tony had dismissed the idea of a conspiracy, but it still niggled at me as a possibility.

I sat musing about it for a long while, then I poured myself a last cup of tea, emptying the teapot, and leaned back with a sigh. Tony had been right, I decided. A conspiracy implied advance planning, and it would be poor planning to commit a murder in a public place and without the preparedness of having a weapon.

If I was going to murder someone at a tea party, I'd drop arsenic in their tea. I shivered at the thought, and realized it had been a worry in the back of my mind. For a moment I wondered if Sylvia could have been the victim of a multiple attack murder à la *Orient Express*. I dismissed it, though. The autopsy would have revealed poison, and Tony would no doubt have bullied me and my staff with obnoxious questions if anything like that had shown up.

So, not Vince and Donna. Maybe Donna alone? But again, if she was in a mood to kill her mother, she could have planned it better.

Vince alone? But why?

Because he and Sylvia both wanted to buy the house where he was planning to open his gallery?

A shiver went down my spine. It seemed unreasonable to commit murder over a house, but then, they'd both wanted it badly enough to bid up the price.

And then the sale had fallen through, and Vince had gotten the house for less money. Because Sylvia had died.

I put down my teacup and fetched my cell phone, sitting back down again in the sunshine to place a call to Claudia Pearson at the Santa Fe Preservation Trust. The receptionist put me through and Claudia answered after a brief wait.

"This is Claudia Pearson," she said, her voice sounding a

bit stressed.

"It's Ellen Rosings. I hope I'm not calling at a bad time."

"No, no. It's just busy, is all, but it's always busy here. What can I do for you?"

"I have a question about the house Mrs. Carruthers wanted to buy for the Trust. I found out who the other buyer was, the one who eventually got the house."

"Oh, yes. Vince Margolan."

"You knew about it?"

"Yes, that real estate man who was at your opening told me. I was curious so I went back and checked Sylvia's file on the project. She'd made notes on a call she received from Mr. Margolan after she made an offer on the house. He wasn't very polite about it, even though Sylvia had assured him we wouldn't raise the rent."

I felt a rush of disappointment. "Oh. That was my question—what did she plan for the Trust to do with the house?"

"Nothing different. Sylvia had already drawn up an agreement for him stating he'd be able to use the house as a gallery. Basically the terms were the same as in the preservation easement we had from the owner."

I knew what a preservation easement was, because I had one with the Trust myself, for the tearoom. It stated that I retained ownership of the property and the Trust would bear the responsibility for its historic preservation.

"Of course," Claudia went on, "if the Trust had succeeded in acquiring the house he was leasing, we'd still have been responsible for its maintenance. Sylvia only drafted the agreement to reassure him that the terms of his lease wouldn't change. It really was a nice deal for him. I don't know why he didn't take it."

"Probably would have cost him less than buying the house," I mused.

"Definitely."

I frowned at the gauze curtains before me, aglow with late sunlight that was starting to get a tinge of gold. Why had Vince refused Sylvia's generous deal? Because he wanted to own the house and not rent it was all I could think of, but it meant much higher costs for him. It didn't make sense that he'd kill her just to own the house when she was willing to let him keep leasing it for his gallery.

"So, now that Vince owns the house, you have the same preservation easement with him, right?" I asked.

I heard a rustle of papers over the phone. "Yes, the easement is binding on all future owners of the property. I haven't gotten around to calling him about setting up the annual inspection. It's one of the things I need to get to. I'm still catching up on Sylvia's projects."

I tried to think of any hitch that could mess up a preservation easement. "What happens if Vince doesn't like the terms of the easement?"

"Too bad. They're recorded in an easement deed that's legally enforceable."

I nodded, remembering the copy of my own easement deed that was filed with the rest of my papers on the house. Maybe I should go find it and read it again, but I was lazy.

"Could you remind me of the sort of terms that might be in the deed?"

"Sure. Basically, in exchange for benefits such as breaks on property and estate taxes, the owner agrees on behalf of himself and all future owners not to make alterations that impact the historic character of the property, and we agree to bear the cost and responsibility of maintaining the property's historic character. We can take any owner of the property to court to prevent him violating the deed."

"Did you say estate taxes?" I asked.

"Yes."

"Does that mean you could have a preservation easement

with a private property owner? I mean, someone who owned an historic residence?"

"Sure. That's one of the reasons for our existence, to help make sure owners of historic properties don't have to sell them to pay taxes. Estate taxes particularly can be a nasty setback for private homeowners. Of course, it all depends on the current policy in a given year."

My throat tightened slightly. *Where were you when Tony's grandparents had to sell their house?* I thought, but didn't say it. It had probably been years after the Aragóns had lost their home by the time Sylvia founded the Santa Fe Preservation Trust.

"Did you have someone in mind?" Claudia asked.

"Uh, no. I was just wondering. Thank you for taking the time to answer all my silly questions."

"Any time, and they're not silly questions. Which reminds me, Shelly pulled the file on your house. There's a note about Captain Dusenberry's murder, but it's very brief. Apparently the murderer was never caught."

Restless ghost. Seeking justice?

Or Willow, trying to convince me of his presence? I kind of doubted that, and despite my discomfort, I was starting to consider asking her what she knew about the captain's murder. It would be faster than doing the research myself, or having Kris do it.

"I see," I said. "Thank you."

"We'll mail you a copy. Thank you for the donation in Sylvia's memory, by the way. I hope the tearoom's doing well."

"So far so good. Drop by when you have time."

"I will, thanks."

We said goodbye and I sat thinking for a while, then picked up my tea things and took them downstairs to wash up. Like Tony, I had pretty much reached a dead end with my speculations. I gave up and spent the evening reading until I was yawning too much to see what was on the page.

The next morning I was up early, before Julio arrived. I was impatient to talk to the staff about what they had seen during the thank-you tea. I passed the time by setting out linens and china in the alcoves, then as soon as Julio came in I pounced on him. He very patiently repeated to me what he'd told the police, which amounted to he hadn't seen a thing.

"What about the window?" I asked, gesturing to the kitchen window. "Did you see anybody coming or going out back? Anybody in white, especially?"

Julio, looking like a chollo with his ball cap—tropical fish print today—on backward, shook his head as he measured out flour for the day's scones. "Nope. Nada."

"Okay. Thanks, Julio."

"Still trying to crack the case, eh boss?"

I snatched a currant out of a bowl he had sitting on the counter. "Yes. Not doing a very good job of it, I'm afraid."

"Maybe it's time to let it go."

I didn't answer, feeling a stubbornness rising in me. For a while I watched him cook, moving confidently around the kitchen. He knew his business. Did I know mine, or was I getting too far out of bounds?

Not yet, I decided. Not until I had at least talked to all the staff. Thoroughness, I thought, wondering what case Tony was working on today. Probably not this one, not unless some startling new evidence had come in.

I grilled Vi and Dee when they arrived. Dee had been waiting on the customers up front and had seen Mr. Ingraham leaving, but hadn't seen any of the other thank-you tea guests. Vi had been in the dining parlor most of the time, though she had started clearing and was back and forth to the pantry when the party was breaking up. She had been with me when I found Sylvia's body, helping to solidify my alibi.

"Who was in the parlor the last time you left it before we

found the body?" I asked her.

"I took the tea trays out first," she said, referring to the three-tiered trays on which the scones and sweets had been served. "When I left with the second one, there were four people in the room: Mrs. Carruthers, her daughter, Mr. Margolan, and Mrs. Hutchins."

"That's what I remembered. Thanks, Vi."

She gave me a slightly anxious look. "The police haven't figured it out yet?"

"Not yet." I smiled to reassure her. "Don't worry, they will."

Kris arrived and I went upstairs with her to ask what she'd seen, even though she had left the tearoom at five on Wednesday. She smoothed her black hair behind one ear and frowned in thought.

"White wool? No, I don't remember anyone wearing that. I would have noticed, I think. A white wool dress would be kind of unusual," she said, looking intrigued at the idea.

"Well, it's not necessarily a dress. Could be a coat, or even a scarf."

I frowned, trying to picture my imaginary killer strangling Sylvia while wearing a white wool scarf. Instead the disobliging killer strangled her *with* the scarf. I shook off the thought.

"You left by the back door, right? Did you see anyone outside?"

She shook her head, generating a slight chiming sound from the earrings she was wearing, long, dangling clusters of tiny silver bells. "No, sorry. I did turn and look back, and I saw the doors to the dining parlor all lit up, but that was it."

"Okay. Thanks, Kris."

"Sure thing."

The only two staffers I hadn't talked to were Mick and Iz. Mick would come in at eleven, when we opened for business.

Iz would be in at one today, to take over for Dee who had an afternoon class.

I passed the morning going through a backlog of messages from over the weekend and writing thank-you notes to people who had sent flowers and other gifts in honor of the tearoom's opening. Just before eleven I went downstairs and started haunting the kitchen, waiting for Mick to arrive. Julio was piping meringue onto a parchment-covered baking sheet in the shape of little seashells. I caught a whiff of almond in the air.

"Those are darling, Julio! Will they hold their shape?"

"That's what I'm going to find out. I think they will. Got a batch in the oven already. No peeking!" he added as I started toward the two commercial ovens.

"I won't open it, I'll just turn on the light. Yes, they look great! Wonderful idea!"

"Thanks."

"When you have a minute I'd like to talk about some ideas for lunch items."

He gave me a quizzical glance. "Lunch? Have you seen today's reservation list?"

"Tuesdays are probably going to be our slowest days," I said, dismissing reservations with a wave of my hand that was much lighter than I felt. "That's why this is a good day for planning. This afternoon, before you go."

"Okay."

I had caught sight of Mick through the window as he parked his mottled car behind the house. I fetched myself a cup of tea to give him time to come in, then sat down with him at the break table in the corner of the kitchen.

"I'm going over what happened last Wednesday, Mick."

"Again?" He glowered.

"Yes. I'm sorry. Could you please tell me everything you saw during and after the thank-you tea?"

"Not much besides china," he said, jerking his head toward the dishwashing station. "All I can see is the little hall outside the butler's pantry and the restroom."

I nodded. The small hallway was the only indoor access to those rooms and to the kitchen. It had an outside door that opened onto the porch, like the kitchen, but Julio had already told me neither door had been opened Wednesday afternoon.

"Do you remember seeing anyone besides me and the girls in the hallway?"

"Well, yeah, when you brought people in to show them the kitchen. Other than that, I saw the lady in the purple dress go into the restroom, and the guy in the turtleneck and jacket came and waited outside it for a while, but he went away again before she left."

"Wait—could you repeat that?"

He did. The purple, or plum, dress had been Claudia's. The turtleneck and jacket had been Vince.

"He waited for the restroom, but then went away again?"

"Yeah. Guess he got impatient."

"Did you see where he went?"

"Back out into the main hall."

So Vince had been in the main hall between the time he left the dining parlor and the time Claudia came out of the restroom. I had been in the hall at that time, too, but I didn't remember seeing him. Of course, I'd been dealing with coats and goodbyes.

"All right, Mick. Thanks."

"Sure. You done with that?" he asked, pointing at my empty teacup.

"Uh, yes."

He carried the cup to the dishwashing station, and I wandered back upstairs and sat by the front window, trying to recall everyone I'd said goodbye to after the tea, and in what order. Mr. Ingraham had left first, then Gina, then Katie. I had said goodbye to Manny and Nat and watched them drive away. Then Donna had sort of stormed out, leaving me and Claudia in the hall.

I couldn't remember seeing Vince leave. I had the impression he'd said goodbye, but I didn't recall watching him out the front door.

When Iz came in I asked her to tell me who she'd seen leaving and in what order on Wednesday, when she'd been at the hostess station. She had been a little distracted with customers in the gift shop, but had seen my guests leaving in the same order I recalled.

"What about Mr. Margolan?" I asked.

"The man in the white turtleneck? I didn't see him go out."

White turtleneck. I sucked a swift breath. Off-white, I'd have called it, but yes. He had worn a light-colored turtleneck under a black jacket. It had looked like cashmere to me.

"You're sure you didn't see him?" I asked her.

Iz nodded seriously. "I figured he'd left while I was ringing up customers. That one lady bought a cup and saucer, and I had to get a box and tissue paper to wrap it. I was poking around under the counter for a while."

"Thank you, Iz."

I walked slowly down the hall toward the back of the house, thinking. Vince had not left by the front door, I was fairly certain.

He could have left by the back hall door, or by the dining parlor door. His gallery was across the street and to the north of the tearoom, so if he'd gone out the back way he could have walked past the lilacs and out alongside the fenced front yard to the street. Little chance anyone would have seen him from the kitchen window.

So that probably explained how Vince had left without being seen by me or Vi. It didn't explain why he would kill Sylvia. I had only a semi-plausible motive for him—ownership of the house where he was planning to open his gallery.

And if his cashmere sweater was the source of the white fibers, why hadn't it matched the sample the police had taken from Sylvia's dress?

I found myself standing in the dining parlor, gripping the back of the chair in which Sylvia had sat. I didn't remember going in. I glanced at the door, standing half-open behind me, and at the chandelier over the table, which for once was dark and absolutely still.

Tony should know this. I had a strong urge to call him and ask what might be a dumb question. What clothes had Vince given to the police? He could have substituted other clothes for the ones he'd worn at the tea.

That would have been risky, especially if anyone had given the police a detailed description of what he'd been wearing. But Tony hadn't asked me about what the others had worn.

I left the room, closing the door with a snap, and hurried upstairs to find my cell phone. I searched back through the calls until I found Tony's, dialed his number, and sat tapping my foot while I waited for him to answer. After four rings I heard the tell-tale sound of a transfer to voice mail. Curbing my impatience, I waited to leave a message.

"Tony, it's Ellen. Please give me a call as soon as you can. I think you need to look at Vince Margolan. He was wearing a light-colored cashmere turtleneck and a dark jacket and slacks at the tea last Wednesday. If that's not the clothing he provided you, then—well, call me."

I hung up and sat frowning at the artwork on my office walls, then got up and went back downstairs, taking my cell phone with me. For half an hour I busied myself around the tearoom, but it was slow and there really wasn't much that needed doing.

Iz and Mick were making more tea samplers at the kitchen break table while Vi watched out front. Julio was baking spice bread for tomorrow, and glared at me the third time I looked into the kitchen.

"You want to talk about lunches?"

"Ah—not right now. Say, that looks wonderful," I added as he turned out a fresh, brown loaf and set it on a cooling rack.

"Want a taste?"

He reached for a loaf that had already cooled, sliced off the heel, and handed it to me. "Good with butter or cream cheese."

"Mm! Wonderful by itself," I said. "In fact, I think I'd like to take some over to Mr. Margolan's gallery. I've been meaning to see how he's doing. Could you cut me a few slices?"

"Sure," Julio said.

I fetched a small plate from the pantry and loaded it with slices of the fresh spice bread. Julio put a chilled swirl of piped butter on the plate next to the bread.

"Want to cover it with something?"

"No, I'm just going across the street. I'll be right back."

No, it wasn't very smart of me. I should have waited until I heard back from Tony, but I was impatient. I should have taken my cell phone with me, but mindful of Miss Manners I left it behind.

As I carried the bread across the street I thought about what to say on my neighborly visit. I'd already asked Vince about what Donna had been saying to her mother after the tea, so I couldn't go there again. I hadn't asked him about Donna's departure, though.

I arranged myself on the front porch, friendly offering in hand, friendly smile on face, before I knocked on the wooden door. After a moment it opened and Vince looked out. He was wearing jeans and long-sleeved t-shirt spattered with white paint, and had a pair of goggles pushed up on his forehead, his hair a sandy spray above them.

"Oh," I said. "Have I come at a bad time? I just wanted to

bring you some of this spice bread."

I looked past him into the house. What had been an empty space was now filled with a clutter of crates, power tools, drop cloths, boom box and painting gear. What had been a series of rooms in an old brick house was now a single, long room. Vince had knocked down walls, a definite no-no in historic preservation terms.

Vince glanced over his shoulder, following my gaze, then opened the door wider. "Come in."

17

Here is where Miss Manners failed me. I should have turned around and left, but not wanting to be rude, I stepped in. Vince pushed the door closed behind me.

"Wow, you've made a lot of changes," I said, the cheeriness in my voice sounding a bit tinny to my ear.

"Yeah."

Desperate for a distraction, I gestured toward the crates, which were large and flat. "Is that some of the artwork you'll be showing?"

"Yeah."

"Oh, may I see? Unless it's too much trouble," I added.

"I've got a couple open."

He walked over to the crates, which leaned against the wall by the fireplace in what had been the front room and was now part of the whole huge gallery space, forming the short foot of a long "L." Vince picked up a pair of latex gloves from the mantel.

"Been painting," he said, looking at me as he put them on.

He pulled a large canvas out of one of the crates and stood it against the stack, then turned for my reaction. The piece was very modern, abstract smears of paint flung across the canvas in what to me seemed random abandon. I confess, modern art is usually not to my taste. This piece looked liked it belonged on Donna Carruthers's living room wall.

"Hmm," I said, nodding. "Very interesting. Not a local artist, I gather."

"No."

"It reminds me of some pieces I saw at Donna Carruthers's house. By the way, I wonder if you saw her leave the tearoom last Wednesday, after the tea?"

"No."

"I see. Well," I said, glancing around the room again. "You're busy. I'll get out of your way."

I started toward the door and Vince followed. I paused to set the plate down on the corner of the work table I'd seen on my last visit.

It was covered with a clutter of hand tools and the boom box weighing down blueprints—I assumed the same plans Vince had been reviewing a few days before. The top one was a drawing of the long room Vince had made by knocking down walls. It showed additional changes—skylights and clerestory windows—the sort of thing I was certain was in violation of his preservation easement.

That was the moment I realized how dangerous Vince was. He could be sued by the Trust for making these changes, but he'd done it anyway, probably assuming they wouldn't put up much of a fight once the damage was done. He'd done it fast, too. So fast Claudia hadn't even found out about his plans. That was the act of a ruthless man.

My brother has always said that I have a terrible poker face. When I looked up at Vince he must have seen exactly what I was thinking.

He grabbed me so fast I didn't have time to fight back. I tried to kick, but he got my arm pinned behind my back and all I could do was squirm. I started to yell for help.

"Shut up!" he shouted, twisting my arm harder. Pain shot through my shoulder and I gasped.

With his free hand he turned on the boom box and cranked the volume. Hard rock music screamed through the house.

He pushed me toward the long room. I stumbled and he pushed me again, knocking me sprawling onto the plastic-covered floor and jerking my arm so hard I was stunned with pain for a moment. I heard the ripping sound of tape being pulled free, then the plastic drop cloth covered my head and a heavy weight fell on my back.

I struggled as much as I could, which wasn't very much. Oddly, I held my breath, as if instinct warned me to conserve air. I got one hand in front of my face and was able to keep a small space within the drop cloth that way, but I knew it wouldn't last long.

Vince was pulling it tighter over my head. I tried to claw a hole in the plastic with my fingernails, wishing I had Gina's long nails instead of my short and practical manicure. My breath made it hot and humid in the tiny space. Part of me was terrified, and another part was thinking, "This is a really stupid way to die."

I was starting to feel dizzy. The loud music was muffled by the plastic to a dull rhythmic thumping. More thumps joined it, then the music abruptly shut off. Yelling, indistinct. The pressure on my face suddenly eased, and the weight came off my back.

I struggled free of the dropcloth, gasping for breath. Just as I got clear I was grabbed again. I fought back, then realized it was Tony, telling me, "Shh, it's all right, you're safe now."

Not Shakespeare, but at that moment they were the most beautiful words I could hear. I turned into a disgusting puddle of jelly, shivering and clinging to Tony.

There were other cops in the room, a lot of them. I didn't see Vince. I was glad. I never wanted to see him again.

"You're an idiot, you know," Tony said after I'd calmed down a little.

"I know. Spare me the lecture."

"You're damned lucky I checked my voicemail."

I looked into his eyes—those dark, intense Latino eyes— and felt a flood of relief wash through me, along with something more intimate that I shied away from examining. I hiccupped.

"Thank you, Tony," I said in a shaky voice.

For an instant his brow creased and he seemed almost as scared as I was. Then he glanced up at the cops moving around the room and transformed into a cop himself.

"Paramedics are here," said one of the uniform cops.

"Good, send them in," Tony said.

"I'm all right," I said, sitting up as Tony released me.

"They'll check you over. Standard procedure. Just sit tight."

He stood up and walked away, joining a couple of the uniformed cops and talking in low voices. I felt excluded and rather let down, but perhaps that was just the aftermath of an adrenaline rush.

Two nice paramedics—a girl with tufty dark hair and a freckled, redheaded farm-boy type—came and spoke gently and kindly to me while they took my vitals. They checked out my arm, which was starting to ache rather badly, and declared the shoulder was not dislocated but that I might have strained a tendon.

"Ibuprofen and a heating pad," said the tufty-haired girl with a businesslike nod. "If it's still sore in a couple days, go see your doctor. You need a ride home?"

"It's just across the street."

"I'll walk you over."

She helped me to my feet. I glanced at Tony, who was still huddled with the other cops. Evidence techs were coming in. I recognized the blond, blue-eyed guy with the wire-framed glasses. He gave me a friendly nod as he carried in a bulky equipment case.

The paramedic walked outside with me into an alien universe. Birds were singing in the late afternoon sunshine. Iris were blooming in Katie's garden next door. People who would never dream of murdering each other were walking up and down the street.

We waited for a lull in traffic, then crossed the street, passing Tony's motorcycle parked at the curb. The paramedic came all the way to the door with me. I opened it, setting off a merry tinkle of bells.

"Thanks," I said, giving her my best Miss Manners smile.

She nodded and left. I squared my shoulders, hoping I didn't look too disheveled, and went into the tearoom.

Vi came out of the gift shop. "Oh, Ellen! We saw all the cops. Are you okay?"

"Ah...fine," I said, glancing toward the south parlor.

"No customers," Vi said. "The last one left just after you went across the street. So what happened?"

Her blue eyes were wide with curiosity. I heard the roar of a motorcycle and glanced through the window in time to see Tony's bike turn the corner. Heading for the police station, no doubt. Probably looking forward to an interview with Vince.

I shivered, then looked at the clock behind the hostess station, which read five forty-five. I locked the front door and turned around the "Closed" sign.

"We're closing early," I said. "Make us a big pot of Irish Breakfast, then get everyone together in the kitchen and I'll fill you in."

18

N o, Gina! Absolutely not. I had enough of that the first time."

"But it's even more important now!"

She leaned against the counter in the butler's pantry, watching me arrange fresh flowers in vases for the parlors, her sleeveless turquoise dress hinting at summertime. The flowers had arrived late Tuesday afternoon, and I hadn't had the chance to get to them until Wednesday morning.

"My face has already been all over the news," I said, tucking another rose into a crystal vase along with a spray of blue mist. "Why do it all over again?"

"Because this time you're a hero! And anyway, people have to see you at least three times before they'll remember you."

"Gina, it's not an advertising campaign!"

"You're right. Like I said, you can't buy this kind of publicity."

I shook my head and picked up the vase, carrying it out into the hall. Gina followed me to the south parlor.

"Remember how worried you were that Sylvia's murder would keep people away from the tearoom?" she said. "Well, this is just the opposite! People who don't even care about tea will come just to see the lady who caught the murderer. Hello," she added, smiling at a pair of middle-aged women who were just leaving the Rose alcove. They exchanged a glance, then bustled out to the gift shop.

I placed the roses on the sideboard that divided Jonquil from Lily. "But I didn't catch him. The police caught him. If they hadn't arrived in time I'd have been in deep—trouble," I said, smiling belatedly at a trio of elderly ladies who had followed Dee into the parlor.

She showed them to Jonquil, where two of them made themselves comfortable at once in chintz-covered chairs. The third hung back to speak to me. Her face was half-hidden beneath a hat buried in silk hydrangeas, but there was no mistaking the stentorian tone of her voice.

"Ms. Rosings, I'm so glad to hear they've caught the man who killed Sylvia Carruthers," said the woman I'd come to think of as the Bird Woman.

I put on a polite smile. "Yes, so am I."

"Now you can open up the murder room again," she boomed, "because her spirit will be appeased."

"Will it?" I said weakly.

"That's what Willow Lane told us. Right, girls?" Her two friends nodded and twittered agreement. "We took her tour of all the haunted places in town," the Bird Woman continued. "Very informative. We're going to go again after she's added the tearoom to the tour."

She beamed at me. All I could do was try to keep smiling.

"How nice," I said, thinking I was going to have a stern discussion with Willow in the near future.

"Well, we'd better sit down, or we won't get our tea, ha ha. Don't forget, we have the murder room reserved for Friday afternoon at four!"

"Oh, I couldn't forget," I said. "You ladies enjoy your tea, now."

"See?" Gina hissed as she followed me out of the parlor. "They love it! They want to hear about it!"

Kris stepped out of the gift shop. "There you are. Messages," she said, handing me a fat bundle. "Mostly from the press."

"You didn't have to bring them down," I told her.

"I was coming down anyway, with revised reservation sheets for this afternoon. Business is booming," she said, flashing me a dark smile as the turned toward the stairs.

"I'll take care of these," Gina said, taking the messages out of my hand. "I'll set you up for appointments between two and three-thirty. First come first served, the rest will have to wait."

"Gina—"

"Ms. Rosings?" said Iz, stepping toward me from the hostess station. She still hadn't adjusted to calling me by my first name.

I took a deep breath. Gina had already darted upstairs after Kris, no doubt to use my office to play talent agent.

"Yes, Iz?" I said, struggling to hold onto my patience.

"There's someone here to see you. Out on the porch."

"The porch?" I glanced toward the front door. "Why didn't you show them in?"

She gave a little shrug. "He wouldn't come in. Said he wasn't dressed right."

She turned back to the gift shop. I went to the front door and opened it.

The sun was high overhead, just beginning to creep toward the house from the garden. A few faded wisteria blooms had fallen to the porch. I'd have to start sweeping every morning, I thought, then I saw Tony Aragón leaning against one of the columns.

He stood up straight as I looked at him. He was wearing his motorcycle duds and his cop shades. Looked very tough. Definitely not right for the tearoom.

"Hi," he said.

"Hello."

I was a little miffed at him. He hadn't called the night before, or that morning. Not that I'd been expecting a call—I knew he was a busy man. But it would have been thoughtful to touch base with me, make sure I was all right. I wanted to be coldly polite in response to this distant behavior, but it's hard to stay annoyed with someone who has recently saved your life.

He took his shades off, which made him seem less tough. He stuck them in a pocket, then reached into his jacket and produced a folded piece of paper.

"I brought this by for you to sign. It's a statement about what happened yesterday, based on what you told me. We'll use it to file charges against Vince Margolan."

"You made some poor clerk type this up before you asked if I wanted to press charges?"

He blinked. "I figured I could talk you into it."

I took the paper and glanced over it while I thought about whether to be angry with him. I heard the scuff of his boot against the porch, and glanced up to see him standing rather close.

"I also figured you wouldn't want to come down to the station," he said in a low voice. "Thought maybe I could do you a favor by bringing it over."

I bit my lip, blinking back confusing feelings. Just when I had worked up to being annoyed with him, he had to go and do something thoughtful.

I looked up and was caught by his dark eyes, by the clean, strong lines of his face framed by still-vivid cascades of wisteria. I didn't want to think about Vince Margolan or the murder case or any of that unpleasantness. I let the paper fold back up in my hands, and was about to lean closer to him when I caught movement out of the side of my eye.

I glanced at the window nearby. The Bird Woman was peering out of it with her bright birdy eyes, smiling and nodding, the hydrangeas on her hat bobbing counterpoint.

"Ah—I've got to go," Tony said, stepping back. "If you want to think about it I can pick that up later."

"No, I don't need to think about it. I'll sign it. Do you have a pen?"

"Not on me."

"Come inside, then. It'll just take a second."

"Oh, I can wait here."

I looked back at him from the door, raising an eyebrow. "You're unwilling to come into my tearoom?"

He hunched his shoulders. "Not unwilling. I just don't

want to cramp your style."

"You haven't cramped it so far."

I pushed the door open. He stood there looking tough for a moment, then one corner of his mouth tweaked upward.

"Yes ma'am," he said, stepping inside.

I led him to the hostess station. Iz was busy straightening the china display. I signed the statement, then handed it back to Tony.

"There you are."

"Thanks."

"See, that wasn't painful."

"No." He grinned. "Grandma says the lady's always right."

I smiled back. "Does she? I think I'd like to meet her. You should bring her to tea some time."

"Bet she'd like that. Maybe I will."

He gazed at me, dark eyes half-lidded in a way that made my stomach feel very unsettled. A small clink of china reminded us of Iz's presence.

"Gotta go," he said, and strode toward the door.

I followed him out to the porch and stood beneath the wisterias, watching him out to his bike at the curb. He glanced back as he closed the gate, but he had his shades on again and I couldn't tell if he was looking at me. He didn't wave.

I remembered lots of things I'd heard about cops, how they were hard to get close to, hard to have relationships with. Some of that was hype from television and movie dramas, but I'd heard enough personal stories to know it was often true.

Tony put on his helmet and swung onto the bike. He started it, gunned it once, then pulled away from the curb. Just before he turned the corner he raised his hand. It could have been to signal a turn, but his fingers formed a victory "V."

The future seemed more promising, all at once. I smiled, then went back into the tearoom, ready for a cuppa.

Ellen's Cream Scones with Currants

(Note: this recipe is designed for 7,000 feet. If you live at a lower elevation, you will probably want to increase the baking powder to 1.5 t for 3,000 feet or 2 t for sea level, and decrease the temperature to 375°.)

Ingredients

4 c flour
1/4 c sugar
1 t salt
1 t baking powder

1/3 c butter
1/2 c dried currants
2 c heavy cream
2 T plain unsweetened yogurt

Directions

Preheat oven to 400°. Mix dry ingredients, cut in butter until crumbly. Stir in currants, making sure there are no clumps. Add cream and yogurt, stir until mostly absorbed, then knead until all the flour is just blended in.

Roll out to 1" thick on floured board. Cut with 2" round biscuit cutter and place on parchment-lined baking pan. Gather scraps, roll out again and cut a few more scones. Brush tops with cream. Bake 20 minutes, or until just tinged with golden brown. Serve warm with butter or lemon curd and clotted cream. Makes about a dozen.

These can be frozen, if you only need one or two (or three...) at a time. Baking directions are the same. Do not thaw.

Julio's Strawberry Puffs

These light bites are Julio's winning dessert from the Wisteria Tearoom's grand opening. Caution: highly addictive. Makes about four dozen.

Meringues
(make a day or two in advance)

(Note: this recipe is designed for an elevation of 7000 feet. At lower elevations you may want to use less cream of tartar, e.g., ¼ t at sea level.)

3 egg whites
1 c sugar
½ t cream of tartar

Preheat oven to 275°. Cover a cookie sheet with parchment paper. Beat egg whites and cream of tartar until foamy. Beat in sugar gradually, then beat mixture until glossy and very stiff.

Place 2mm tip in icing bag and fill with meringue. (If you don't have icing tips/bags, an easy substitute is to fill a food storage bag with meringue, then snip 1/8" off one corner.)

Pipe meringue into cups by piping 1¼" discs (about three turns piping as a spiral outward from the center), then piping two turns on top of the outer edge to make a wall. The diameter of the cups should be about the size of a half-dollar. These are meant to be eaten in one bite or two, so don't make the cups too big! Bake for 45 minutes to one hour, then turn off the oven and leave overnight.

Filling

1 c whipping cream	2 pints fresh strawberries
2 T powdered sugar	¼ cup strawberry preserves
dash of salt	2 T orange liqueur

Wash strawberries and cut 1" off of the tips of the best-looking 18 berries, set tips aside for garnish. Coarse-chop 1 cup of the remaining berries, then put into food processor and pulse 3-6 times until more finely chopped.

Blend powdered sugar, salt, and whipping cream, then whip to stiff peaks. Fold in chopped berries. Place in pastry bag with ½" round tip or in large food storage bag and clip ¼" off one corner.

In a small bowl, stir orange liqueur into preserves; set aside.

Garnish & Assembly

Hold a berry tip by the point and make a vertical cut toward the point but not through it. On each side of that cut, make similar partial cuts so that you have three slices, each about 1/8" thick, on each side of the middle. Finish the middle cut, resulting in two halves of the berry, each with three connected slices. Spread each half into a fan. Repeat for all the berry tips.

Spread a thin layer of preserves in the bottom of each meringue cup. Pipe cream/berry filling on top. Garnish with berry fan. Serve immediately (or may be refrigerated for up to 4 hours).

About the Author

Patrice Greenwood was born and raised in New Mexico, and remembers when dusty dogs rolled in the Santa Fe plaza. She has been writing fiction for over twenty years.

She loves afternoon tea, old buildings, gourmet tailgating at the opera, and solving puzzles. Her popular Wisteria Tearoom Mysteries are informed by many of these interests. She is presently collapsed on her chaise longue, planning the next book in the series.

Made in the USA
San Bernardino, CA
02 August 2017